About the author

Susan Lyons was educated in North London and at Homerton College, Cambridge. She also holds a humanities degree from the University of Leicester. Susan followed a successful teaching career, embracing primary and adult education, with a focus on French for young learners. Her interests include walking, art appreciation, entertaining and international travel. The latter was the inspiration for her first novel. Susan lives in Leicestershire and is married to Arthur. They have two daughters, one living in London, and the other in Australia with a young family.

THE MAP OF CHOICE

Susan Lyons

THE MAP OF CHOICE

Vanguard Press

A CIP catalogue record for this title is
available from the British Library.

ISBN 978 1 84386 6503

*Vanguard Press is an imprint of
Pegasus Elliot Mackenzie Publishers Ltd.*
www.pegasuspublishers.com

First Published in 2010

**Vanguard Press
Sheraton House Castle Park
Cambridge England**

Printed & Bound in Great Britain

Dedication

For Arthur and his positive encouragement.
For Claire and her loving support.
For Elizabeth, the perfect travelling companion.

Acknowledgements

I would like to thank all those who have been so generous with their encouragement – my loving family and supportive friends, especially my sister Jenny and dear friend Ann. Thank you too, Rosemary, for the proof-reading.

I am grateful to the team at Pegasus Elliot Mackenzie, who guided me through the publishing process.

The quotation from 'The Other Side of You', is reprinted by permission of HarperCollins Publishers Ltd. © 2000, Salley Vickers.

'On the map of human choice, there are highways and by-ways, crossroads and narrow tracks and cul-de-sacs.'

Salley Vickers, *The Other Side of You*

Chapter 1

She died before she got round to opening it.

So the letter was still there on the coffee table when the nurse knocked gently, then more insistently, at the bedroom door before opening it just sufficiently to enable her to peer in. She knew immediately what had happened.

Helen had been at the nursing home for a decade and had witnessed many arrivals and departures. But at such times, for even the most troublesome of inmates – and Margaret had certainly not been one of those – she always felt the tenderness and compassion that distinguished her as a true and loving carer.

There was just sufficient pale and insubstantial light for Helen to see her head positioned in the middle of the pillow, slightly to one side. Unlike most other residents, regardless of the season, Margaret would never allow her curtains to be fully closed and so the slow dawning of a November morning with its dampness and dankness was gradually infiltrating into the room. Normally in such circumstances, Helen would now shut the curtains and check her patient more fully, as her professional role dictated, by the additional light of one of the small lamps. But the nurse had understood her patient well, so she moved quietly and respectfully to open the drapes a little further, careful not to dislodge the letter and packaging on the coffee table. She stood in quiet contemplation overlooking the garden that had brought such pleasure to Margaret in recent years.

The nursing home stood within large grounds on the outskirts of a large and expanding village. It was a substantial

Victorian house that had been much changed over the years both in architectural style and usage. However, it had been sensitively modified and extended and its present purpose suited it well. Its exclusivity was both a product of its undeniably attractive setting and the personal finances of its residents, and was easily the most appealing, certainly the most expensive, of the residential establishments the family had inspected. All the rooms were large and airy, sympathetically converted to form self-contained units and although some were of necessity on the first floor, there was lift access. In addition, the communal rooms – a large lounge, a television room, a quiet room or library and an attractive dining room – were pleasant and well furnished.

But for Margaret, the grounds were the deciding factor. As the car turned into the drive on that morning in early summer, she scrutinised the substantial front garden with keen interest, finally resting her gaze with evident pleasure on a magnificent eucalyptus very much in the centre of the recently mown lawn. There were rose bushes and colourful borders with the country garden flowers she so loved – delphiniums, lupins and clumps of fragrant pinks. It looked cared for and loved but not suffocated by unnecessary attention to detail. She was immediately delighted. She felt at home.

The house too looked inviting, pleasantly proportioned and approached by a series of three wide steps and an accommodating ramp to one side. Here they were met by the manager, who welcomed them, explaining that two apartments had now become available, then introducing them to a member of staff who proceeded to show them round.

The family was quick to point out the advantage of the ground-floor flat with a particularly large living room and a southerly aspect. But Margaret, shunning the lift, was already on her way up the impressive staircase to view the upstairs flat, aware from the information she had already gleaned that it must have an uninterrupted view of the front garden. It was even better than she had expected.

Entered from the spacious first-floor landing, with a small bathroom to the right and a well-appointed kitchen to the left, the main living space had been knocked through from front to back.

Margaret made first for the large window to her left where she stood to survey the scene. The splendid eucalyptus was in full view. She clasped her hands together, nodding appreciatively. Next, she turned to the window at the far side of the room, partially separated by a partition, which screened the bedroom alcove from the main sitting area. This overlooked a large tract of land, well tended in the immediate vicinity of the building, but which appeared to extend to an orchard and woodland beyond. In the distance was the outline of low hills.

'Does all this land belong to Orchard House?'

'See that arch set in the old wall beyond those fruit trees? That leads into a small wood, not that extensive, but big enough. There are bluebells in spring and wild garlic. I'll show you the way out when you feel you've finished up here.'

Margaret returned to the front window.

'So west is over here and the back is to the east?'

'Yes. That's about it.'

'The ground-floor flat faces south,' pointed out her daughter. 'And do look at the internal layout very carefully. You're hardly going to live in the garden. You've barely even been into the kitchen and bathroom.'

However, Margaret had no need to look further. 'Such a vast expanse of sky! That tree! And grass, orchard, fields, woods and low hills!'

The son and daughter were pleased and relieved by her evident delight, but felt compelled to outline what they saw as possible drawbacks. They wanted her to be certain. But she was not to be dissuaded.

And within the month, she had taken up residence.

Helen, saddened, remained at the window. It was now light and she could see into the distance beyond the well-tended garden to the rear and past the remains of what must once have been a flourishing orchard. Several apple trees, a couple of plums and a crab apple remained although none had been pruned for some while. A few fallen apples merged with the blown autumn leaves and wet grass, rotting and partially camouflaged. Mostly, the fruit remained unpicked, some still clinging to the unclothed branches, although some of the residents had evidently gathered and enjoyed what they were able to reach. They were good crisp eaters and she and Margaret had shared a few together over the years. Beyond the unkempt orchard was a short length of wall that disintegrated towards each end, but probably when first erected made a feature of the curved central arch, ablaze in June with masses of white roses, but now just a vast entanglement of overgrown branches. It too was clearly in urgent need of pruning. But it was a big arch and, even now, the way through was unhindered. To the left side was a niche, with sufficient room for a stone seat where Margaret had often sat with a book. She had always said that it was in need of its twin on the other side, but there was no evidence that another such niche had ever existed. Further off were the woods and then the low hills over which the rising sun would first appear, today, however, rather wanly as if it too was sad. But on many occasions that self-same sun had risen in the greatest of splendour, eagerly anticipated, viewed from this very spot where the nurse now stood. Like many elderly people, Margaret was an early riser and Helen had often found her fully dressed at the window when she gave her early morning knock.

But this morning, it was not to be. Slowly and with a heavy heart, Helen turned back to the bed to undertake what was now necessary. She bent to kiss the forehead with the utmost tenderness, and then straightening up with a sigh, made her way from the bedroom recess through to the large window that gave on to the front of the house. For Margaret had been equally captivated by the expansive views to the front.

Helen next opened the front curtains just a little further. The view was again extensive and far-reaching. This aspect overlooked the approach to Orchard House and the garden towards the impressive front door was regularly well tended and colourful particularly in spring and summer. Now the borders were possibly a little bedraggled, but the area of lawn had recently been given what was probably its last mowing of the season and the gravel drive was weed free, crisp and crunchy as it curved its way to the perimeter beech hedge. The view was mainly of agricultural land but being an area of mixed farming, there was livestock too, and a few farmhouses and outlying buildings could be seen. Far to the left was the edge of the recent new housing estate. To the horizon was the slight incline of gentle hills. The self-same sun now struggling to make its mark on a damp autumn morning came to rest here at the end of each day. The favourite chair was positioned in readiness, by the tea trolley, waiting in the window.

'I don't know which you like best, your sunrise or sunset!' Helen had once commented. But she wasn't really asking a question and Margaret, turning to smile, hadn't replied.

Helen left the room. The necessary arrangements would now have to be made. She went straight to Eileen Edwards' office.

Eileen sat back in her chair in contemplation. 'Such a lovely old lady.' Then, leaning forward, she placed her elbows on the table to rest her chin on clasped hands. The clock ticked.

Eileen's room to the far side of the entrance hall overlooked the same easterly aspect that had so delighted her patient in her upstairs room. The large old oak table at which she was seated was angled so that she half faced the door at which Helen had quietly knocked some short while previously, but could also swivel to the right on her chair and enjoy the back garden. She now raised her lowered head from her hands, sat back with arms loosely across her lap and slightly adjusted her position.

Dan Armitage was shuffling his way round the perimeter path as he did every morning.

A door to the right of the office led from the welcoming and well-proportioned hall on to a wide paved patio. This adjoined a gravel path that continued in a northerly direction for some fifty yards or so until it turned to cross the grass and follow the line of the old wall. It passed the solid and overgrown arch that led into the wood and Margaret's beloved niche. Eventually it wound its way back to skirt the first-floor bedroom, where now lay a body, and then curved its way past Eileen's window where some low level shrubs were planted.

The women observed Dan's slow, labouring progress.

'We must let the residents know. Perhaps it would be kinder to alert him first.' Then, turning to Helen, 'I'll get on the phone to her daughter straight away. The family were all here last weekend, weren't they? They are going to be so grateful for that.' And then, scrutinising the face of the younger woman beside her, 'Don't be too sad. Lives end, Helen and it was a good life. You have been a loving friend to her and that has enriched both your lives. But you are also a nurse and death, as you well know, is a part of your working life. You know that I have the greatest regard for everything you do here and that Orchard House is truly fortunate to have you. When you feel ready, let the others know and I'll alert the family and speak to Dan.'

Eileen rose, and with an arm around Helen's shoulders, escorted her to the door.

She was truly appreciative of her younger colleague and spoke in all sincerity. It was not always easy to find staff and Helen had been a great asset during her ten years' service. She had not, Eileen recalled, been the strongest candidate for the post at the time in terms of relevant experience, since she had undertaken only a modest amount of agency work in the nearest appreciably sized town since qualifying. Additionally she had had very little experience with the elderly and none at all within the context of residential care. But she had had no hesitancy in her offer of employment. So Helen had stayed and proved more than simply a colleague. Although the distinction in their roles was professionally observed at all times, the two women shared an understanding that went beyond that of employer and employee. Each was sensitive to the mood of the other especially at a time like this.

Eileen sighed as she rose from her desk. She had a sad phone call to make, but it would not take long. The initial call, unlike those that would inevitably follow, never did.

She then turned her attention to Dan who had been a close friend of the now deceased.

Dan Armitage had paused at the niche and despite the cool morning was resting on the stone seat, stick in hand and legs apart. Eileen's most recent conversation with Dan had related to the condition of the gravel path. The fine gravel suited those who were mobile quite well, but was less helpful to wheelchair users, particularly in the winter months. Dan, as Chairman of the Residents' Association had been in recent discussion with herself and other members of staff concerning possible alternative surfaces. Surprisingly, since a number suffered mobility problems, there was a considerable degree of resistance to change. Even those who found it a little difficult to negotiate the wet gravel in winter were supportive of retaining their path.

'It looks right and the little flowers grow through,' claimed Sylvia. The fact that the favoured flowers were actually weeds was immaterial. Still, something needed to be done. Eileen thought that on the pretext of further discussion about paving or asphalt, she could inform Dan of the passing of his friend and companion of recent years before those who wanted breakfast downstairs assembled in the dining hall.

With a jacket pulled around her shoulders, she made her way across the wet grass towards the stone seat. Dan watched her coming. He moved his bulk to one side as she approached and patted the space beside him.

'A bit on the cold side, but you can sit on my scarf,' he invited. Eileen shook her head and managed a smile. She sat down beside him and paused for a moment. But before she could speak, Dan raised his stick towards the upper window.

'You don't need to tell me. See that curtain?'

Eileen looked to where he was pointing. The drapes in Margaret's room were not quite fully open.

There was a silence.

'It was in her sleep and perfectly peaceful.'

Dan turned his head away for a moment, lowering his eyes to the ground. They directed their gazes towards the path.

'Well,' said Dan at length intercepting her line of thought. 'You'd better get it paved or whatever. That's what she felt really. Better for those who find this old gravel a bit tricky at times. She was thinking of the likes of me, though deep down, mind, she would have chosen to leave it as it is, like the rest of them.' He drew a few patterns aimlessly with his stick, disturbing the stony surface to reveal a layer of hardened earth. He paused, contemplating the effect and then poked slowly and desultorily at the ground as if attempting to reinstate the path. Then, without looking up, he gravely and attentively drew a letter 'M' in the gravel, and raising his head to face Eileen commented, 'She wasn't so good yesterday, you know. Seemed agitated. I'm not really surprised.'

Perhaps, Eileen considered, his years as a GP had given him a certain sixth sense, for she herself had had no such inkling. Indeed, only the previous weekend, Margaret had seemed in particularly good form when the family visited.

'I'll be sitting here for a bit. I'll not be in for breakfast. But when the family's been, I'd like to go up and say my own farewell.' She patted his hand and left him. There were others to inform.

22

Dan sat for a while recalling how he and Margaret first met. He'd been more mobile ten years ago and happened to be sketching in the wood behind when the recently arrived resident approached. The narrowness of the path forced Margaret either to pass closely or to turn back, both options, in her opinion, appearing somewhat intrusive. However, the artist resolved her dilemma by lifting his pencil from his pad to indicate the forking of the tree he was trying to captivate. 'See that,' he'd said, by way of introduction, 'those leaves are dancing. How is one to capture that?'

'Movement, light and shade,' mused Margaret by way of response, and so began a friendship that brought great pleasure to them both. Margaret often joined Dan as he sketched but despite his encouragement, could never be persuaded to try drawing herself. At that time, he was an enthusiastic member of a local art class in the village. 'Good to escape all the other oldies,' he often commented, and in the first couple of years of their friendship, Margaret had been very happy to accompany him on his group's coach outings to various art galleries until, sadly, this became too problematic. The last visit had been to London to an exhibition entitled 'Sketches – Flora and Fauna of the Dresden Group', which meant little to either of them, although the advertising poster looked interesting. There they were both struck by a couple of exhibits exquisitely capturing the interaction of light and dark on the leaves of a forked branch of eucalyptus, since Dan frequently looked to the specimen in their own front lawn for his inspiration. He shuffled forward to peer more closely at the exhibit before them.

'Reminds me very much of that sketch of yours on your wall,' he remarked, after lengthy scrutiny.

Margaret peered with renewed interest.

'Can you make out the signature?'

'Not really. Possibly something like Schwarz, although the end of the name is very indistinct.'

'First initial a W, I think,' added Dan, as he turned away.

But Margaret, suddenly transfixed, remained for a while, and visibly jumped when Dan called her.

Later, by mutual consent, they found themselves in the National Gallery. It will have to be the Impressionists, they agreed.

'Do you have a favourite tree?' asked Margaret, as they paused before the most majestic of pines, its strong columnar trunk rising from the ochre sun-baked earth in contrast to its wind-blown leaves.

'At this very moment, it has to be this one, of course. But see here! I'll go for this line of poplars. Just look at those slender trunks, how lithe they are!'

'Dawn and dusk, the most fragile times of day,' commented Margaret, moving on, as her eyes charted the progress of the sun over the river.

Their visit ended with carrot cake and coffee before the return trip, a coachload of elderly tourists dozing the way home after a satisfying day out.

And as this was the last of the art group's excursions they were able to share together, it remained firmly etched in their minds.

Dr Daniel Armitage would greatly miss his companion.

Chapter 2

Thursday was usually her shopping night. On this particular Thursday, there were two things very much on her mind, in addition to the normal end of term demands and activities.

One concern related to the forthcoming weekend and her retirement celebration. Maggie knew that her daughter Kate, driving up from Ealing, would have everything in hand, but had been requested to stock up with a few extra items for the birthday gathering that had been planned with family and a few friends. With Kate's list in her hand, she pushed the uncooperative trolley along the insufficiently wide aisles, scanning the shelves for balsamic vinegar, oregano and sun-dried tomatoes.

But she was also thinking about her colleague, Lyn. They had been together now at Ridge Road School for some twelve years or so, often teaching parallel classes, and had come to enjoy each other's company. With their respective husbands, they met from time to time at weekends for local outings and, on a couple of occasions, enjoyed trips away together. A particularly memorable one had been to Paris, where Bill, following an especially good supper accompanied by several glasses of wine, allowed a persuasive artist in Montmartre to sketch his wife. The resulting portrait was quite dreadful, but relatively inexpensive and Bill had bought it largely because it caused both women such merriment.

'It's ghastly!' laughed Lyn.

'Afraid so,' agreed her friend, equally amused.

Then Lyn was totally unexpectedly diagnosed with a brain tumour, and was dead within two weeks.

All this had happened some few months back, but Maggie was painfully conscious, as she made her way through the supermarket, that there would be no retirement party for her friend, who had been of similar age to herself.

Lyn's death affected them all at school. Maggie, in her efforts like the rest of the staff, to be strong for the sake of the children, felt she had had little time to grieve herself.

The funeral was a sad and sobering affair. Bill stared straight ahead as he followed his wife's coffin flanked by his two lads, grim faced with heads bowed. Vicky, grieving for her mother, sobbed openly as she grasped the arm of her grandmother.

When the service was over, Vicky stood miserably beside Kate looking at the flowers.

'Those are mine,' she sniffed.

Maggie bent forward to examine the posy more closely.

'They are just right for your Mum. She loved the woodland flowers.'

Maggie suddenly realised that she had come to a halt and was causing problems for a young woman with a toddler in her trolley trying to reach the frozen vegetables. She started abruptly and with a quick apologetic nod moved forward a few paces. But before returning to her current train of thought, or perhaps more practically and productively to her shopping, she gave a further glance to the child now on her left, wriggling in the trolley seat. Dressed in pink shorts and top, with wispy fair hair fastened to one side of a wide forehead by means of a somewhat insecure pink slide, she was clutching a slightly soggy toothpaste packet to her chest. She gazed directly and quizzically at Maggie. Her baby freshness and her obvious openness to all new experiences contrasted starkly with Maggie's earlier contemplation of finality and loss. She reminded Maggie of Kate at a similar age. There was no knowing what Tina would have looked like. She too had had fair hair.

Maggie completed her shopping and made her way to the checkout. With bags packed haphazardly into the boot, she negotiated the sharp descent from the car park, and, once out of town, gathered speed for the final run home.

The straight, slightly undulating road passed through unremarkable agricultural countryside, except that on this particular day, in late afternoon sunshine, it looked decidedly attractive. Waving cornfields rose and fell in the slight breeze.

Strange to think that soon she would drive home from work along this road for the very last time.

There had been so many children, she mused, as well as quite a number of schools, and it was indeed sobering to think that her first pupils must now be approaching their fiftieth birthdays! Yet she could still see class 3A in her mind's eye as clearly as when she first stood before them, in nervous anticipation on that bright September morning.

Her first teaching post had been a large well-organised primary school in what was then a leafy London suburb. It fronted the main road, with the parade of shops opposite and was bounded on the other side by a sizeable park with flowerbeds, an avenue of impressive horse chestnuts and a play area with a formidable slide and creaking witches' hat. Although the school had substantial grounds itself, the park was well used by the children, for those were the days of nature walks and impromptu activities, later to be stifled by imposed, rigid timetabling. Maggie had been happy there and made good friends amongst her new colleagues.

After their marriage, she and Richard moved to a flat in another suburb, where Maggie felt less comfortable with her new post. The brand new building looked enticing, but there were practical disadvantages to the open-plan classrooms, for the children were incredibly noisy and easily distracted. The staff struggled loyally to promote the new learning environment, but felt increasingly exhausted at the end of each day.

Then came the first pregnancy, escape and later the home at Woodbridge Lane. After that, once Kate was at nursery, there was supply teaching, the village school, the inner city school that she had loved – but the travelling defeated her – and finally, Ridge Road.

There was to be a retirement party for her at school at the end of the final week and she was now getting used to being asked about her future plans and whether she was looking forward to this next stage of her life. Of course, she never mentioned her immediate plan, but began to give more consideration to the other frequently asked question. In her view, growing older had long since ceased to be an attractive proposition, and as time passed, there did indeed seem to be fewer and fewer compensations. Yet one huge bonus of retirement appeared to be the ability to choose what one did with one's time.

Richard was totally absorbed in his work, the children now adults, her parents in reasonable health and she was about to become a senior citizen.

She left the main road, the plastic carriers in the boot shifting a little to one side, and slowed at the approach to the large sprawling village where they had lived since the arrival of the family. When they first left London, they had not anticipated so many years in Woodbridge Lane, but the house and location had grown on them all.

Her spirits rose as she turned into the drive. It was indeed a fine June evening and perhaps there would be time for a cup of tea in the garden after unloading the shopping and before starting on supper. The weekend ahead promised well. The end of term was within reach, and all the major headaches associated with the end of an academic year were beginning to diminish in intensity. Her reports were finalised, which meant she would be able to relax and enjoy the celebrations planned for her, and it looked as though the family would be together for a couple of days – although, of course, there was always Tom's unpredictability to contend with. He was supposedly arriving at Heathrow on the Friday night. Maybe the plan was to have a lift up with Kate and Martin.

At some point during the weekend, she would have to tell them of her plan. This thought both excited and unnerved her. She had no idea what they would all think.

Richard had arrived home first and came to help her unload the car.

'You're a bit on the late side, aren't you?'

'I didn't get away as quickly as I had hoped, and then there were a few extra things to pick up for Kate.'

'Well, it looks set to be a fine weekend. We'll be able to eat outside, which is what Kate had hoped, I think. Cup of tea?'

After desultory talk of possible college mergers, Richard disappeared indoors leaving Maggie alone with her thoughts. How would she tell them?

Half dozing, with the warmth of brick behind her, she found herself once again thinking of Lyn, whose early, unexpected death seemed so unfair.

Way back in the past, when she was herself a small child sitting in a school classroom somewhere, she remembered listening to the magical stories of the Three Fates. The teacher had held up the book, pointing out the large pictures and the children jostled and strained to see. The illustrations were arrestingly colourful, particularly that of Atropos with her scissors gripped between furled fingers. Now, so many years later in her garden, Maggie reminisced as her head nodded forward.

It is calm in the classroom of a suburban school, with the enveloping, deadening mistiness of a late November afternoon. It is story time and soon it will be four o'clock. Slowly, gradually the walls are erecting themselves around her and she sees the paintings mounted on dark blue card, many heavy in texture with a satisfying over-abundance of thick, comforting powder paint. A door is taking form, blue paint with scuffed kick marks, so many comings and goings. To the side is the old square wooden table, ready for the delivery of tomorrow's crate of milk, and the battered cardboard box of straws next to the monitor's rota. The teacher is young and alive – she has not forgotten Miss Turner – and now she can see that it isn't just mist. It's the drizzle and the whining of the rain. She is hearing 'Atropos'. Some raindrops are wiggling their way up the window, rather than down. She is watching one very carefully to see how this can be. Do not lose sight of it. It must be followed in its intricate dance, or else she will not know whether this apparent ascent is really possible or not. But it is still Atropos, Atropos of the beautiful name, who can make the scissors go snip snip. Now she is side-tracked and fingering the ingrained desktop with its deep grooves and empty, unused inkwell filled with pencil sharpening and shreds of pink, ink-stained blotting paper. There's the little hole too in the bottom of the desk. She is poking up her finger to the exercise book with the maroon cover and its soft, furled edges.

Maggie's head jerked against the brick. It was cooler now. She must have dozed off. She went indoors to find Richard and prepare supper.

Then the phone rang. It was Kate confirming that she and Martin would be coming up by car on Friday evening but she was unsure of her brother's arrangements. She had offered a lift up from London, assuming Tom's flight was to Heathrow, but now it appeared that he would be arriving in Birmingham.

'So when will he get here then?'

Richard shrugged.

Unlike her mother, Kate never worried about her brother; his vagueness, indiscretions, abstractions and occasional insensitivity caused her no undue concerns. Theirs was sibling love, unconditional and undemanding. The love of father for son was more muted, certainly affectionate, but there was between the two of them an unspoken understanding that their ways had somehow diverged and that there were now invisible barriers which both of them chose not to cross. Maggie sensed this and it made her uncomfortable, but any attempt to share her thoughts with Richard were unfruitful and she came to see this apparent lack of depth in the relationship between her two men as somehow a fault of her own.

So husband and wife sat down to supper. Then Richard went to his study whilst Maggie quickly made up beds for the family. Kate's room was little changed, apart from the double bed with new quilt and curtains. However, her wardrobe had become a store for much family paraphernalia and it was now difficult to create enough hanging space for the visitors; not, reasoned Maggie, that much would be required anyway for a weekend visit. However, Tom's old room looked decidedly shabby, still bearing the evidence of posters he had discarded in his teenage years. He too still stored many of his personal possessions at his parental home and the shelves Richard had erected some twenty years ago were full of long-since discarded music and computer equipment. Maggie cast a final eye over the room as she turned to close the door. Perhaps, in due course, redecoration could be a retirement project. In fact, come the day when Richard chose to retire too, although she sometimes wondered whether there would in fact ever be such a time, they might then even choose to move: This was a new idea to contemplate. But what struck Maggie most significantly as she quickly sorted out both rooms was how speedily the years had passed since there were two small children asleep here. She found herself wondering whether the retirement years would pass equally speedily. This was an uncomfortable thought and she began to feel a little anxious about the years ahead, fearful too lest she should miss the rhythm of her working life more than she had imagined.

Later over coffee, they sat together on the settee and before long both had their eyes shut, oblivious to the television and the evening news. Richard's mind was full of college politics, possible mergers, staffing issues and dissident students. Maggie dreamt of a rugged valley with a deep ravine from where she could hear the voices of children. There was a route to follow and she left the valley to climb upwards, panting, out of breath, following narrow, untrodden, indistinct paths. Then finally reaching the summit and realising that the valley had become narrower, rockier and more steeply sided as she climbed, she edged forwards, cautiously, carefully, lying on her stomach to dare to look back down. The dizziness of the drop made her gasp: There were rocks and foliage and a hint of river beneath. But she was deeply fearful for it was now dusk. She knew she had to return, for no one would wish to lose their way up here in the dark.

The news ended. She awoke and switched on the light.

Chapter 3

'It's just that it's so very unlike her,' explained Kate, kicking the duvet away.

'Good luck to her is what I say,' commented Martin, stretching out somewhat lethargically. They were now back in their flat, the weekend behind them with another working week looming ahead. It was again a warm night, and the combination of excess food and drink, a trying return journey down the motorway and Kate's concern for her mother's plans all contrived to keep sleep at bay. Martin had enjoyed his weekend. Although a confirmed city dweller, a couple of days outdoors in an attractive garden had proved a welcome change. At any rate, wine and beer flowed quite freely and Kate produced a great spread. The celebratory lunch was eaten in the garden on one of those perfect and never to be taken for granted days that June in England can sometimes pull out of the hat. And Richard, undoubtedly an excellent host, was always most forthcoming in a switched off from work mode. Tom was easy company and Maggie always made him most welcome. And then, of course, it had been most interesting to observe the family reactions when Maggie dropped her little bombshell!

After lunch and a leisurely session on sun-loungers, a walk down the lane and across the fields was suggested, the usual loop being vetoed, due to overindulgence at lunchtime. There was very little traffic on the lane, and they soon turned off through the awkward-to-open five bar gate on the right that led down through a couple of fields with some dozen or so cows, seemingly acceptant of the buzzing flies around their eyes. The area by the gate was deeply rutted but very dry and Maggie and Kate picked their way carefully in their summer sandals. Richard, Tom and Martin were ahead, and paused by the somewhat sluggish ditch that Tom and Kate had called Slip Slop stream as children.

'Turn around at Slip Slop,' called Kate, and the little group ambled their amicable way back to the house and garden.

It was when they were all assembled again later that afternoon, ready for the cutting of the cake, joined by their close friends Judy and Karl from the far end of the village, that Maggie decided now was time to announce her plan.

'Here's to you, Maggie!' smiled Richard, raising his glass, as good wishes were expressed by them all. 'All the best for your retirement.'

'Make a wish!' called Kate, carrying out the cake she had brought up from Ealing and handing the knife to her mother. The white iced cake with its trellis pattern and roses reminded Maggie of the many past Christmases, when both children had helped to beat the thick royal icing and make their own individual contribution to the decoration. She turned with a smile towards her daughter.

'Perhaps I'm allowed two wishes on this special occasion,' she began. 'The first one will have to be my usual wish!'

There had been so many years of celebratory cake making, particularly the baking of the Christmas cake, possibly Maggie's favourite, as small sticky children's hands laboured with the thick, unyielding mixture, clinging stubbornly to the wooden spoon. Then the ritual, supposedly secret, wishing took place. Tom and Kate, like all small children, found the concept of secrecy too difficult and their wishes were usually speedily divulged. Not so their mother, who smilingly took her annual turn at the final stirring, announcing, 'It will be my usual wish,' and what it was, was never told. Then one year, when Kate was about nine years old, she too ventured, a little hesitantly at first; 'It will be my usual wish too!'

'But you don't have a usual wish!' retorted Tom, who although he felt rather too old for wishes had kept the custom going for the sake of tradition and his sister.

'I do now!' claimed Kate. And that had been the beginning of the end as far as Christmas cake wishes were concerned.

Then came the year when Maggie made and decorated her cake alone, both children away at university. She enjoyed the ritual wrapping round of the cake tin with new, strong brown paper and the warm kitchen smell. She dug in her skewer several times as always, to ascertain exactly when her cake was ready. She was pleased when it lay cooling on the wire tray covered with a fresh tea towel. But of course, it was not the same. For a start, there was no one to lick the bowl or to fight over the last scrapings, and although Richard was called to have his wish, they both knew the magic had evaporated. Maggie, determinedly undaunted, made her usual wish anyway, but the next year a supermarket cake was purchased.

So Maggie was in her garden on a Saturday afternoon in June, poised to cut her cake. 'It will be my usual wish!' she reaffirmed to the accompaniment of some good-natured heckling from Tom. She placed her hand on top of Kate's and together they completed the cutting of the first slice. The cake was dark and thick with luscious fruit. She turned to face them all. 'But I also have one other wish.' Her voice was steady and resolute. 'I'd like to share it with you all now. I wish to celebrate my retirement with an adventure of my own. When term ends, I'm off to the other side of the world. I have booked a flight to Australia and I'd like you all to wish me good luck!'

Martin leant back on his pillow, head on hands, and thought back to that moment in the garden.

An uncomfortable air of incredulity, disbelief and uncertainty amongst family and friends followed Maggie's announcement. Kate was clearly very surprised, even alarmed, casting anxious glances from one parent to the other. Tom seemed amused. But Richard was clearly confused and troubled, slow and reluctant to grasp the fact of his exclusion. Judy and Karl wondered initially if they had in fact been informed of some travel plans which they had either not fully registered at the time, or had very embarrassingly forgotten.

Maggie too felt confused. She knew her plan would surprise her family, but she had not expected to feel such intense disillusionment and disappointment. She thought back to her husband's reaction and began to wonder whether, after all, she should have discussed her planned venture with him. Yet, she reasoned, Richard had been more than usually preoccupied in recent months with his own increasingly onerous commitments at college. Had she suggested the possibility of an extended holiday or a new activity, she knew in her heart that he would have found numerous excuses. She had also acted in uncharacteristic haste, for the whole idea had only come to her as the result of a chance comment overheard in the staff room some two weeks ago.

Maybe, she thought, glancing again at Richard, her act was one of treachery and she should have known better than to nurse a secret. She had not anticipated the price to pay for the pleasure it had afforded her. Even in childhood, she reflected, secrets mutate at the moment of their conception, for the very nature of a secret implies that for those who are in the know, there are those who are left in the dark: Tom used to torment Kate with secrets he would not share.

Martin turned to one side, as the duvet slid to the floor, to put his arm around Kate. But she was not in relaxed mood.

'So very unlike her,' she repeated, as she wriggled from his embrace to set the alarm.

Maggie too was finding it difficult to get to sleep, for an undercurrent had been set in motion, predestined by its very nature to run its chosen course.

Richard lay beside his wife, his body now curved away from Maggie into a foetal position.

Earlier he had drawn his wife to him, pushing the thin strap of her nightdress aside as his hand slid between her breasts. Maggie turned towards him pushing back the damp straggle of hair that had flopped forward on to his forehead and running her fingers across his brow and over a roughened cheek to fondle the lobe of his ear. 'So you don't mind about me going?' she quizzed tentatively.

'Well,' confided Richard, 'I was surprised initially of course to think you had planned something like this without me knowing and that it involved only you, but I suppose, since I am somewhat committed over the summer to the Liverpool project, it's not that unreasonable. You could alternatively have waited till we were both free to do a special trip of some sort.'

But when would that ever be, had thought Maggie privately. Richard withdrew his hand, quite gently and not at all brusquely, but Maggie knew that there would be no further intimacies that night. In a way, she was almost relieved. It was actually quite late and they both had busy working weeks ahead and there was now something within that relationship between them that she felt was slightly ruffled. But Richard had recovered from his surprise for he was not one to hold grudges. There could even be some advantages in his wife's extended holiday plans, for he foresaw his own fully demanding work schedule in the immediate months ahead. And in contrast to Maggie, who tended to lie awake planning and worrying, Richard's mind, when claimed by sleep, was compliant and accepting.

So Richard slept, a deep uncomplicated sleep, his sonorous rhythmic breathing punctuated by the occasional short snort, whilst his wife lay awake.

Somewhat reassured by Richard's apparent acceptance of her plan, she once again began to feel more positive about her venture. It was not unreasonable, she concluded, at this particular stage of her life, to pursue her own path for a while. Certainly she had acted uncharacteristically, without any of the careful thought she would normally give to any project but would return in due course with a sense of fulfilment and renewed purpose. However, sleep still eluded her for some length of time.

Tom too was still awake. While Kate tossed and turned in London beside Martin and Maggie lay wide-eyed beside a sleeping Richard, Tom's Sunday night was not yet over.

Although he had given his parents the impression that he was returning to Paris that night, he actually had no such plan. He allowed them to assume that he would be in work on Monday morning and had merely been economical with the truth – one of the phrases to which his father had a particular aversion. He needed some time out without the knowledge of his present company – clearly a couple of days 'indisposition' would suffice.

There was an old school friend he wanted to look up, now living in a flat towards the city centre – a much revamped area since Tom had last visited, and this was an opportunity to renew contact and discuss the joint business proposition that was under early consideration. Both men were entrepreneurial by nature, not averse to risk taking, keen to exploit the technological shift that had seen the computer become a virtual household necessity. Once they had casually toyed with the video game market, but now they wondered whether they had missed that particular boat and that maybe online security was an issue worth serious investigation. Having brainstormed some of the possible unanticipated hazards of modern technology, Tom and Kip visited a few bars and were now back at Kip's place. Tom recounted events of the weekend.

'So what's your mum up to then?' yawned Kip.

'Some bee in her bonnet about doing her own thing, I think,' was Tom's response. 'Retirement and all that – focuses the mind a bit, I should say. A lot to do and less time to do it. Dad's busy as usual so perhaps she feels she'll go for her own adventure. At any rate, she has no set plans for what she'll do there or even any set date for a return. When you think about it, it's very unlike her. Anyway, good luck to her. She'll be fine.'

'Not something I could ever imagine my mum doing,' mused Kip.

Tom genuinely believed, as he said, that his mum would be OK. But Kate was more cautious, more practical. Whereas she fervently, earnestly hoped that her mother would be all right, Tom was easily able to assume that she would indeed be so.

Each thought they knew their mother so well.

Chapter 4

Boarding for the second leg of her long-haul flight, Maggie settled herself into her aisle seat and took stock of her fellow travellers. There still seemed to be a never-ending progression of passengers, searching out the small, allocated private space that was to be theirs for a considerable number of hours to come. There were couples, families, a few larger groups and a not inconsiderable number of small children, clutching new toys and bags, as yet fresh and excited at the prospect of the flight. The adults on the other hand appeared to be a creased and baggy representation of humanity, anxious to lay claim to the most readily accessible locker above their numbered seats, staking ownership to as much territory as could possibly be thought to be a reasonable entitlement. There was much pressing of bodies to one side and heaving and squashing of bags into compartments.

'No, I told you to leave the water out. We don't want it up there,' barked a large tracksuited woman to Maggie's left. Her thin, sinewy husband was clearly used to obeying orders and leapt to her command. The bottle of water reappeared from the locker causing yet another minor traffic jam in the gangway. 'Where's my magazine? Here take my jacket! Now you've dropped the pillow.'

Maggie was relieved when a particularly bulky male, having minutely scrutinised the seat beside her, moved on to the row behind, leaving the two seats immediately adjacent to be occupied by a young couple, who looked as though they might be reasonable neighbours to share enforced proximity for the journey ahead.

Maggie thumbed through the flight magazine, having decided as a result of the first leg of her journey that to while away the hours with as many films as possible helped the seemingly endless time to pass. She had not really felt in the mood for her book, which was a disappointment, as she had anticipated a good read.

The meals were supposed to relieve the boredom, but in Maggie's eyes they merely contributed to the tedium, since they were both bland in appearance and extremely tedious to manipulate. The arrival of a tray on her flapped down table also accentuated her feeling of being trapped and ensnared, for as soon as her food was in front of her, she felt a great urge to move, either to the toilet or along the gangway to stretch her aching limbs.

Unable to concentrate on any one activity, she found herself mulling over the uneasy thoughts she had tried to quell with such determination and vigour over the preceding couple of weeks. She flicked half-heartedly through the entertainment channels whilst these clamouring thoughts emerged for an airing, to fly in random but restricted fashion, then rebound and finally to re-circulate endlessly through the fetid cabin air.

But still she did not know as yet what she really thought.

By contrast, she was quick to formulate an opinion of Sydney. It was, Maggie thought, quite the most incredibly beautiful city she had ever visited. From Circular Quay she was magnetically drawn to the Opera House and the way in which it gleamed resplendent beneath a clear blue sky. She sat on the nearby wall to absorb the warmth and the architectural splendour of a building that had the character of both an old friend and a new idol; so it was in reverence, as a believer clad in a toga, that she climbed the steps of the temple-like forecourt. She drew close to examine one of the hundreds, thousands, surely even millions of apparently lack-lustre tiles that magically conspired as a whole to be a brilliant edifice. Maggie felt herself to be miles away from her old life, as indeed she was in every possible way. She felt refreshed, alive, in total contrast to the discomforts of her fatiguing flight of a day or so ago. She was in fact beginning both to appreciate and to relish the fact that she had only herself to please. But perhaps as yet this was not quite the case. She realised she needed to find an internet café to let Richard and the children know of her safe arrival in Sydney, the perfectly acceptable accommodation that had been surprisingly easy to find and the fact that she was well, in good form and ready for her Australian adventure. She must, of course, ask the family to pass on her news to her parents who were of an age to allow certain aspects of technology to pass them by.

So Maggie did the tourist thing for the next three or four days. She frequently found herself down on the waterfront on Sydney Harbour, for it was enough to watch the sun on the water, to view those two structures, the Opera House and the bridge, from different viewpoints and at varying times of the day, and to eat satisfyingly in one of the numerous outdoor cafés. The whole world seemed to be in Sydney, clearly a most cosmopolitan city, but although the areas Maggie often frequented were busy with tourists and also business people, there seemed to her little of the urgency and bustle of many city centres she had known. There genuinely did seem to be that atmosphere of friendliness, of the laid-back life, of the ready acceptance of others that epitomised Australian culture to the British back home.

A local lad from Manly, who must have heard her English accent, joined her on one occasion, somewhat to her surprise, as she ordered a beer. He quickly seated himself at her table and proceeded cheerfully to ask her a considerable number of questions, relating mainly to the UK, her home-town and her visit to Australia; but what really impressed Maggie was that this unknown young man seemed both genuinely interested with a desire to be of assistance. She supposed that back home she would have thought him impertinent or suspect in some way. Tom came into her mind since he was of like build and probably of similar age. She couldn't quite imagine him striking up a conversation with a middle-aged woman, so evidently a tourist, on her own in London.

Her new friend was making suggestions about further trips that she should make. A surfing addict, he obviously spent much of his own time in the sea, as did a large number of young people Maggie assumed, and he recommended his own Manly as well worth a visit. He described the rich sea life in the rock pools north of Manly and recounted some of the inevitable stories of the dangers associated with the sea. He was a good storyteller and Maggie was both a captive and interested audience. Predictably his stories of the sea centred on sharks, naming species which Maggie recognised, such as the great white pointer, hammerhead and bull shark, but some, such as the mako, previously unknown to her. Death as a result of a shark attack, she learnt, was by no means a daily occurrence in Australia, but some advice was offered, none the less, should she be sufficiently unfortunate to find herself face to face with one of these splendid big fish. In the case of a great white, a well-aimed kick or punch in the eye was the recommendation, and staying calm – which would probably be somewhat difficult in the circumstance – was general advice for all. But crocodiles seemed even more ruthless, particularly the salties, the advice here being again to poke them in the eyes in the case of the imminent approach of horrendous jaws. It would not be wise, counselled her friend, to have too many beers and find oneself staggering somewhat on the banks of a crocodile infested river. Maggie made a mental note to curtail her alcoholic intake in such circumstances. Box jellyfish, stingrays, stonefish, and bluebottles – how did anyone survive the perils of the water, thought Maggie, as her storyteller returned to his original topic of surfing and those waves?

Maggie was vaguely aware of his final story, having seen a recent television documentary, of a calm day in the 1930s at Bondi when a series of freak waves crashed their way on the shore, dragging out to sea some couple of hundred swimmers, a handful of whom lost their lives despite the selfless efforts of some fifty or so lifeguards. Since the topic of conversation had moved to that most renowned of beaches, he expressed surprise she had not yet visited Bondi with the result that the next day, Maggie found herself sitting on that very same beach.

Although Maggie arrived quite early in Bondi, she could see, stepping down from the bus, that one particular area of the beach was already active with surfers. This was hardly surprising in Maggie's eyes, since she knew this large curving sandy beachfront to be synonymous with surfing and a focal point for the backpacking fraternity. She decided to have breakfast at one of the cafés along the front in order to survey the scene. Bondi was clearly past its sell by date, she thought, with its somewhat tacky small shopfronts and the pavilion building reminiscent of English seaside holiday resorts, relic of a bygone age, but the expansive promenade, the crescent of pale sand fringing those famous waves enabled it to retain a certain appeal. The black-suited youngsters in the sea, mainly male, were endlessly preparing for the biggest ride of their lives, doggedly persevering in the quest. How adroitly they seemed to recover from each spill, turning boards skilfully seawards to dive through oncoming breakers, ready for the next attempt. Maggie's eyes moved along the beach, taking in the flagged area, to be patrolled later by the lifeguards, perfect in form, like bronzed Greek gods and goddesses, caught in a time warp of ripe sexuality. As yet, there were few other people on the beach, and Maggie was happy to people watch and write a few postcards home.

An unexpected gust of wind caused her to bend to retrieve one of her cards, but already she was too late. She noticed first the hairy and tanned arm of the rescuer of her mail as both she and he resurfaced. There was steeliness about the blue eyes now staring at her that she found a little disconcerting.

'So, how's the holiday?' he asked, in the direct, forceful manner that seemed to be the norm.

'Good,' replied Maggie, 'I'm really enjoying your country.'

'And where are you from?' came the next predictable question. Maggie explained that her home was near Birmingham in the UK, ready to expand upon the exact location of this Midlands city, but her new acquaintance, already seated at her table, needed no clarification.

'I've been to Birmingham and to London and to Cornwall,' he stated, 'and I really enjoyed your country. London was great. I loved it, Buckingham Palace, Trafalgar Square, Big Ben, Houses of Parliament.' Her new contact paused to eye her slowly and his narrow lips elongated into a smile. He was in need of a shave. 'You sure have some fine buildings.' Maggie acquiesced with a nod and a smile, wondering how, without being impolite, she could escape, for on this particular morning she was enjoying the pleasure and luxury of her own company.

'On your own?' he asked, nonchalantly.

'Yes,' replied Maggie, but immediately regretted her spontaneous and honest reply, realising that it would now be a little more difficult to extricate herself from the present situation.

For some unknown reason she had the presence of mind, for which she was later to be deeply grateful, to modify her response, suggesting that she was only on her own whilst waiting for her husband to come down on the beach. Even as she spoke, she was aware of the incongruity of the situation in the abandonment of a real husband and the creation of an imaginary one.

'I think I'd better find out where he's got to,' said Maggie, as she rose from the table. She felt his eyes following her as she crossed the promenade on to the beach and the feeling was an uncomfortable one. The brief contact, unlike that with her Manly friend of the previous day, left her without those earlier buoyant and positive feelings and she decided to leave the beach for a while to follow a coastal path recommended by her guidebook.

She soon found herself at a small bay, from where she continued to the cemetery. Here she stopped for it was simply such a splendid view. She looked out to a blue-green sea dotted with small yachts and occasional white breakers and then walked slowly round some of the tombs and monuments, noting the various epitaphs. It was, she felt, both comforting and inspiring to have a sense of elation in such a place. She paused for a moment before a memorial to a young child. Here she stood silently, in thought.

How rudely and viciously was the quiet moment shattered!

The hand landed roughly, abruptly and painfully on her shoulder.

He was not smiling now.

He approached from behind and to her right side.

She screamed.

Everything subsequently happened so quickly that Maggie was later unable to recall the exact sequence of events, but it was his right hand that moved fast to grab the front of her lower neck, with a pincer like movement of thumb and forefinger, squeezing flesh as she struggled to cough.

She writhed.

She tried to push him off.

His other hand, fist clenched, lunged into her lower spine causing her back to arch. What she was most conscious of was the closeness of their two faces side by side and his heavy breathing behind her right ear. She could see the bristles on his chin.

She needed to think speedily.

Despite the hold on her neck, she managed to call out.

And despite the leering closeness of his face, she was able to gather her wits together in order to make it appear that help was at hand.

She somehow found the strength to yell out to the husband who was not actually physically present, 'I'm over here Richard!'

To her gasping, immeasurable relief, her attacker let go.

It was finished.

Maggie found herself unable to move.

She then became aware that there were voices from nearby in the cemetery, not totally surprising, for the path was quite well used. Perhaps someone had heard her shout. She looked round fearfully, but her assailant had fled.

It was over.

Perhaps nothing had happened at all and everything had been in her imagination. Except that she knew it not to be so. Apart from the voices in the background, there was the same stillness in the cemetery. The earlier breeze had dropped. The sky was as blue as ever. But Maggie's heart was racing and her blood pounding. Her knees gave way beneath her and she collapsed to the grass. She made herself take some deep breaths. Then she raised her head, moving to a sitting position to clasp her knees close with her still shaking arms. She was certain now that she could hear other voices in the cemetery, a family perhaps, as there were children's voices too. The proximity of others was her salvation, enabling her to recover and regain her confidence. A little family was indeed now in sight, following the path that led to the next beach. Amazingly, it seemed that her cries had not been heard.

Maggie felt very unsure as to what she should do. The family was disappearing and she certainly did not wish to be left alone. Apart from being dishevelled and probably bruised, she was unharmed. Had she unwittingly invited this attack, she began to wonder? She thought back to her earlier encounter with her attacker. She had certainly been more forthcoming with a stranger than she would have been at home, but the culture, although by no means alien, was certainly different and maybe it was because she hadn't really understood the rules? At any rate, she felt disinclined to tell her story to the family group who had obviously not witnessed her dilemma; thankfully she realised she could use them as protection to continue her route.

And so she arrived at the next beach, subdued and still confused. The little family she had followed made their way to a café and Maggie did the same. She ordered a coffee, sipped her drink and realised her hands were now steady. A gaily-coloured parrot flew high into the nearby palm with much squawking and raucous sound. Nothing had changed.

Gradually her spirits returned and she took more notice of her surroundings, even able to exchange a nod and a hint of a smile with the mother of her family as the children struggled with choices of drinks and ice creams. The fact was that nothing had actually happened to her. She was quite safe. And on an even more comforting note, she began to feel reassured that she had not in reality been misled by the relaxed attitude of those with whom she had come into contact since arriving in Sydney. She should, of course, have heeded the slight misgivings she experienced when talking with the man who joined her at breakfast. The intuition or sixth sense that so often points the clear warning finger was still very much with her, requiring only that she observe it here in her new surroundings as she would at home. She would learn from this lesson and an unfortunate experience would not be allowed to deter her from her adventure. Only later did the uncomfortable voice of conscience hint that an alternative course of action might have resulted in the warning of others.

Maggie's optimism revived. She had been away for nearly a fortnight and needed now to concern herself with the ultimate focus of her trip. Sydney was a wonderful city, of that she was readily convinced, and she knew that she would be very happy to spend further time sightseeing. But there was a deeper purpose to her enterprise and she needed to discover what it was. She would give herself a few more days to discover it.

Chapter 5

When Maggie called her husband's name on her ill-fated walk, it was her daughter who stirred. She and Martin were having a lie-in following a Friday night pub meal with friends. Kate thought at first that Martin had woken, but quickly realised that he was still deeply asleep, so she lay still, listening to the rain. The recent week had been rather a wet one, regretfully for their night out, as they had hoped to eat in the pub garden, or at least to have drinks outside before the meal. The earlier spell of uncharacteristic warm and sunny weather, such as they had enjoyed for the retirement party, had been quickly forgotten and there was now much general grumbling about the British summer. Kate resented the fact that she was now awake. She knew she would not easily get off to sleep again, so she did what her mother did on such occasions, which was to allow free rein to her roaming thoughts.

That morning, she had her mother very much in mind and as the driving rain hit the bedroom window, she found herself more than usually anxious about her well-being. Inwardly she thought the retirement trip quite an undertaking for someone who had not travelled alone for many years, a view not shared by either her partner or her brother.

However, there were also other issues very much on her mind, as she lay wide-eyed in bed, that related to her own situation.

Kate's dilemma, if he could be thus described, was in fact asleep beside her. She and Martin had been partners now for some six years and were a couple in the eyes of all their friends and relatives. But Kate felt ready for a more formal commitment in the relationship and Martin appeared very disinclined to speak of marriage. Kate wondered whether her hints in this direction had been too obscure. Her mother had once intimated that Martin lacked initiative, but in what context Kate could no longer remember. Such a criticism could not be applied to his working life, where he was well regarded by his company and appeared to be following the anticipated career path. Kate was undoubtedly the driving force in terms of their social life, but although the entries in the diary were hers, the activities they recorded were shared. Did her mother think they were well suited? Kate thought so, but she was not there to be asked.

Kate turned from her back on to her side to contemplate her sleeping partner. Martin's head was squarely positioned on the pillow, his somewhat sharp nose in clear profile and his rather large nostrils flaring slightly as he breathed. He was thin in face as he was in body and due to his height, well over six feet, his feet were sticking out from beneath the duvet. Although she could not see them, Kate knew that his socks would be lying inside out by the skirting board and his underwear, in some disarray, half on and half off the upright chair beside the window. She stretched out a hand and tentatively stroked the bare upper arm with its fair curly hairs and slight suggestion of freckles. Martin's eyes flickered, then opened and he rolled over to face Kate, curving his body around hers, his knees pressing on her legs as he caressed her thighs. With gently probing fingers, he fondled her lower body, teasing the dark curly hairs, and circled his way to rest on her shoulder pulling her insistently, firmly towards him as her body relaxed and softened to meet his. His hand travelled further to explore secret contours, rises and falls, finally caressing and then propelling the small of her back to pull her to him, fastening his mouth on to hers. He was indeed a satisfying lover, thought Kate, as she rolled back, moistened, with the sweet pungent scent of their sex now between them. As always, she felt the bewitchment, the fascination of her man, the enticement that caused her to be totally captivated in their most intimate of moments. Here was her soulmate. Martin's own emotions must surely mirror hers, thought Kate. This man loves me as I love him and he must now be strongly persuaded to do something practical about it.

Later, over breakfast, they mooted various plans for the day. Martin was after some particular DVDs and Kate had planned to meet up with her former school friend, Sarah, who had been working in London for some while, and had recently acquired a small flat in preference to her commute from Brighton.

So Martin and Kate arranged to go their own ways and then to have a stay at home evening.

It was over coffee at Sarah's that the conversation moved to their men. Sarah, in the travel business, which frequently took her away for lengthy periods, could always be relied upon for a lively, robust account of her latest date. She was an inveterate collector of the male species, enjoying to the full each relationship as it came her way, and then moving onwards, cheerfully optimistically and honestly in her deeply held conviction that another delightful romance was around the next corner, as it invariably was. Her latest admirer was a young Greek whom she happened to have met in Crete whilst officially on business. As her work schedule somewhat cramped her style, they both readily accepted that the relationship would be brief and entirely without a future. Consequently, together they shared one of those magical days forever engraved deeply and pleasurably into the memory, creating a warm glow for years to come for both of them to rekindle very much later on occasions when the cause of the fire's origin was long since lost. It had started with warm bread from a traditional bakery accompanied by hot strong coffee, and progressed without plan or forethought to include a long scooter ride through the mountains of eastern Crete, with helmets strapped to the handlebars and Sarah's hair blowing freely in the wind.

There was the harshness of craggy, rocky mountain landscape with nimble-footed, bearded goats and the occasional wearily obedient plodding donkey, accompanied by an elderly weather-beaten man. Sometimes they would pass a black clad woman of indeterminate age, clutching at her lower back and moving slowly in a laboriously swaying motion in a manner that spoke of physical toil. Then there had been the magic of ancient civilisations, and the delight of a remote and scruffy taverna with its fish and ouzo and the swim from the rocks of a deserted small beach. The sky was so blue, and the water so clear and refreshingly cool as it caressed young bare flesh, seemingly making all things possible.

'A brilliantly romantic day,' concluded Sarah. 'He even went down on one knee pressing his lips to my hand to say his farewell. A couple of onlookers raised a cheer. They must have thought he was proposing!'

Kate laughed. She could imagine the scene so well and Sarah's stories were always well embellished and delivered in lively and entertaining form.

Romance being the topic, Kate thought it opportune to share her own thoughts with her friend.

'So you see! A proposal is actually what I'm after myself!'

Sarah listened sympathetically as her friend sought support and advice.

'Of course,' concluded Kate with a wry smile, 'a romantic proposal would be an added bonus.'

'Well surely he knows how you feel,' responded Sarah, who viewed Kate and Martin as an excellent match. True, Martin could be laid-back at times, whereas Kate was the go-getter, the maker of happenings, but this would seem to be, in Sarah's eyes certainly, a positive point in a partnership. And the sex, by all accounts, was pretty good.

'Have you told him you're expecting to be asked?' pursued Sarah.

'Sort of,' replied Kate. 'I can't really believe that he hasn't got the message.'

'Oh, men like him need some pushing,' assured Sarah. 'You've made life too easy for him; it's all there on a plate. Just ask him, 'When are we getting married?''

Kate tried to think whether she had been quite as direct in her hints to Martin as her friend clearly thought she should have been. 'I want *him* to ask *me*. I've been waiting for his initiative,' she concluded. 'Perhaps I've really wanted to be reassured that what *I* want is what *he* wants too.'

'Well, of course it is,' affirmed Sarah, who saw them, as did other friends, and indeed their own families, as an ideal couple. 'There are three possibilities. You tell him to propose, propose to him yourself or push him into a situation where he realises he's on to a damned good thing, and he'd bloody well better not miss out.'

Kate considered her friend's suggestions. The first two were relatively easy to dismiss. But what of the final other option?

'You show him what he's missing, of course,' explained Sarah. 'Oh you don't need to go as far as having an affair, stupid,' she continued, aware of the expression on her friend's face. 'You're just not quite so readily available, that's all. You go away for a bit, let him think you're having quite a good time without him, but could have enjoyed it with him – delicate balance – and leave him to pick up his socks, remember to bring in the milk and notice the lack of sex.'

Kate sat contemplatively, considering this way forward. Was this part of her mother's thinking too?

'So what's she doing now, your mum?' asked Sarah after Kate had described the events of the recent retirement gathering.

'Still in Sydney,' replied Kate. 'She's been gone about a couple of weeks. We've had the occasional email and my grandparents had a phone call from her last week. Actually, she was very much on my mind this morning when I woke. I could perhaps give a ring – I have a number for the holiday apartment – although I couldn't be sure of finding her in. The rather surprising part of her venture is the lack of any pre-booked flight home and her total disinclination to give any indication of when this might be. There seems to be some grand design to all this that has yet to be unravelled.'

Both girls paused to consider this in the light of their recent discussion.

'Dad's fine,' added Kate, pre-empting Sarah's next question. 'He's OK at looking after himself and very involved at the moment in a project in collaboration with a colleague in the English department, something to do with gypsies in literature for which Dad is researching the historical background. Must make a change from his medieval manuscripts. I wouldn't really know how much he misses her at the moment – it's early days yet and he will be lost to the world in his work. In any case, I can't quite imagine him doing the Shirley Valentine act.' Sarah required some ingenuity to fathom the reference, for Kate, familiar with one of Maggie's favourite films, had mistakenly assumed that it would be within Sarah's own repertoire.

'So, what's the decision?' demanded Sarah. 'You have a few days in Paris with your brother, accept my offer of joining me in Greece, since I'm owed time off and there's an apartment there we could use, or go off somewhere totally by yourself?'

Kate was not at all sure she wanted to go off on her own and Tom, although always good company, would not understand the delicacies of the venture. She felt drawn to the girlie holiday, but it was with some pang of regret that Martin would not be there to share it.

Sarah was beginning to show signs of impatience with Kate's lack of decision.

She must make up her mind.

The practicalities could be sorted.

She would go away to enjoy some sun with her friend and Martin would ask her to marry him upon her return.

The two girls, in good spirits, set off for a little of Sarah's favourite retail therapy, passing first through the market with its amazing array of continental breads, luscious olives and colourful fruity jams. They had earlier consulted the A to Z to see if they could manage a visit to the other member of the school trio, now living in Essex with husband and baby, but it appeared to be further than they had realised. Jen was, in any case, tending to drop out of the picture, for motherhood, to which she had looked forward immensely, was proving to be much harder work and far more time consuming than she had imagined remotely possible.

'Don't take Martin to visit Jen and Matt in the immediate future,' counselled Sarah. 'Perhaps his apparent reticence to tie the knot is that he's not into kids.'

This thought had also occurred to Kate and she knew that here was an issue to be well aired before the cementing of any relationship. She herself felt that she would like to have children and although Martin had never made any positive declaration in this direction, he was a great success with the young offspring of friends and relatives.

Although Martin was surprised to hear of Kate's plans later that evening, he was sufficiently charitable to wish her well, and managed to contain the slight aggravation that rose within. It occurred to him later that perhaps he himself should have got his act together and made holiday plans for the two of them, something he acknowledged that he tended to leave to Kate, since she arranged things so well.

And, of course, it occurred to both of them that they were in some way re-enacting the scene in the garden of some couple of weeks ago.

Richard, when phoned, wished Kate well for her holiday trip with former school friend Sarah without reading any subtleties into the weeks away. Tom made a few jibes about being fancy-free and commented as to what each of them might get up to without the other. Maggie, returned from her disquieting walk, had to wait until the next afternoon for her phone call.

She knew it to be Kate even as she was called to the entrance lobby. So Kate was going to Greece with Sarah. And Maggie had walked from Bondi to Coogee.

Each heard the other's news, and knew it to be incomplete.

Chapter 6

Maggie was sitting in the yard of her holiday apartment and feeling much better than she had the previous day. She fleetingly contemplated whether yesterday's assault should be reported to the police, but another day of sunshine – albeit one she was using to catch up on washing and letter writing – was restoring her sense of well-being. Also, she still felt that in some undefined way, she had been to blame. And there again, nothing had actually happened.

She returned to her spot in the yard after her phone conversation with Kate and cleared away papers, pegs and coffee mug. Although the days were bright and blue, mornings and evenings were fresher, and she retreated indoors to fetch a cardigan and the pizza she had bought earlier for her supper. She also collected a pile of brochures and a couple of well-thumbed guidebooks.

Eating and reading at one and the same time was, she thought, a luxurious prerogative of the single traveller. Regularity might eventually dull its appeal, but for the moment, it was a relatively new found and pleasurable experience. It accounted in some measure for the state of her guidebooks, with the odd water mark and coffee stain adding further character to an old friend, with its loosening pages and furled corners. She looked up from the text to catch a drizzle of cheese from her supper and found herself thinking of her family in general and Kate in particular.

So Kate was off to Greece with Sarah! Mothers are often more perceptive than their children imagine, and Maggie found herself well able to read between the lines and to realise that herein lay a message for Martin. Not that Kate had given any indication of this, as the loyal girlfriend, but the mother approved of the daughter's positive move. She too, whilst very fond of Martin, had sometimes thought that where the relationship with her daughter was concerned, Martin required the 'kick up the backside' so eloquently recommended by Judy when they were having one of their conversations about their offspring. Martin was eminently likeable, a tall somewhat gangly young man, possessed of those social skills particularly welcomed by his parents' generation, easy in company, but could never be described as dynamic. In his job, something to do with logistics, Maggie imagined him to be perfectly capable in all his dealings but, in her eyes, he was no prime mover. Able and competent, undoubtedly, but not forcible, energetic or vigorous. A little pressure applied by Kate would do him no harm.

She also wondered how Richard was coping. Her conclusion was that he would manage perfectly well on his own. After all, she had only been away a couple of weeks, and many conferences in the past had taken them away from each other for far lengthier periods. She knew in terms of household management exactly what would be done and what would be left undone. And despite this, the place would manage to look much the same. Did they miss each other? Well of course each was aware of the other's absence, for it could not be otherwise in a long established relationship. But Maggie had to admit that all her new experiences had fully occupied her mind. Yes, it was true that she had just now been thinking of Kate, but in reality, she had to acknowledge that thoughts of her husband, son and daughter had only fleetingly surfaced since her departure from home. And, on reflection, that very much surprised her.

She drew her cardigan round her shoulders and returned to one of her bookmarked pages.

There it was, staring her in the face!

Maggie's guidebook had been her constant companion, suggesting, inviting, persuading, encouraging, cajoling, even insisting that certain locations, particular activities, special events were awaiting her exploration. And her guide had not disappointed her, opening her eyes to this most exquisitely beautiful city.

What she now saw was an amazing, stunning photograph of breathtaking grandeur and beauty.

It stood alone on the page, that splendid monolithic, red rock, immediately familiar even to those who had never set eyes on it and Maggie, fascinated and trapped, knew this to be her quest, her passion. She desired with an intensity that surprised her to experience this territory, to feast her eyes upon the strongly delineated outline of this magical, mysterious monument and to savour the mysteries of the remote centre of the vast country in which she now found herself. Her adventure would be connected with this place. This was why she had come to Australia.

What was it she wondered, scrutinising a series of photos in great detail, that inspired such fascination? Perhaps it was the very remoteness of the interior, she thought, recalling the last stages of her flight to Sydney, when bright clear skies offered views of endless nothingness as she gazed dumbfounded upon vast emptiness. And then there had been the apparitions – immeasurable, irregular tracts of mysterious grey and silver, frequently dull and opaque, but occasionally erupting into translucent, crystal lakes.

'What are they?' she had asked another passenger. But he didn't know.

The mind cannot grasp such a landscape. It is unreal. It is the backdrop to a mythical drama.

Her next consideration was how best to explore this remote outback. As a woman on her own, and by no means youthful, solo exploration of what was essentially unknown and clearly forbidding territory was not an option. However, her book indicated several possibilities of small scale guided camping expeditions around the Red Centre visiting Uluru, and these seemed to offer a reasonable compromise. She continued to pour over her maps and guides until darkness fell, later taking her reading matter to bed with her, until she put out the light and pulled the sheet to her chin. She felt too excited to sleep.

The young Margaret is lying in her bed, unable to sleep. But this time there is no thunderstorm, such as they had had a couple of nights ago, which had taken her into her parents' bed.

She is snuggling down between them, but still she does not like it at all. Her mother does not like it either, but is seeking to explain and reassure. 'The clouds are arguing and grumbling,' her mother is saying. 'They are chasing the sky away because they are cross and in a bad mood. They are making as much noise as they can. They are lighting fireworks to make even more noise. Soon the show will stop because they will run out of light and sound, and tomorrow the blue will be back.'

Nor is it because of the dark face with the horns that is lurking on the landing near the bathroom, lying in wait for a small barefooted child who is leaving her bed. 'There's nothing here!' her father is saying, 'See!' And he's switching on the landing light.

This time there is no storm.

This time there is no monster.

She is excited and the small heart is racing in anticipation.

The cases are packed and her own little bag is ready.

She is bringing Big Bear and he is ready too, sitting at the end of her bed.

Sleep will come eventually and when she wakes, she will be happy because something special is about to happen.

Maggie finally fell asleep, excited as a small child looking forward to the summer holiday.

The man in the travel agents was both knowledgeable and helpful.

'Lots of organised trips, and August is a good time to go. It'll be warm by day, but watch out for freezing nights if you are camping.'

He produced a selection of brochures, pounced on one and thumbed speedily through the pages.

'Now this trip here – bit longer than many, gives a taste of the real outback and you'll hardly get on to a tarmac highway. Let's get you a map.'

He dived under the counter to produce a map of the Northern Territory, which he spread out in front of her.

'Here's Alice Springs, just about right in the centre of the continent and there's Uluru National Park.'

'It doesn't look that far,' commented Maggie.

'Don't you be mistaken, lady! It's quite some trip, particularly when you follow the somewhat indirect route taken by the expedition I've just pointed out in the brochure. Of course you want to see the rock, that's why most people go there, but there's a whole world out there that's quite amazing. It's a fantastically spectacular area and with this trip you'd get to see a lot else besides.'

Maggie examined the map.

'So where exactly does this trip go?'

'You'll find you get off the main tracks, so I can't show you on here and anyway, your 4WD driver will use his own judgement. The situation can change rapidly out there and he'll have the latest info on the state of the tracks.'

Maggie returned to the original brochure with its eye-catching photo of the rock itself. There was the monolith, immediately recognisable, rising dramatically from the arid landscape.

'The layers are of hard, coarse grained sandstone,' continued the travel agent, observing her fascination. 'See, it's the shape of a huge loaf rising vertically from the hard baked earth. Not that it doesn't rain sometimes, for it sure does! And when it does, you know it! Waterfalls stream down, so you get these irregularities, like these cracks and caves.'

Together they examined the irregular grooved surface.

'It's some size,' he continued. 'Some mile and a half long. Course, there are those who want to climb it, and although the Aboriginals request that they don't, as the place is sacred to them, many do.'

'It's just awesome!'

'Are you a camper?'

Maggie thought back to the days of family camps in Devon and Norfolk. These now seemed so far removed from what she was considering that she was no longer sure.

'Yes,' she replied after a slight pause.

'Well, you go for this, and you won't be disappointed. The pick up is in Alice where there's quite a bit to see. You should get yourself up Anzac Hill for the view and then there's the telegraph station and the Desert Park. That park really sets the scene for you and you'll understand the desert better when you've been there. That's where my uncle works, so I have to promote the place! You'll see a very diverse range of birds and desert animals in the enclosures. There are lots of places to stay in the town and you could do some shopping if you feel in the mood, as Alice is the centre for art and crafts produced by the Aboriginals. You could even buy yourself a didgeridoo!'

By now, Maggie was only half listening. All these attractions were a bonus, but the focus for her was the rock. She left the travel agents with flight, motel and camping trip booked and went down to the beach with her map and her new brochure.

She tried to trace the expedition route for herself, but as she had been told, there was insufficient detail in the description. Highways were clearly marked and Alice appeared to be at a crossroads, but there was an indistinct network of lesser tracks, some seemingly dead ends.

She looked at her watch, for the time had passed quickly, and there were practicalities to attend to.

She phoned her parents to assure them of her safety, and Richard to warn him that her planned expedition would probably make communication difficult over the next couple of weeks or so. Though the call was brief, she sounded in good form, Richard reported later to Kate.

Richard too was examining a map.

After the call from his wife, he found an old atlas and located Uluru, or Ayers Rock, according to his out of date information. He searched out Alice Springs and to his surprise too, realised that Uluru was some distance from Alice Springs, which set him thinking about the scale of such a huge country. It was simply vast. It looked as though nothing much happened in this huge centre, so many miles from the well-separated cities fringing the sea. He traced some of the highways with his finger – Stuart, Lasseter, Plenty and Ross. Then there were the lesser routes, the old tracks. He traced those too. But although he could pick out many of the places his wife had mentioned, he was unsure of her precise plans.

For neither of them knew as yet the chosen route.

Chapter 7

Maggie found herself with a couple of days to spare in Alice Springs before joining her expedition. She booked herself into her inexpensive motel on the outskirts of town, unpacked and went down for dinner. She decided to eat in, because upon making enquiries about restaurants in town, she had been advised, much to her surprise, not to go in the vicinity of the Todd River after dark.

Later, in conversation with a couple she discovered to be from Sheffield, she mentioned the warning she had been given.

'So what is it about Alice Springs?' queried Maggie.

'It's the Aboriginals,' replied Geoff. 'They're the problem. It's the drink.'

Maggie pondered the response. It occurred to her, that in the time she had already spent in Australia, she had been singularly unaware of the original occupants of this vast and ancient land. In fact, she doubted whether she had seen a single Aboriginal in Sydney.

'It's a sad story of misunderstandings,' continued Pat. 'The white man arrives to impose his superior culture and beliefs. Yes, there is a particular problem in this town because disaffected Aboriginals seem to be drawn here. And Geoff's right. I wouldn't advise the Todd River after dark on your own either. I would also steer clear of the topic with the Australians. They all say it's a problem and then either don't know why or don't want to say why.'

'What makes it even more odd,' added Geoff, 'is that all the white lot are a pretty random mix of ethnic groups anyway. You'd think that would be a big plus for cultural diversity. No it seems an odd set-up in what should be more enlightened times. It's probably best to do what the Australians do – say it's a problem – and then wipe it from your mind.'

Maggie felt both ignorant and humbled. A personal mission drew her to the red rock to satisfy her own indulgence; she had now been made uncomfortably aware of her poor and shallow understanding of those for whom it had deep spiritual significance.

Next morning, she accepted Pat and Geoff's invitation to join them for a leisurely breakfast in Todd Mall, catching sight on the way of the dried-up bed of the Todd River. It seemed inconceivable that torrents of water could ever gush and swirl their way over the hard, rutted and cracked surfaces, but the pictures back at reception in the motel witnessed otherwise. By day, in contrast with the previous night's discussion, the whole area looked completely unthreatening, although there were clearly large, somewhat noisy groups of Aboriginals gathered on some of the open spaces as they approached the pedestrianised part of town.

Maggie sat back, enjoying her breakfast in the sunshine, wondering as always what it is that makes eating out of doors such a particular delight. Pat and Geoff, with a morning to while away before an afternoon flight from Alice Springs airport, offered to walk with her to Anzac Hill, from where, once again, Maggie marvelled at the amazingly isolated position of the town. Her eyes were drawn to the surrounding, awesome, rugged ridges and her thoughts to the imminent adventure ahead. Gaps in the ranges suggested a never-ending emptiness of dusty red earth, frightening in immensity and quite beyond the grasp of an outsider. The visible exit points of the town pulled and clamoured compellingly at Maggie as she stood on the hill in the morning breeze with a sense of heightened anticipation coursing through her whole being. She gazed from on high, her billowing skirt outlined in profile, momentarily unsure as to whether she was there by chance or design.

Some twenty-four hours or so later, Maggie certainly felt that good luck was playing a key role in her journeying so far. For a start, her first impression of her travelling companions was decidedly favourable. Since the pick-up from her holiday motel had been a very early one, she, as the first member of the group to be collected, had chosen to sit at the front of the 4WD, so was able to observe her fellow travellers as various locations in dark, abandoned Alice Springs were visited. First to load their minimal luggage into the trailer were a couple of men who appeared to be in their forties, the younger of whom gave a particularly cheery greeting and smile to Maggie as he made his way past. Although they had spoken to her in English, Maggie was not surprised to hear them conversing behind her in German owing to their European appearance and the particularly blonde hair of the younger man. Then came a couple of Australian women, to Maggie's relief quite evidently and reassuringly in their fifties – for she had wondered whether her companions would all be youngsters. It was not a possible age difference within her fellow travellers that had slightly worried Maggie, for she enjoyed the company of young people and generally related well to them. She had been more concerned about how strenuous the camping safari might prove to be, but upon observing her new companions, her initial thoughts were that she would be able to hold her own. Next pick-up was of a young lad who kept his head down somewhat as he made his way to the back of the vehicle, closely followed by an older man whose 'Good mornings' sounded very English as did the greetings of the married couple behind him. A further drive of some ten minutes or so saw the final member of the party aboard, a cheerful and very attractive young girl whose 'Allo' seemed to suggest she could well be French. So ten of us in all, registered Maggie, feeling that that appeared to be a very satisfactory number for a group of strangers who were to share an experience together. That left their guide and driver, who turned to introduce himself as Brad once all passengers were collected. He outlined the initial plan, that of driving into the outback, first leg towards Uluru, when a comfort stop would be made when daylight dawned. As so often on such expeditions, it was not long before most participants fell asleep.

With daylight came an opportunity to stretch legs and to make initial introductions. However, the general mood, somewhat to Maggie's surprise, was a little subdued. Partly, it had been a very early start, but additionally, as various travellers had awoken, there had been that first opportunity to contemplate the outback. Maggie was awestruck. There was nothing, she felt, neither the amazing photograph in her guide book, none of the publicity, nor even any previous knowledge of the semi-arid interior of Australia, that could ever have prepared her for her first glimpse of that huge expanse and remoteness. It was a place where anything might happen, or indeed may already have happened, a place that defied normal understanding and expectation. Maybe the visual scene could be described in some small way, but the internal tearing of her soul was beyond description. In this place she felt very, very small.

The programme outlined by Brad was first to spend a couple of days camping in the outback, visiting Uluru, with walks investigating the flora and fauna of this seemingly inhospitable, immense land area planned from a further range of sites.

They drove on leaving the surfaced highway for endlessly straight red, corrugated dusty roads with rarely another vehicle in sight. Only occasionally did they meet another 4WD, heralded by a cloud of dust on the horizon and only at the last minute did the drivers bother to relinquish the centre of the limitless road for the rougher less defined rutted edges. Nevertheless, the greetings between drivers were cordial, with much hand waving and cheerful shouting. At least if you were stuck, thought Maggie, something might come along in the course of the day, but waiting for any required help could be a long, anxious and somewhat frightening experience.

The vista was of dry spiky spinifex, scattered thorny bushes and occasional silvery grey trees with surprisingly green foliage. The passengers in the 4WD began to relax, to exchange first comments relating to the landscape, with the incredible intensity of the blue sky contrasting with the russet redness of the dusty terrain, moving then to pleasantries of a more personal nature. Arrival at the campsite, where on this first occasion they were treated to the luxury of ready erected tents, offered further opportunities for the travellers to get to know each other.

Small green, basic tents were arranged in a rough semi-circle on bare hard baked earth in the middle of which was a circle of rough stones edging the blackened evidence of a previous camp fire. Entrances to the tents were tied back, and apart from the fact that each tent had a groundsheet, they were visibly quite empty. All kit was stowed in the trailer from where each traveller collected a thin mattress, a bulky sleeping bag, an inner sheet sleeping bag and his or her own minimal baggage. Maggie surveyed the location. To her surprise and somewhat to her amusement, the actual choice of tent seemed of utmost importance to some members of the group. Eric and Werner were quickly off the mark, conversing urgently and loudly with each other in their native German, seizing upon the tent to the extreme left of the semi-circle, still bathed in the last rays of fast fading sunshine. The two Australian women speedily opted for the tent at the far right. Since they had already shown themselves to be veteran campers, in the sense that they had elected to bring their own well-filled luxurious looking sleeping bags and seemed to know exactly what was expected of them, Maggie supposed there must be some significant advantage to being on the fringe of the camp. She was bemused by this initial rush, since it brought to mind the first day of a new school year and the concern of pupils – at least the confident ones who knew the ropes from the previous year – to 'bag' desks in close proximity to friends. This always proved to be a fruitless manoeuvre, since any teacher with five minutes' experience was quick to make major readjustments, but the children, of course, remained ever hopeful. She half expected Brad to appear and relocate his team, but he was busy with the trailer. Since there were thirteen tents in all on this occasion, there was clearly room to space themselves out, which is what the British couple did by moving their gear into the next tent but one to Eric and Werner. So Maggie made her way to the right, heaving her belongings into the tent which was next door but one to the experienced Beck and Jo. A smiling Henriette settled into the adjacent tent, which left ample choice for the other two men and their guide. Maggie's nostrils quivered to the smell of warm, musty canvas, reminding her of early family camping holidays.

She's kneeling on the ground, adjusting the guy rope and keeping a watchful eye as the two children run round the tent in a state of heightened excitement. Everything is looking good, for of course, it is the beginning. All that is to happen hasn't happened yet. The children are sniffing the canvas approvingly. He is giving a final swing to the mallet. There's the trailer now to unload and she is calling them to help. But there they are, running away down the slope towards the hedge. She is leaving them to it. She's unpacking on her own. She needs to get a move on, anxious to sort things out before it gets dark.

Maggie bent to enter her tent, aware that light would fade fast. There was, in actuality, very little to organise. Since there was nowhere to put anything, there was little point in unpacking her bag, which anyway only held the absolute basics recommended for the trip. She had the foresight to look out her torch and her night things, including an extra jumper and her long johns, for Brad had most pointedly reminded his group on more than one occasion of the strongly contrasting temperatures of day and night. She straightened up, which was almost possible in the middle of her tent, to find Henriette by the open flap wanting Maggie to find the shower block with her. Brad indicated the direction to them with a nonchalant wave of the hand, reminding them that the preparation of supper was a team effort and that he had already got the campfire going. So with a whiff of smoke rising from the circle of stones and a sense of well-being, Maggie and Henriette linked arms and followed a small hardened earth path to a rough wooden shack beside some thorny bushes. The young French girl's eyes opened wide as she surveyed the two compartments. The facilities were clearly extremely basic, for which Maggie felt mentally prepared, but it was obviously a shock to her companion. However, the earth closet was clean, as was the one shower, but it was the practicalities of using the latter that most concerned Henriette. Daylight was indeed fast disappearing and neither of them had thought to bring a torch. The wooden door to the shower cubicle was somewhat rudimentary, being only really half a door at mid height, with an annoying habit of swinging open and no apparent means of keeping it shut. Maggie promised the young girl the necessary help, so Henriette showered first, bemoaning the lack of pegs and a light whilst Maggie kept guard at her companion's request. Both wrestled with the two taps trying to cajole hot water out of them, finally settling for a temperature that at least was tepid rather than cold. Then Maggie took her turn, in happy acceptance of the primitive conditions, for she felt a delightful sense of bonhomie and pleasurable anticipation within.

Back round the fire, a communal meal was shared, and when all had been cleared away, everyone relaxed in a comfortable circle, appreciating the warmth of the dancing flames beneath a night sky alive with a myriad of stars. The group relaxed, for a common purpose united them. Tongues loosened as wine and beer brought from Alice were handed round in plastic beakers and the anecdotes and storytelling began. The extroverts within the group emerged quite speedily and showed themselves to be Werner, the blonde German, possibly the younger of the two friends and the middle-aged Australian women, Jo and Beck. Werner told tales of exploits mostly in Europe involving numerous canoeing expeditions and the inevitable accounts of rapids encountered and near misses with rocks. His animation and enthusiasm were evident and he expressed himself very well in English. His companion was far less vocal, but supported his friend's accounts with approving nods. This was their first visit to Australia and the start of a year of travelling, both having taken unpaid leave from their occupations, as a PE teacher in the case of Eric and from some sort of secretarial role in Werner's case. Jo and Beck, however, had never left Australia, but had travelled widely within their own country and this was far from being their first visit to the Red Centre.

'We just adore this place,' confided Jo, 'and we've been coming here for years. It's magical! We can't get it out of our systems. We've usually done the camping safaris, but sometimes we've stayed in the homesteads. This way is best – you really get the feel of the place.'

'People say it's all red and flat, uncomfortable when hot and uncomfortable when cold, but we can never have enough of it,' added Beck. 'It's always different. The colours are always different. These night skies are never the same.'

The gazes of all focused on the heavenly display above. Maggie, with some disbelief, had once heard it said that there are more stars in the sky than grains of sand on the earth and she now began to think it possible. There was a silent pause in the conversation, as there must be, when there are no words to be said.

Henriette shivered, drawing closer to the fire and Maggie too became conscious of the fact that although her face was burning, her back felt chilled. The penetrating cold of the winter night was beginning to make itself felt. Talk became a little more fragmentary. Eric moved closer to Werner and Henriette to Maggie. Mike and Dee, the English couple, described their travels to date. This was their second visit to

Australia as their first, some few years back, had centred on cities and beaches. Henriette, in heavily accented English, described it as her first. She too was taking time out to travel and had been in Thailand prior to the current expedition. Maggie and Jim, the remaining participants, also acknowledged this visit to be their first.

It was getting cold. Brad, helped by Maggie and Henriette, made some hot drinks to refuel the now empty wine and beer mugs, and as hands were warmed by the clutching of the plastic, the last embers were prodded to produce a brief flaming. Brad brought the evening's conversation to a close by recounting a few outback tales, some from way back in time, some centring on more recent tales of strange happenings in camps and mysterious encounters on the rough roads. Finally, all made their way to their tents for it had been a long day.

Maggie's tent struck her as cold and damp. It was also incredibly dark and despite the fact that she thought she had left her torch and necessary items for the night readily to hand, she found herself groping her way around awkwardly, as was Henriette, judging from the stumbling and 'oh mon dieu' coming from her near neighbour. Her planning needed some readjustment, she realised. She should have her torch with her at supper and needed to be already clothed in long johns and extra jumper before the evening meal. Niceties such as teeth cleaning would have to go by the board. At last, feeling very well padded, she crawled into her sleeping bag. 'Are you OK Henriette?' she called softly to her companion.

'I am managing,' came the muffled response, and Maggie assumed her young friend was now well tucked into her bag, probably with as much of it as possible pulled well over her head.

And Maggie suddenly realised that she was totally exhausted. It had indeed been a long day with so many new faces and experiences. Had she really been in Alice Springs only that morning? Visions of the preparation of bags, waiting in the cold morning air, the loading of a vehicle with bodies and luggage, weariness, redness and dust, dust and redness, the smell of damp canvas, conversation, laughter, awe, eating and drinking and a sense of restriction in too many garments entered her thoughts, jostling with each other and competing for attention. 'My restless mind,' thought Maggie. 'Sleep as usual will elude me, and I crave it so desperately.' But sleep came almost instantly. And she must have slept soundly for two or three hours, before waking with the sudden realisation, that despite all she was wearing, she was in fact cold. She felt for her anorak on the ground beside her and managed with difficulty to extricate herself sufficiently from her sleeping bag in order to put it on. Sleep then was more spasmodic, probably, as is frequently the case, longer than she imagined it to have been when she woke the next morning, as the night gave way to the first signs of dawn, reasonably warm in a fashion, but also rather damp.

A shower – the water was hot to Maggie's grateful surprise – ensured that the physical discomforts of the night were quickly forgotten and the group began to assemble for a substantial breakfast. Jo and Beck, assisted by Mike and Brad were engaged in fire lighting and Dee was sorting out beakers and prepared to boil up the water. Maggie, together with Jim, was unravelling sausages and cutting up copious amounts of bread. Henriette had not yet reappeared from the shower shack, the Germans were nowhere to be seen and Luke – the only one, Maggie reflected, who had contributed nothing to the previous night's conversation, hung about awkwardly at the fringe of the rough shelter which acted as their store. Maggie who enrolled him to be chief chopper up of chunks of bread rescued him, but even then, he was barely able to utter any comment or to raise his head from his task. Brad had earlier explained that today's highlight was to be the exploration of Uluru after a morning hike into the surrounding area. Later, they would find a spot for a barbecue before driving back to Uluru for the sunset.

And thus the scene was set. The required props were all in place ready for the plot to unfold. How strange the actors could be so unaware.

Chapter 8

In contrast to some planned early starts, departure to the canyon, which they were to explore on foot, was at a highly civilised time, appreciated by them all, as even the veteran campers had found the previous day to be sufficiently long and tiring. Brad suggested they regularly changed places in the 4WD, ostensibly to give every one a chance to sit in the front seats that gave a clear and uninterrupted view; but in reality, as Maggie suspected, to give them the opportunity to get to know each other and to ensure that the solo travellers were not always on their own. So Maggie found herself beside Henriette, and Mike left his wife to occupy the seat next to Jim, perhaps expecting that either Beck or Jo would join her, but the two friends seated themselves together, as did Werner and Eric. That left Luke with the option of joining Dee, but he passed her seat with lowered head to position himself at the rear. Dee smilingly shrugged her shoulders to Maggie, who happened to be glancing in her direction at the time.

On the short drive to the start of the morning's hike, Brad gave a brief outline of Australia's history touching on the Aboriginals, the penal settlements and the invasion of the white man. It was just as he was describing the use of camels by early explorers that the first viewing of a wild herd was seen. Maggie had not expected camels, for in her mind, Australia was synonymous with koalas and kangaroos. Brad pulled up for a camera session and use was made of the unscheduled stop to gather firewood for the next campfire. Jo and Beck made a hearty contribution to the efforts of the group, but Maggie and Henriette were more tentative, worried as to what might be lurking in piles of dead wood and broken branches. Mike was more interested in his photography, but after only a short while a sizeable amount of firewood was collected. Brad loaded the wood on to the roof rack of the 4WD, tossing quite large branches on to the growing pile and tying all down firmly with a strong cord with movements that were both supple and effortless. With his bronzed skin, casually dressed in long, khaki shorts, navy T-shirt and sporting a cowboy hat, he was indeed a most attractive man and Maggie was interested to note that her own observations were clearly echoed by those of Henriette, whose eyes rested on the rippling arms, shiny with sweat, with obvious admiration. So Maggie was not surprised later, as they set off scrambling first over rough stones and then following a small path through a rocky terrain punctuated by scrub, to find Henriette very much at the front of the group, keeping up well with their guide.

It was now quite hot and the party found themselves shedding some of the warm clothing they had been wearing earlier, which made all their packs somewhat heavier and more cumbersome. However, the ascent was quite easy, despite rather loose stones that were readily dislodged and after a couple of hours of relatively undemanding climb, they found themselves at a point that, they were assured, would give an amazing view of the gorge below. To enjoy this view, informed Brad, it was of course necessary to approach right to the edge of the canyon. Here the group paused to mop brows and drink from their water bottles. Rucksacks and other belongings were offloaded on to the rocks and all eyes followed their leader as he strode ahead confidently, turning to encourage the others and extending a hand to Henriette, who approached cautiously hanging on to his arm as she advanced nervously to the edge of the gorge. She lay on her front beside Brad, manoeuvring forward slowly until she reached the edge. Her gasps of amazement and admiration emboldened the rest of them and they were soon all struck by the awe that such a sight inspired. For far below them in the narrow chasm edged by gigantic rocky cliffs was a verdant lush and green landscape with water and palm trees. It was an oasis, a paradise seemingly promising abundance, in contrast to the ascent, which had emphasised harshness and scarcity. It was so beautiful as to be almost threatening and Maggie, crouching beside Jim, found herself shuddering involuntarily. Jim put an arm round her shoulder.

The train is rattling through the tunnel. Now she is standing close beside him. She is keeping her balance by gripping the pole with her left hand. He is half behind her. His jacket is brushing against her new coat. He is grabbing at the strap. Now come the advertisements flashing by speedily, still speedily, less speedily and now more slowly. But they are still stopping too abruptly at the station. She is lurching forward. He is unsteady on his feet too. But he is more prepared than she. He is already gripping the strap more firmly. He is ready for her. His left hand is now seizing the pole, just above hers. His right arm is dropping to her shoulder. Her whole being is tingling. She is trying to pretend she is not noticing. But she is noticing and she knows he is too. They both half turn, smiling. They are feeling so conscious of this first touching. They are both sixteen. And this is a beginning.

Brad led his party to a spot suitable for their picnic and they relaxed in the sunshine to enjoy lunch. Everyone spread out to find a comfortable location and Maggie found herself sharing a rock that served conveniently as a backrest with Jim.

Until their arrival at the gorge, Maggie had not been overly observant of her companion. Neither Jim nor Maggie had played a significant role in the previous night's conversations, although both had been interested listeners, contributing readily and appropriately to the topics under discussion without offering much in the way of personal information. Maggie had been very surprised by her acute awareness of Jim's physical presence at the gorge when his protective arm had given her the confidence to look down upon the view. It must be, she thought, that her senses were aroused and heightened by the grandeur of the surrounding landscape, or that the perpendicular drop to the water below gave a sense of dizziness and disorientation to the viewer. There could be no other reason. Nevertheless, she cast a decidedly more inquisitive and interested glance at the man now beside her.

Jim leant back upon the rock, munching his roll, with his face slightly uplifted to enjoy the warmth of the midday sun. He was possibly of similar age, fair skinned with a rather thin face and severely receding, almost sandy hair somewhat reminiscent in style of a medieval monk. Maggie thought it to be a kindly and approachable face, a little wrinkled and now beginning to show signs of the effect of the sun. His long legs were drawn up, supported by his rucksack, his feet encased in sturdy sandals sticking up at right angles to the stony ground. He turned to smile at Maggie.

'Not bad this,' he commented, indicating his roll. 'How are you doing? I must say I have enormously enjoyed this morning's expedition. It's been a great walk to a spectacular spot. If this is a taste of what is to come, it will more than meet all expectations.'

So they chatted together about the trip so far and shared some additional background information. He learnt that the slim, tanned, dark haired woman beside him, whom he reckoned to be in her early fifties, was travelling on her own, having left a husband and family in England. He was not surprised to learn she was formerly a teacher, specialising in PE, her trim figure witness to her lifelong involvement with sport. She, on the other hand, discovered that Jim, long since divorced, without a family and now living in London, started, then abandoned medical studies, and later spent many years in the States. He was now retired from an administrative post in the NHS and indulging his desire to travel.

There were signs that the lunch break was coming to an end and soon the group found themselves on the downward gravel path, ready for the next and highly significant item on the agenda, their first sighting of that awesome red rock, for Maggie especially, the focus of her travels. They drove for about an hour, over the now familiar terrain, stopping only once for Mike to take a photo of some termites' mounds.

'They are just huge!' he commented.

'Everything here is larger than life,' said Jo. 'Just you wait till you see the rock.'

As they approached Uluru, the group fell silent. Were some of them now perhaps anticipating a sense of possible anticlimax, fearful lest the reality of the experience would not match their expectations? However, Maggie, now seated beside Jim, did not suffer such anxiety, remaining confidently certain that this was to be especially meaningful in some way that she couldn't yet fully grasp. Neither did Beck and Jo share these qualms, for they had already seen the gigantic rock in a huge variety of its tantalising guises. 'It's never the same,' they had so frequently reiterated.

And then, there it was, rising stupendously, gigantically, from an immense stretch of nothingness. And it wasn't only its size, its arresting colour or its immediately recognisable shape. It was its representation of the spiritual, the magical. It was a visible portrayal of concepts way beyond understanding. The unfathomable. A solid, certain connection with antiquity. Maggie was both awestruck and at peace. If nothing else came of the trip, this in itself was sufficient. Simply to feast her eyes on this sublime rock. She felt, as one can so easily in such circumstances, that sense of well-being and contentment, that elusive and rare accompaniment to a once in a lifetime experience. And through her whole being there throbbed a muttered half forgotten rhythm, a long lost incantation, as though it were an ancient tribal murmuring growing, re-echoing, a clamouring from the deep centre of the universe, this deafening, resolute affirmation that all should be well.

She jumped as she heard Brad's voice. 'So there you have it. Now you see it! We'll go closer, round the rock in the 4WD and then I'll drop you off for a couple of hours or so to savour the place. Your options are to walk around it – some five and a half miles or so – or, in theory, to climb up it. But of course, as I said yesterday, to the Aboriginals it's a sacred rock and to them, climbing it is offensive. I'll be happy to lead a group round, or alternatively please feel free to make your own way if you wish.

Luke hurried away quickly from the 4WD, but the others descended in more leisurely fashion, still mesmerised by the first sighting. Maggie felt the need to explore on her own, so after indicating her intentions to Brad, made her own purposeful way along the well-trodden path to the base of the rock. Here she paused to look upwards, marvelling at its height as she stood in solitary contemplation of its many rugged features, the nooks and crannies that had been less apparent in the guidebook picture. Seeing the others – and quite a few of the party chose to join Brad – set off in an anticlockwise direction, she elected to go the opposite way. It was not that she felt particularly antisocial, but rather that she wanted to savour this particular experience on her own.

Various boards along the way gave details and illustrations of the Anangu culture and at first Maggie noted the information as she made her way round. However, she soon ceased to read the notices, wishing simply to revel in the majesty of the monolith and to delight in her solitary observation at close quarters. It was near vertical with evident signs of erosion and marked and pitted by grooves and indentations, with clear evidence of the effect of running water descending in errant fashion to the base. Some weak trickles were still visible, creating patterns and shapes that the imagination could form into strange creatures and faces. Some of the fissures were large enough to be described as caves and after a while she sat down for a brief pause beside the entrance to one of the smaller openings. It was very quiet with no other visitors visible. Maggie sat on the bare earth with her arms wrapped around her knees, and fixed her gaze once more on the base of the rock, allowing her eyes to move slowly upwards then downwards, almost as if she were searching for a particular pattern or formation. Then she scrutinised the monument once more, in like manner, and her final gaze fell this time on to the hard baked, sandy earth where her heels were resting. To the left, nearer looser earth and scrubby vegetation, were some huge ants purposefully engrossed in their never-ending task. Nothing was allowed to come in the way of the long line, pebbles, larger stones, small pieces of bark and larger twigs; all were surmounted with unswerving, rigorous determination. Some walked over others in their resolution, unwavering and undeterred. She leant forward to observe more closely with the warm sun on her back.

They are watching mesmerised and with childish fascination. They are asking so many questions. The adults are amazed too. If these were the equivalent of people, then each piece of leaf would equate to ... well what would it equate to? He is struggling to find some comparisons. Now he's suggesting big, concrete paving stones like the ones he is using for the path at home. But they are making other suggestions. Perhaps a car. Perhaps a train. Can you lift a car? Can you lift a train? He doesn't think he can. But the ants can! The adults don't want him to poke one with a stick and neither does she. He's going to spoil it all. She is making to grab his stick and he is running off.

Thus Maggie's thoughts moved to her family, so far removed from her in time and space. But her thoughts were not with Richard, nor Tom nor Kate, well perhaps only fleetingly. No, the very dear face of her beloved Tina came to mind as though emerging from a recess in the rough sandstone before her. And Maggie smiled softly in her contemplation. Here she felt totally at peace with thoughts of her little daughter, whilst remaining fully aware that even thirty-four years could not wipe out the vision of that dark and dismal late afternoon in February. Those moments would be graven forever in her consciousness as clearly and everlastingly as the markings and carvings now before her eyes. She knew that she would forever hear the hideous squealing of brakes and her own distant wailing cries, as though belonging to someone other than herself, far away in the gloom and drizzle. She would forever be conscious of the knowledge that in the fraction of a second an event of great magnitude, of unspeakable horror and terror, a single split instant when lives are changed forever can actually be played in front of one's eyes before the inevitability of the actual event. And all this in unbearable, slow motion. It is that moment in dreams when action is imperative, movement vital, and legs are rooted to the spot.

In any case, there was no way in which Maggie could have reacted differently to avoid the nightmare of the inevitable. The car would hit the buggy. It would happen. No one, nothing could possibly intervene.

So Maggie contemplated her cave, entertaining thoughts of her little daughter, able to smile at the memories of the baby face. She saw through the blood to the dimpled cheeks of an infant, felt the soft malleable flesh and marvelled again upon the pursed, little mouth angling haphazardly, randomly for the breast. She heard too other sounds, sounds of contentment, the chuckles, burps and snuffling breathing of a sleeping child.

The Australian sun with strong dependable rays, warmed Maggie's now upturned face and stirring soul.

There was a rustling movement beside her. She looked up to see Jim.

Aware that they had both chosen individual, rather than group exploration of Uluru, Jim was a little hesitant to invade Maggie's privacy. Yet it would seem somewhat unfriendly to pass her without any comment.

'As you see, I took the other route too,' he said. 'I was unaware you were ahead of me as I didn't see you set off. Now I've caught you up.'

He paused and they both contemplated the cave ahead. He turned to smile at Maggie then with a slight nod of his head, made as to move on. But Maggie returned his smile indicating the patch of ground beside her. They then sat together in companionable silence, turning after a short interval at precisely the same moment to look at each other. Maggie, comfortably relaxed, half turned again and stretched her long legs. Once more they sat without speaking.

Jim sensed that Maggie was far away in her own thoughts. He was happy to do the same.

'You look miles away,' he commented eventually. 'You seem at one with this rock.'

Thinking back in the years yet to come, Maggie was to consider this moment in their developing friendship as one of deepest significance. However, at the time, she simply responded dreamily and almost vaguely, 'I was thinking of my beautiful baby. She was two months old when she died.'

There was again a silence between them. Jim tried to focus on what he had just heard. When Maggie had spoken earlier of her family as they shared their lunchtime picnic spot, she had referred to her two adult children and there had been no mention of another child. He had the sensitivity to realise he was privy to some very personal information.

He turned again to face Maggie, who appeared in no way distressed. In fact, her stance seemed totally to have changed. After the stretching of her legs, her back had straightened and she now sat upright, her hands behind her resting on the ground and legs fully extended. Her head was slightly tilted backwards and it was as though her face shone.

'I'm so very sorry,' he said quietly,' and his hand moved gently to cover hers.

And Maggie felt uplifted and at ease in the sharing of her thoughts with her new friend, conscious now of the hand upon hers; Jim increased the pressure briefly then gently withdrew. He turned to face her. 'Shall we continue round together?' he asked quietly, and they both knew that she would agree.

He too understood the pain of sudden inexplicable bereavement and knew that one day he would share his own experience with Maggie.

However, this was neither the time nor place for further confidences. He raised himself up and stretched out a hand, helping her to her feet. They both brushed the dust from their clothes, bent to retrieve their backpacks and continued round the perimeter route.

Back at the 4WD, the party gradually reassembled to enjoy further cold drinks that Brad produced from a cool box and to recount their various impressions of the rock. No one seemed to have done the somewhat perilous climb to the top, although Jo and Beck, mistakenly as it turned out, thought they had observed Luke descending the last steep gradient with great difficulty.

'Wasn't me, 'he said, raising his head as he spoke and managing to eye members of the group. 'I was ahead of the rest of you and went part way round again. There was this cave…' and here he paused, aware as were the others that he had hardly been heard to speak at all so far on the trip. He even looked almost animated as though he was becoming alive, and his pale skin had begun to freckle in the sun. This has been a positive experience for our Luke too, mused Maggie, in buoyant and rejuvenated mood, as they climbed back into their vehicle.

This time, they did not travel very far, just far enough to reach a pre-planned barbecue spot for a fairly speedy supper before returning to Uluru to watch the sunset. Brad was meticulous in his organisation, effectively ensuring that all members of his group played a part in the preparation and clearing away of the meal. Maggie, Henriette and Werner found themselves in charge of the burgers with an opportunity to exchange their experiences of the day. Henriette was bubbly with excitement and Werner, noted by

Maggie, seemed to be paying rapt attention to all the details the young French girl furnished about the walk round the base of the rock, for she had evidently benefited from Brad's repertoire of stories and anecdotes as they circled the monolith. As the two women finally took their paper plates to join the others, Maggie hinted to her young companion that perhaps she now had another admirer in the form of Werner. Henriette clearly found this suggestion to be hugely amusing and totally inappropriate.

'But, Maggie, I think it is not me, not me at all! Soon as those two men are here, I see at once! No, Werner is not liking me at all as girlfriend.'

Maggie looked over to where the two Germans were sitting next to each other in the circle. No, she had not been aware of the nature of their relationship, but in any case their sexual inclinations, in her view, could be of little significance to anyone else. Nevertheless, she found herself observing them more closely.

As usual, Werner was the livelier of the two, recounting a meeting with a fellow German as they had toured the rock, with Eric giving his usual nods of assent or occasionally prompting his friend. Watching Eric, and his supportive concern for the story his friend was telling, the glances he threw to his companion and his clear approbation of the account, Maggie suddenly recalled Stuart, one of Tom's former school friends. Stuart never disguised his obvious adoration of her son and Maggie, for some reason she was never fully able to justify, had strongly disapproved of Stuart, thinking him, in some undefined way, unsuitable company. She had therefore tried to discourage the friendship, which naturally inspired Tom, wayward in his teenage years, to flaunt it and further develop it. In the end, the friendship had died a death with the advent of a series of equally unsuitable girlfriends, and, more particularly, Maggie's decreasing preoccupation with the question of her son's liaisons.

Maggie concentrated on the plate in front of her as she made her way to the space beside Jim which he had reserved for her, whilst continuing to think about Tom. She realised with a jump that Jim was talking to her.

'You OK?' he queried kindly, with concern. He was highly conscious of the fact that Maggie had earlier made him party to some precious and personal information that she was not in the habit of sharing generally. She sensed what he was thinking. 'I'm fine,' she answered, anxious to reassure him. 'I seem to have another member of my family on my mind. Sometimes I worry about Tom, quite needlessly I'm sure. May be I'm beginning to feel a little guilty about the fact that until that moment at Uluru I've hardly thought about the family at all. I suppose I have an excuse, out here, where communication anyway is something of a non-starter.'

They sat together, quietly. Jim, reassured, noticed that Maggie had been watching the German boys. 'Well,' he said, as he glanced over in their direction, 'they are a well-matched couple in my view.'

So he had noticed too. Perhaps everyone else had as well.

Their conversation ceased at that moment, as one of those periodic lulls came over the group. Brad took the opportunity to goad them into action. They needed now to return the short distance to Uluru in order not to miss the spectacular sunset and witness the dramatic, rapidly changing play of light on the red rock. He apologised for the fact that they would not have the permitted viewing points to themselves, but explained that, with a little ingenuity, they could isolate themselves sufficiently to feel that the experience was unique.

And it was. As Brad had earlier indicated, they were not alone at the chosen viewpoint. There were indeed a number of vehicles of various types, including a couple of coaches, but the area was quite extensive, and they were able easily to spread themselves out, with their party keeping fairly much together towards the extreme left-hand side of the clearing. Other groups were making something of a party of the occasion and the coach parties had even set up a couple of tables on which wine bottles and glasses could be seen. At this point Mike indicated that he would like a group photo, setting his camera up on the convenient stump of a nearby tree, ready to sprint back to join Dee. 'Move up, move up!' he called, 'I can't get you all in!' So they dutifully squashed together, Eric with his arm around Werner, Jo in-between Beck and Dee, hugging the three of them closer together and Maggie and Jim at the extreme left, Jim's arm around Maggie's shoulder, pulling her into the photo. Mike's race back from the tree stump caused some amusement, as he made a dramatic recovery from a near mishap in the form of a stubbed toe in his anxiety to reach Dee, but they were all in place ready for the flash after which the happy group dispersed to take up their positions. A two-strand wire fence marked the extent of the viewpoint, which Mike chose not to observe, ducking under, with Dee in pursuit, ready to take up a strategic location for further photography.

So Maggie and Jim, at the far extremity of the site, waited together to view the magnificent and unforgettable descent of the sun. It was an amazing and awesome show, the climax to a day engraved forever in the mind of each and every spectator.

No words were adequate after such a display, so Maggie and Jim stood silently and peacefully together in perfect communion.

It was some while before either of them moved and when they finally turned to face each other, it was no surprise to either of them when Jim took Maggie into his arms.

This first kiss, maybe, was perhaps initially intended as one of tenderness and compassion. But the magic of the moment and the rejuvenating, energising experiences of the day drew them ever closer together and the embrace lingered far longer and more passionately than either of them could ever possibly have anticipated.

Chapter 9

Of course, Richard had been thinking of Maggie, more so recently as the weeks had begun to pass. In fact, as chance would have it, he happened to have her particularly in mind at the very moment at which his wife found herself in front of her cave at Uluru. For Maggie, as those momentous past events emerged from the depths of a deep crevice of course-grained sandstone and somehow took new form in her strangely stirred and reinvigorated consciousness, it was mid afternoon. For her husband, it was the start of a new summer's day.

Richard hadn't heard from Maggie for some time, but was not unduly worried. After the first of the emails, which arrived soon after she landed in Sydney, there had been somewhat of an interlude before a couple more emails arrived, followed by a brief phone call. And anyway, he knew that Maggie was currently in the outback where her mobile would be of no use. He had also been very much occupied with his research, spending considerable time in his office at home and some pleasant evenings with a beer in the garden. But now, he needed to know where the overnight case was normally kept. Was it tucked away in the large wardrobe that was in Kate's former bedroom or was it to be found in the garage or the loft, for it was his wife who normally occupied herself with such mundane matters. She would have located it instantly and the clean shirts and underclothes he now required would already be folded on the bed.

He needed the case because he planned to visit a former colleague, now based in London, in order to have further informal discussions relating to the Liverpool project. He was now well immersed in his gypsy culture and literature, but the scheme was very much in its infancy, and his initial brief of contributing to the integration of Roma issues into a broadly based, as yet largely to be devised modular humanities programme needed some sort of focus. Indeed, the whole emphasis seemed to be shifting, as one or two of those who had initially expressed interest in taking part had now, for various reasons, decided to withdraw. Richard felt, as a result of researching the specialist areas of the remaining participants, that there would be a shift of content that would significantly affect the nature of his own contribution. It seemed possible that his area might relate to a narrower field than he had originally anticipated restricting him possibly to the nineteenth century. This in itself was no problem as Victorian society's hypocritical attitude toward gypsies, its prejudices and romanticism could be abundantly illustrated in literature. What was less clear was the anticipated student profile. Herein lay one of the problems that had dogged Richard during the course of his working life, for he was an academic in a modern world of widening student participation. It was indeed, he felt, a great pain, and one that had to be forever concealed, this attempted sharing of his expertise with an audience he sometimes felt to be, at best, singularly unappreciative and, at worst, hopelessly inadequate and ill prepared. However, currently involved only in his preparation and aware of an interesting sounding exhibition of nomadic lifestyles in London, the project was viewed thus as a further incentive to visit the capital.

Since the loft would require a bit of an effort, Richard first tried Kate's wardrobe. He hadn't realised quite how many of her personal belongings were still stored in her parental home. There seemed to be a considerable collection of old shoes and bags, some in almost new condition and Richard reasoned that they must have been sorted for a charity shop and then possibly forgotten. There were also a number of old shoeboxes that appeared to be full of family photographs with a particularly battered one tied up with string, indicating Maggie's hand. However, Maggie had evidently been over ambitious in her packing, with the result that the box didn't quite stay shut, spilling out some of its contents as he dragged it forward to see if his case was lurking behind. He glanced at the photos as he tried to stuff them back. One that landed face up on the carpet was of Maggie as a student and he scrutinised it more closely. It suddenly occurred to him that this was one of the earliest photos he had of his wife, taken possibly in the Lake District as she posed by a bridge. There was very little from their school days apart from a few formal groups, sports teams and the inevitable annual whole school photograph. Maggie looked so very young and Richard smiled to himself. They had weathered quite a lot in their years together, he reflected, certainly with more good times than bad. He had fallen for the pretty fifth former on a school theatre trip to the Old Vic and had been determinedly unswerving in his subsequent pursuit, unaware that she had already admired him for some length of time. Another photo caught his eye, Kate as a baby, probably. But wait. Of course, it was not Kate. He scanned it urgently as his heart missed a beat. Some moments in time are carved as though on rock; the wind and the rain may play their part, the sun may daily run its course, but such moments can never be eradicated.

The father is preparing his camera. They are both laughing. The little eyes are closing again. This is always happening when they try to take a photo. The mother is tickling the soft, arched, dimpled foot. Now come the jerk and the shudder. The eyes are flickering. Now the eyes are opening. Quick, quick! Now she's yawning. They are laughing again. Quick, quick! He isn't quick enough. Too late! Now she is yawning once more. Now the hiccups are coming. Her hand is wrapped around the mother's finger. She is holding it tightly. The mother is moving the finger up and down so gently. The mother is tickling so softly, so softly.

The eyes are closing. They are both laughing for it always seems to be so. He is pressing the button. But of course, he is too late again! He's putting the camera back.

Richard's gaze rested on the half-closed eyes of the small form well cocooned in its shawl. It was a black and white photo so the half-shut eyes looked dark, but Richard was struggling to recall their exact colour. Didn't babies always have blue eyes, he wondered? He was no longer sure. He'd always thought Kate's eyes were similar and hers now were certainly dark brown, whereas Tom's had more of a greyish hue, and were initially, he thought, a mid blue. He carefully studied the photo with its furled corners, first sitting back on his heels between the bed and the wardrobe in Kate's room and then rising slowly to take the picture downstairs into the kitchen. Here he drew up a chair and pushing the photo gently to one side, placed his elbows on the table, clasped his hands together and rested his chin on his knuckles.

It was all such a long time ago. How long ago? It must have been a couple of months after Christmas, for she could easily have been a Christmas Day baby. But she wasn't. She was an early present. And, of course, everything had been so very different. Christmas Day, he remembered, had been unusually bright and sunny and the new buggy and new baby had taken their first airing with the new parents.

But on that most hateful, most tragic of all days, it had been dank and drizzly. It was dark early and some of the streetlights were already lit. And to think she had only gone out for some milk! They hadn't even needed milk, for there was some still left in a bottle in the fridge – traitorous and hateful milk, curdling cruelly when stirred next night into the endless cups of tea which were so despairingly rejected. Tea. He remembered the tea. Endless cups of tea. The tears. Endless, despairing tears. And then the flowers.

'Why do they all keep sending flowers?' asked an uncomprehending Maggie in a drugged stupor.

'It's to show that they care,' responded her equally uncomprehending mother, who had come straight away to be with her daughter.

Her daughter stared, then turned away and went straight back to her room.

Then there were more flowers and an absurdly tiny coffin.

And Richard, who had not cried at the time, so many years ago, found tears in his eyes. They coursed down his cheeks and a grown man sat at his kitchen table and sobbed.

And then he made a cup of tea and after he had drunk it, went again to Kate's old bedroom and collected the particularly battered box from which the photos had escaped and lived again the early years of family life. There were a surprising number of pictures of Tina considering her very short life, some where she even had her eyes fully open. How sad to admit to himself that he could hardly really remember their first child. What would have become of her?

Tom was born a year later and his progress was well documented with photographs. Maggie had been an anxious mother, relaxing only when Kate was born some couple of years later and she found herself too busy with two toddlers to worry about every possible eventuality. And now, with the aid of all his visual cues, Richard found himself recalling family events that had long lain deeply buried in his subconsciousness. There were, in addition and somewhat to his surprise, many faces and events of which he had absolutely no recollection whatsoever. He remembered those early years with his young family as being demanding in establishing his career. There had been many evening meetings, many trips away. But that was how it was then.

He gathered up all the photos, tied the string more securely round the old box and stuffed it back into the rear of the wardrobe.

Then he wandered into the garden, thoughts of packing and his London trip far from his mind. He had been very struck by the furled, well-handled appearance of the photos of

Tina. His survival strategy had been to put the unbearable from his mind. He could hardly remember whether he had ever looked through the box of family memorabilia, whilst it was abundantly clear that someone else had frequently done so.

What he did recall, however, with great clarity, was being at work on that fateful day when the phone had rung.

The phone rang. He was suddenly aware that it had probably been ringing for some time. He gathered himself together, and went back indoors. It took him some time to realise that it was Roger Carter speaking and that the purpose of the call was to finalise details for meeting in London.

'Are you OK?' queried Roger, feeling that his old friend seemed somewhat distant and vague. Richard was able respond adequately to his friend's evident concern and the necessary arrangements were made.

Later in the afternoon, Richard felt able to return to the task in hand and immersed himself once again in the world in which he felt secure – that of his books and papers. Later, with a sandwich supper balanced on his knees, it occurred to him that he might as well see something of Kate and Martin whilst in London and that his daughter and partner would most probably suggest he stayed with them overnight rather than put up at a hotel. It was Martin who answered his call.

'Sure,' responded Martin. 'But Kate's not here at the moment. She's just gone off to Greece with a friend.'

Richard suddenly remembered his last conversation with his daughter. 'Of course, I'd forgotten. Yes, she did say something about a holiday last time we spoke. Well, if it's OK with you I'd still quite like to come down on the Wednesday and stay overnight to give me the opportunity of seeing a highly recommended exhibition on the following day. Perhaps you'll let me take you out for a curry or whatever on the Wednesday night.'

Thus what was later to be recalled as a memorable summer day – a winter day for Maggie – came to a close, as days inevitably do. Indeed, the sun had long set for Maggie as

Richard switched off his bedside light. Unusually though, sleep eluded him as thoughts of his family jostled his mind, this time focusing on Kate. Slightly surprising, pondered the father that she should be holidaying with Sarah. Perhaps Martin couldn't get time off. Where was it Martin said she had gone? It must have been a sudden decision anyway, thought Richard, since as far as he could remember no future holiday plans had been mentioned by either of them at the time of the party in the garden. So the father, who had woken that morning thinking especially of his absent wife, who had then spent much of the day stirred by memories of his little daughter, and who now on the verge of sleep was occupied by thoughts of his living daughter, finally and a little fitfully found sleep.

But sleep still eluded Martin. He was, of course, also thinking of Kate, who had sent him a brief text earlier that evening confirming her safe arrival. He was still at somewhat of a loss to understand her sudden decision to have a couple of weeks away with Sarah and did, in fact, feel rather put out by this arrangement, although he had pretended not to mind at the time. Additionally, he had sensed a certain reticence on Kate's part before she set off, as though she too was not totally convinced by her planned course of action. Martin lay awake for some while, but by the next morning, most uncharacteristically, had already decided on his own immediately to be implemented course of action that inevitably surprised just about everyone in time to come.

Kate lay awake too, thinking naturally of Martin. But she had had a long and eventful day which had only just come to an end, following a night of eating, drinking and dancing in the company of some of her friend's work colleagues. So yes, she thought of her boyfriend, but fell asleep much sooner than she had expected.

However, her brother Tom was not yet asleep, for he was still very much occupied by the girl in his arms as she lay beneath him, their bodies moving as one.

Nor was his mother at that very moment asleep. For Maggie it was then the dawn of a new day. Yesterday, that long and amazing day of so many surprising awakenings, had been the longest day of all. Unsurprisingly, she was at that same moment very far from thinking of any of them at all - but yesterday, of course, it was her dear Tina who had particularly occupied her thoughts.

And Tina was thinking of no one, for she had been dead for thirty-four years.

Thus, delicately suspended, swayed a tangled spider's web of interconnected threads, the intricate, purposeful patterning disturbed by the continuing, ongoing struggles of a small defenceless insect. Nature will favour the spider. But what if the web should be disturbed?

Chapter 10

Maggie lay in Jim's arms.

When they first arrived back at the camp that night, there had been the usual gathering around the fire for drinks and reminiscences of the day's activities. Maggie and Jim sat close together sharing one of the spare blankets around their two shoulders for extra warmth as did Mike and Dee. At first, as if by common consent, there was little conversation. The thick, velvety darkness of the sky was backdrop to the myriad of stars, a star bright night, and a magical night. Brad followed the star struck eyes of his group and in a softly spoken voice pointed out some constellations to those now drawn together around their fire, having already shared so much since they first met. Maggie's eyes gazed ever heavenwards, transfixed, as Brad spoke of cosmology and the galactic system whilst the Milky Way stretched away, above and beyond. The very age of the stars seemed to defy human comprehension, mused Maggie as she attempted to register the scale of a number such as one hundred thousand millions.

There was movement around the fire as more wood was added. Then came sudden and intermittent flares as new branches caught alight, briefly illuminating the faces in the circle. It seemed as though every one was glowingly alive, senses heightened by fire and firmament. Brad was loathe to break the spell, but when it appeared that Dee was about to retreat to her tent, needed to remind them of plans for the following day. He explained that the morning would be for their own individual exploration, since there were plenty of short walks well indicated from the campsite. In the afternoon, after a short drive, he planned a walk involving modest scrambling over stony ground adjacent to a dried-up creek. He went on to suggest that a fitting conclusion to the present day might be to bring their sleeping bags around the campfire which could be further stoked up. There was in any case, he reasoned, very little difference in temperature within or without a tent, and there was certain magic in sleeping beneath the stars. Every one was very readily persuaded, even Dee when cajoled by Mike, so eventually eleven relative strangers settled down together, a tiny huddle of humanity in the back of beyond.

They are begging, pestering incessantly, never-endingly, to be allowed to sleep outside in the garden. It is so warm this evening. They are in their play tent. How they are enjoying it, this tent of theirs! There is hardly any squabbling at all this day. They are even sharing the cake out amicably and fairly. Amazing what a new toy will do before the novelty wears off! 'Please, please,' they are clamouring. But she is not feeling too certain about this. If he would stay too, it might be possible. But he isn't really wanting to. And in all honesty, neither is she. But she is trying to persuade him, as they are trying, like them, only so much more subtly. He is giving in, she is realising. They are realising too. How much excitement is there now! They are racing indoors for pyjamas. He is not so keen, but she is pretending not to notice. Anyway, they will be giving up before midnight, but no one knows that yet. For the moment, it is pure magic.

By midnight, some had abandoned the fire for their tents, despite Brad's comments about the relative warmth or otherwise. Werner and Eric stumbled away in the dark, as did Dee, followed a little later by Mike. Henriette had by now realised that whilst Brad was in charge of his group, she was to be shown no overt favours, although she secretly nurtured to herself many of his gestures and comments. These she thought she would take to her single bed – if her sleeping bag could be so described – to dwell upon and cultivate in privacy. Being a young, attractive and sensible girl, she was not dismayed by his outward lack of response to her discreet advances: In fact, she respected him all the more for this in view of his position as their leader. She knew there were many hidden ways of paving the road ahead. The trip would in due course come to an end and she was in no especial hurry. Therefore she decided she would curl up in her tent – although a comfy bed and a magazine would be a welcome bonus – and nurse her own secret thoughts, which, thus entertained, could be correctly routed along the desired channels.

From time to time, Brad replenished the fire, and Maggie and Jim continued to lie side by side, half-awake and half-asleep, for the events of the day had been almost more than they could comprehend. Maggie's eyes flickered as she drifted into sleep. In her dreams a host of heavenly, fleeting, disjointed images spun around her and she felt light-headed, empowered, and favoured with unique and exceptional experiences. It was hot. She found herself at the entrance to a tomb and cautiously descended the decaying, damp, uneven steps. Bending low she entered the narrow tunnel, blocked by slabs of solid stone. She held out a hand and the wall dissolved before her, to reveal a world of dazzling, golden artefacts. 'What can you see?' called a voice from the mouth of the tomb. 'Wonderful things, wonderful things!' But now she was walking along a dusty track, looking downwards, scuffing the dirt as she trod. Her foot disturbed a gigantic ant's nest and unleashed a brave new world of swarming, agitated creatures, whose relentless march was already pre-ordained. There was a huge box. She felt that she knew this box and had seen it before. She opened it and from it there sprung all manner of things. What things were these? She struggled to recall. Of course, she could remember now. Many had flown, but wasn't there one left? Wasn't it hope that was left? It had to be hope. Maggie stirred and was aware of Jim moving beside her. 'Shall we go in now?' he asked.

That was how Maggie found herself in Jim's tent, lying in his arms.

Suddenly, they both felt very much awake. Together they grovelled in the thick blackness to unzip sleeping bags and to pull a further mound of blankets over the two of them. They helped each other to extract themselves from a variety of extraneous clothing, able in their newly shared intimacy to acknowledge and enjoy the inevitable element of absurdity in the act that followed.

Then they lay together like young lovers, sleeping the deep, fulfilling sleep of blissful contentment to wake together the next morning at much the same moment just as darkness was fading. Jim, turned, smiled and pulled Maggie ever closer to him. She responded by snuggling further into the crook of his arm and with upturned face, caressed and traced the lines of his brow with her left hand. His body rolled over on to hers as their lips met again and they shared once more that most intimate of acts. They turned to their sides each of them satisfied and content as they lay facing each other. Both were absurdly happy. Both were astonished at what had taken place between them, that it had been so utterly pleasurable and delightful, that they had been such willing partners, that what had happened had occurred so spontaneously. They were both practised lovers, of course, and experience in all things brings certain advantages. But sex has generally come to be seen as the preserve of the young. And neither Maggie nor Jim was young.

Gradually, as the sun struggled to make a rather weak first appearance, as though its energies had been fully spent on yesterday's spectacular performance, the campers emerged from their tents and made their various ways to the shower shack and to breakfast. Maggie and Jim felt no compulsion to pretend that they were now anything other than a couple, presuming that it would inevitably become apparent that they had not spent the night in their separate tents. Henriette was first to make this observation, when she pulled back the tent flap of her older friend looking for company down to the shack. But if anyone else had noticed there were no comments, no judgements. It mattered not to Maggie and Jim and mattered not to anyone else. It seemed later when Maggie and Jim looked back to this particular morning that all of them were in some way beyond the normal rules of society, way beyond the wider world and that its way was no longer theirs. They now existed together, the little group, in their microcosm, this tiny speck hardly visible on the map of a huge continent, of no significance whatsoever when searched on the globe.

Even so, Maggie felt that her very appearance announced her night of rapturous lovemaking. She felt as though her face shone, as though she walked within a radiant glow that must surely dazzle others as she passed. She felt hungry for her breakfast, and fell to her task of cutting up hunks of bread with energy and relish. The odd crust found its way to her mouth as she worked away beside Luke, and the smell of sizzling sausages wafting their way was tantalising in the extreme.

The campfire breakfast transformed them all. Dee, who back home normally breakfasted on yoghurt and coffee, returned to the trestle table for extra sausages and then downed hungrily the somewhat singed toast now dusted with a little ash that still edged the fire from the previous night. Mike, negotiating the tree trunk that served as a bench, joined her, balancing his even more copious breakfast carefully on his knees. Luke climbed into the small space between the English couple and Jim and finally Maggie made her way over from the table to collect the well-piled plate that Jim had saved for her. From the other side of the circle, Henriette waved a cheery morning greeting by means of a sausage balanced precariously on the end of her fork. She was totally unconcerned when her sausage fell on to the hard baked ground, and merely picked it up with her fingers and bit into it ravenously. Gradually, over breakfast, groups were formed for the morning's activity. Luke, who seemed to have found both a tongue and some confidence turned to Mike and Jim and explained that as a result of a suggestion from Brad last night, he had a short walk in mind and would be happy to act as their guide. Dee and Maggie also acquiesced, both aware that the young lad's willing incorporation into the group was of significant importance for him, although Dee would have preferred a foursome and Maggie a twosome for the morning's expedition. Werner announced that he wanted to do some drawing so he and Eric would make their own way just beyond the perimeter track till a suitable subject was found. This declaration gave rise to further comments and questions, as there had been no mention as yet of Werner's artistic skills. 'Werner is very good,' pronounced Eric. 'Already he has exhibitions in Germany. It is plants and natural forms he likes. Later, he may be showing his sketchbook for you to see.' Henriette had been invited by Jo and Beck to join them for the morning and although she had secretly been planning a session of hair washing and general beautification, knew that she should make the most of her Australian adventure. Besides which, Jo and Beck were really good company. She had had slight misgivings initially, as had some of the others, fearing that the two Australians might become the self-appointed experts of the camping trip. However, their enthusiasm for the outback had infected everyone and they were both generous, rather than ostentatious, in the sharing of their knowledge and expertise. Brad, aware now that all members of his group were well sorted, was grateful to have the opportunity for a quick run back to Ayers Rock Resort for basic provisions and for the opportunity for some forward planning in view of moving camp the following day.

Had they been on home ground, it is possible that Maggie and Jim, in view of the generation to which they belonged, might now have certain reservations, even misgivings concerning the previous night. But as they began with Mike and Dee to follow the route from the camp planned for them by Luke, neither felt the slightest need to reflect upon any issues of morality.

No more did Tom as he slept with Michelle. For Maggie's children and their contemporaries, the concept of an affair had ceased to exist. Rather, the world had become one of relationships and partners, which seemed in a simple and uncomplicated manner to absolve one from moral responsibilities. Maggie and Jim were now enjoying this new taste of freedom. This meant that although their preference might have been to share the morning together, since they found themselves in complete accordance, without any issues requiring discussion, they were contentedly happy with the events of the morning.

Werner's sketches were, in Maggie's eyes, surprisingly good. Although for some reason a little reticent to show any earlier pages, his pencil sketches of stones and twigs captured the spirit of place. Maggie wondered if he had made any sketches at Uluru, but before she had the opportunity to ask him this, Brad spoke urging them to assemble for the afternoon exploration of the creek. They were now beginning to be accustomed to driving in the outback, but the experience remained quite awesome. 'It's always different,' Beck had said earlier when speaking of Uluru and now her comment was more appreciatively understood. So conversation was a little disjointed as eyes scanned the sandy red expanse that eventually gave way to a rough dirt track beside what at times was presumed, with some difficulty, to be a rushing torrent. Suddenly, Brad swerved, grinning as Henriette let out a shriek, and turned on to the course of the creek. Stones were punctuated by rougher and larger boulders, which Brad navigated with consummate ease, eventually coming to a halt by a river red gum, where the light played tantalisingly on the silvery white trunk. Here they all disembarked and followed Brad along the narrowing creek. The route, although ascending slightly, was not physically demanding, but did require their full attention, simply because of the unevenness of terrain. Rounding a rocky outcrop, they eventually came upon another of the outback's surprises as barrenness gave way to a small area of relatively lush growth surrounding a small pool of water. It was here that Brad sat down with his companions to talk about the way in which the Aboriginals dig for water along dry creek beds and collect grass seeds, such as their native millet, and firewood. Their group, he explained, would be visiting a more significant waterhole the next day, an example of one that would remain a valuable source of water for many months following a season of good rain. Here too in the shade of the rocks Werner made the sketches that Jim was to acquire later and Eric surprised every one by suddenly standing on his head. Jo and Beck, always adventurous, scrambled a little further up the narrowing gorge. Dee told Mike she thought they ought to emigrate. Luke quietly decided he would become a botanist and disappeared off on his own. Henriette stretched out by a boulder and surreptitiously eyed Brad, whilst designing cave drawings in the dust and Brad surreptitiously eyed Henriette when he thought she wasn't looking. Maggie lay drowsily beside Jim whilst he gently caressed her breasts.

Chapter 11

Back at camp that same night, Jo and Beck opted once again to sleep beneath the stars as too did Luke. However, the others gradually made their ways back to their tents, all of them in buoyant and anticipatory mood as a result of the happy activities of the day and the planned early start for the viewing of the sunrise over Uluru. They would then return to their present camp for breakfast, after which they would pack up and leave for the further exploration of the Red Centre, this time pitching their own tents by the waterhole of which Brad had spoken earlier. Over conversation around the campfire at supper time Henriette voiced her concerns relating to the likely even more primitive nature of the next encampment and the probable difficulty she herself felt she would encounter in managing to pitch a tent at all. Brad promised a ready and helping hand and assured in addition that one could shower very well by means of a bucket on a string. With a disarming grin, he relaxed somewhat from his leadership role to offer help in that direction too.

'Happy?' asked Jim as he and Maggie snuggled closely together. But of course, it was not a question, simply an affirmation for them both. Jim's arm lay protectively over Maggie as they burrowed together in joined sleeping bags to talk over the events of the day. They spoke first of the morning's walk, the exploration of the creek and the awesome landscape, moving on to discuss their travelling companions, for in this respect too there had been many unexpected discoveries. Mike's earlier somewhat banal comments, for example, and his almost over effusive use of his camera initially masked the later perceptive and thoughtful comments. His wife too had shown herself to be particularly generous and sensitive to the needs of others, Luke clearly having benefited from her concern for his well-being. Barely able to look his fellow travellers in the face at the outset of the trip, Luke now appeared to be in his element. Had he not offered his services as a leader that very morning? On a humorous note, Eric had surprised them all at the creek when he followed his expertly executed cartwheel with a proficient handstand. Up until then he had always appeared to be very much Werner's shadow or echo, but the display of physical dexterity, although totally unexpected, had found Werner in the role of supportive admirer.

'What made him suddenly do that?' mused Maggie.

'No idea,' responded Jim. 'Weren't you a PE teacher? You could have done the same! I don't know. Perhaps it's just the magic of this place. Maybe we'll all end up acting inexplicably.' They lay together quietly, both possibly realising the implications of Jim's last comment.

'As for Werner's artistic talents,' resumed Jim, 'I was very struck by a couple of today's sketches. He'd really caught the effect of light and shade on the branches of that red river gum. A wonderful juxtaposition with those boulders and rocks behind. I must tell him how much I liked it. And then tomorrow there's our sunrise!'

Brad too, back under canvas, was also thinking of the group. Each expedition with which he was involved always had a similar effect upon him as he observed unfailingly and with quiet fascination the way in which the disparate personalities who clambered aboard his vehicle in the early morning hours became a supportive and involved little community. And whichever group was current was always his favourite. Of course, there had inevitably been characters he had preferred to others and he supposed there must have been tourists he had possibly even disliked. He tried to recall the faces of some of these. But Brad was both a born optimist and a man who loved his job, so he saw rather the faces of those for whom horizons had broadened immeasurably as a result of the experience he was able to share with them. However, he was also practical and a realist so knew that after their couple of weeks of magic, when all things seemed possible, normal life for most of them would probably resume. Dee and Mike were unlikely to emigrate and would most probably return to live their lives in the UK, for upon reflection, they might concede that a better and more satisfying life is not necessarily associated with a particular place. Werner and Eric had a framework in which they could flourish, or not, for they were still young and there were many connections still to make. Jo and Beck would in all probability continue to indulge their passion for the Red Centre and visit on many future occasions, for the red sand now coursed through their veins. Luke would return home, or elsewhere, but now able to view the world with less bitterness, knowing that there was perhaps a place for him somewhere. Maggie and Jim? Here Brad found himself less able to predict the future. There had always been holiday romances on expeditions such as his but he knew very well that they rarely survived. Like the fragile habitat around them, only plants and animals incredibly well adapted to the environment, only tribes that have hunted and gathered for thousands of years, only those in full understanding of relationships and connections had any chance whatsoever of survival. And that led him to thoughts of Henriette. She was undeniably pretty and lively with a great sense of adventure and Brad had by now met many such women on his tours. Early on he had learnt not to mix business with pleasure, not an easy lesson, but one he had been forced to take to heart. And with knowledge came responsibility. The very Aboriginal land they were now exploring was created by ancestors who passed the law down from generation to generation to provide the focus for daily life and behaviour. Brad might not be an Aboriginal, but this much he understood: He knew about the sanctity of rules and respect for harmonious living. He wanted his group to understand this too and he demonstrated this not only in the opportunities of exploration he offered, but also in his professionalism as their guide. So, apart from an earlier light-hearted comment directed towards Henriette in terms of showering with bucket and string, there was nothing in his behaviour towards her that might cause her to think he found her extremely attractive. Which he did.

'We've talked a little about the others,' said Maggie, 'but we don't know a great deal about each other.'

'No,' agreed Jim after a slight pause. 'But we know that we are happy to be sharing this holiday together. Perhaps that's enough for the moment.'

'Maybe, but you could tell me a little about your life before we met. You know some of mine.'

Jim reflected briefly. In actuality, he felt equally that he knew very little about Maggie either, with the exception, of course, that she had shared the moment before the cleft opening at Uluru with him. Then she had entrusted him with the knowledge of the loss of a baby daughter. He had not, however, chosen that moment to divulge the death of his brother.

'OK,' capitulated Jim, 'here comes my story – well some of it anyway – we have an early start in the morning.' He thought for a few moments, wondering quite how much of his story to tell. He pulled the sleeping bags closer around them.

'Recently, as I think you know anyway, I've done quite a bit of travelling. I'd had some twenty years or so of the NHS in administration and suddenly woke up one morning thinking I had had enough. Not an unusual feeling, I'm sure, in any walk of life, even one that might have been more enjoyable than I had begun to view mine, but I had no family ties. As I lay in bed that morning, I realised that I didn't really have any financial ties either. I was a free agent and could do anything I liked. That's really quite a frightening thought in a way, almost more restrictive than the alternatives: If you can in reality do anything, the temptation is to do nothing. But I suddenly felt resolute, firmer, stronger.

I did what still seemed quite impetuously brave at the time, but was really one big opt-out. I simply went to work and handed in my notice. I came home, felt pleased with myself and wondered what to do. That sounds very easy, but it was followed by a fair degree of panic. I had to take myself in hand quite severely and consider what it was that I *really* wanted to do.

It was then that I started travelling in earnest. Of course, I'd already done lots of the usual sightseeing and tourist things that might have been expected, but they had often been with groups or friends in my student days or with Marlene in the early days of my marriage. At first, I relished being on my own to explore first Europe, visiting many new locations I had never been to before, such as Prague, Copenhagen and St Petersburg. Then I revisited old favourites, Florence, Rome, Barcelona and Paris – many times to Paris, perhaps my favourite capital. I revelled in doing exactly what I wanted to do at any one time. I could be quite selfish. It took me a while to realise that I no longer had to make the most of every single moment away. If I wanted to read a book in a hotel room instead of tramping the streets in pouring rain so as not to miss any opportunities, I would read my book. I remember I once had a magical week in Pembrokeshire in the most appalling weather conditions, staying inside my rented cottage with only brief outings to a village library and a local pub where I chatted with people whose paths I would never normally have crossed. I would light a fire in the evening, open a bottle of wine, and doze, read or just go upstairs where there was a fantastic view to watch the rain form into torrents in the rutted lane.

Then I became a little more ambitious and joined an organised trip to India, thinking I might find it difficult to travel around solo. At about that time anyway, I was probably beginning to notice one of the things I did actually miss about my paid employment was my colleagues. I might have grumbled about some of them at the time, but work gives you that regularity of contact that's not necessarily so easy to find once you're retired. I have to say that I enjoyed sharing those experiences in India with others. If you see something like the Taj Mahal, you really need someone around with whom to share the experience.'

Jim paused, 'That's rather what I feel about this present trip,' he said, searching for Maggie's hand. She responded with a tender, affectionate kiss, then lay back, obviously expecting a continuation of the story.

'As for earlier times,' continued Jim, 'I'm jumping back now to before my NHS job and the ten years I spent in the States prior to that. I returned to England in my late thirties at the time of my mother's untimely death in her late fifties. I suppose I may well have stayed in America, but my father at that time was absolutely heartbroken. You see, he had lost his wife, but he had also already suffered the loss of a son too, my brother Gary when he was only a young man of twenty-one and should have had his whole life ahead of him.' He paused. 'The loss of a child is a bitter experience and one you sadly understand only too well.' Here he hesitated once more, uncertainly as if waiting for a cue.

Maggie drew closer and stroked his shoulder. She waited expectantly.

'My parents never recovered from the circumstances of Gary's death,' he continued. 'I think somehow they had invested all their hopes and aspirations in my brother. He was seven years younger than I was and possibly, looking back now, they had had to wait longer for him than they had for me. Also at that time, I sometimes wonder if I had begun to disappoint them in some way. They were sorry to see me abandon my medical studies, and though reasonably supportive of my marriage to Marlene once they realised it was definitely going to take place nevertheless made it clear that they thought I had made a big mistake. They were right, of course, and I think I sensed this at the time. But somehow their lack of approval of my girlfriend seemed to make it almost more inevitable that I would marry her. Telling you this makes it sound as though I should have been jealous of

Gary, but in all honesty, I shared in my parents' obvious adoration and was as delighted as they with his academic and sporting prowess. And Gary and I got on very well together. We shared many things together, chief of our delights being our many walking and camping trips. Being older, I was frequently entrusted with my younger brother, so whereas some of his classmates were felt by their parents too young to be off on their own, the two of us could find ourselves out on the hills and moors. Yorkshire was a favourite location and we had many an expedition there when I was seventeen or eighteen and he was only ten or eleven. He was seventeen when I married Marlene and he at least had no reservations about his sister-in-law – those I was beginning to have, I kept initially to myself. He admired her more bohemian lifestyle and when he saw that it diverted me from my medical studies, could see no harm in living more for the moment. Marlene was fond of him. He seemed blessed with the sort of happy and endearing personality that makes a friend of everyone. Marlene did say, however, that I spoilt him and I think that we all did. She said that again on the day he took the car. 'You spoil that boy. You'll be the death of him.' And of course I was.

Maggie was now lying very still beside him. She willed him to continue.

'When he took the car,' resumed Jim, unsteadily, 'my marriage to Marlene was already shaky. That's nothing to do with the fact that I took no notice of her comments, so I don't really know why I'm telling you. I only know that when Gary passed his driving test, he came round to our flat and I threw him the keys of our car in celebration. 'Go have a little spin,' I said. 'You could pick up Karen.' Then Marlene's words, 'You spoil that boy. You'll be the death of him'.'

'It was a horrible night in every way, misty, dull, murky. It was not a night for any driver to be out, let alone a newly qualified driver and I should never have made the suggestion – totally irresponsible on my part. One of those foggy days you used to get in London. Anyway, he didn't get as far as

Karen's. It was said later that he wasn't even driving excessively fast. He just lost control. He wasn't up to those conditions. But unaccountably, he didn't stop. Neither he nor any of us ever quite knew why he didn't, for despite what his solicitor told him to say, he knew he had hit something. There was even some compassion for him in court, but for some reason, there was a pretty stiff sentence.' Jim sighed heavily. 'He got three years.'

Maggie and Jim lay immobile.

'He was out after two,' continued Jim, haltingly, 'but it killed him anyway. He was haunted by it all. He committed suicide at the age of twenty-one, by which time I was already divorced from Marlene. It was all quite indescribably dreadful. My mother never came to terms with his death and effectively then died too, although she went through the motions of living until I was called home from America. Dad could take no more and he died some six months after my mother.'

Jim stopped, but there appeared to be something else he was struggling to say. 'The horror of it all didn't stop there.'

Now he could hardly speak. Maggie held him closer. There was the silence of the thick dark night around them. 'You see, there was another death that night. There was a child. A little child in a pushchair.'

Maggie froze and time stood still.

She managed to mouth the questions.

'Where, when?'

Jim, uncomprehending, told her where and he told her when.

Eventually, emotionally exhausted by the telling of his tale, he fell into restless sleep.

Maggie withdrew her arm, turned on to her back and stared wide-eyed and paralysed into the void.

Chapter 12

Richard had spent the day in London with Roger Carter whom he had known and respected for many years. Their paths had first crossed at university, although they had not known each other well at that time. However, contact was re-established when they both found themselves working in a similar field and therefore attending some of the same conferences and seminars. Roger had already established a course in his department similar to the one now envisaged for the Liverpool project and Richard hoped to capitalise from his friend's experiences. It quickly became evident that Roger, associated with a highly prestigious university, was able to recruit students whose academic attainments and capabilities were considerably higher than those of the students at Richard's institution. As old friends, they felt thus able to discuss the vexed question of the 'dumbing down' of courses in a manner that would certainly be ill-advised and inappropriate in a more formal context. It was difficult, they agreed, to have a productive debate about something that is not openly acknowledged to be happening. Not only did Richard envy Roger his students, but he also coveted Roger's relationship with those to whom he lectured. The truth was that Roger enjoyed working with young people and Richard did not. Having once again discussed this issue, for this difference was one of which they were both fully aware, they again expressed their usual fanciful conclusion, namely that they should swap institutions. Richard could spend more time on his research and forget about students as far as possible.

Roger could take pleasure in focusing more on his students and publish fewer papers.

Their business was efficiently and speedily concluded. Roger handed over documents relating to his own course together with student feedback questionnaires. He also highlighted some of the shortcomings of his own programme of which he himself had now become aware and together the two men had the opportunity to see how these could be addressed. Richard felt more confident with the framework of his own proposed input and began to see how such a module could be viable within the outlined constraints imposed by the faculty. Under the influence of his friend, he even began to feel a degree of enthusiasm at the thought of imparting his information to his as yet unknown students. The question of course content reminded him of the decidedly pleasurable item on the agenda, that of visiting the 'British Gypsies' exhibition the following day. He was hoping Roger would be able to join him so was disappointed to hear that his friend had a prior pressing engagement. There was time, however, for a drink before Roger made his way home and Richard made his way to Kate and Martin's flat.

The two men first raised their glasses to the successful, eventual implementation of the new course and then to their respective wives and families. Richard learnt of the successful promotion of Roger's wife Jill and of the whereabouts of their three boys, the eldest of whom had recently made Roger a grandfather. The youngest lad was currently travelling; an activity, agreed the two friends, that seemed nowadays to occupy an inordinately large percentage of the population at any one time. Roger was very interested to hear that Maggie too formed part of this number and found himself asking various questions about her enterprise. He knew that Jill would want all the details.

'How unlike her!' he could already hear his wife saying.

Of the two wives, Jill was by far the more likely to set off on an expedition of the sort Maggie seemed to have undertaken, but had she done so, Roger would have undoubtedly been party to such a decision. He was unable to fathom, for the sake of his wife's curiosity, why Maggie had set off in such previously unannounced fashion. Indeed Richard himself seemed unable, or possibly unwilling, to explain this and Roger began to feel that his enquiries were becoming too personal. Jill, of course, would have plenty of theories of her own.

'She's leaving him,' she asserted later, as they got ready for bed. 'Why else would it be an open-ended trip?'

But Roger didn't know and anyway he was tired. Additionally, he was not quite so interested in the situation as was his wife. He certainly wouldn't wish domestic problems upon his friend and found it difficult to agree with his wife's immediate assumption. Maggie and Richard had a very well-established marital relationship as far as he was concerned, but nevertheless he found himself mulling over Jill's comments before he finally fell asleep.

Richard, once he had extracted his Oyster card from the torn lining in his trouser pocket, finally found himself at Kate and Martin's flat, a little later than he had perhaps originally envisaged. He negotiated the narrow path between the dustbins, and climbed the few steps to the front door, thankful that he had remembered the spare set of keys in case Martin was not yet back. Their flat was located on the first floor and after ringing and getting no response, he inserted his key in the lock and turned it twice anticlockwise.

'Hi there!' he called, just in case there was a response but as expected, there was none, so he dumped his case in the small square hall and made his way into the living room. This was a large and pleasant room with a westerly aspect, which meant that on this particular day it was still catching the last rays of the sun and was somewhat warm. Richard crossed over the rug, remembering how Kate and Martin had struggled back from Turkey with it only to discover they liked it less than they had anticipated once it was in place. It was supposedly always about to be replaced, but somehow this had never happened, and Martin and Kate had grown accustomed to it. It was actually delightfully soft and welcoming for a frolicsome cuddle. And so the rug had stayed. Richard tussled with the sash window and managed to open it fractionally. He then went back through the hall to put on a kettle in the tiny kitchen. This room, though certainly small, was very well planned and had all the conveniences one could possibly need, perhaps more than one might ever require, reflected Richard as he glanced around at the wide range of electrical appliances waiting for his kettle to boil.

It was then that he began to be a little more observant. There was evidence of a meal eaten in haste and more than a couple of unwashed saucepans. The door of the washing machine was slightly ajar and he bent down to see a few shirts and various other items awaiting transfer to the tumble dryer. A tea towel lay discarded on the floor. Whilst Kate and Martin were busy working people, and niceties such as washing up featured, he knew, less prominently upon the agenda of the young than of his own generation, he was confident that Kate, in anticipation of his visit, would have had what she termed 'a thorough whisk round'. And then he remembered. Kate, of course, was off somewhere with that friend of hers. He concentrated hard to recall where and with whom. His mind still grappling with this question, he found a tea bag and took his mug back into the living room, relaxing on to the low-level couch and balancing his drink on top of some magazines on the coffee table. Finally he remembered. She was on some Greek island with Sarah. Why hadn't Martin gone, he mused. Was he supposed to know? He couldn't remember. Thinking of Martin, it was now high time he was back. Weren't they expecting to eat out together? Richard looked at his watch and then settled back with his tea, reaching out for a nearby paper, quickly realising it was two days old, but reading it in any case.

Time passed. He quickly exhausted the newspaper and turned briefly to the magazines, flicking the pages at random. He began to feel first a little impatient, then slightly annoyed and finally somewhat concerned. It was just as he raised himself from the couch once again in order to look out of the window that the phone rang. Martin, loud and verbose at the other end, initially sounded so agitated and incoherent that Richard thought there was a major problem of some sort.

'Slow down, slow down!' urged Richard. 'Start again. I haven't the vaguest idea what you're on about. Is there a problem of some kind?'

It transpired that there was. Richard finally understood Martin to be that very moment at Gatwick, about to board a flight to Greece. Apparently, he had made a sudden decision to join Kate for the last week of her holiday and had totally forgotten the previous arrangement. He was full of apologies, particularly sorry to let Richard down, for he was appreciative of Richard and Maggie's unfailing concern for their daughter and therefore for him too. There had been many occasions in the past when this love and support had been demonstrated in practical terms for the young couple and Martin would certainly have preferred to let down almost anyone other than Kate's father. He also remembered in the course of his explanation that he had left the flat in rather a hurry and that there would be much evidence of this. He proffered many apologies and Richard tried valiantly to reassure him that this was no major calamity. It was clear that Martin had little time left for further conversation as he requested Richard to make use of the flat in any way he wished, adding that he was so grateful that he had obviously remembered his keys.

'Hang on! We're actually boarding now. Gotta go. So sorry. Please make yourself at home.'

And Richard responded to the farewells, replacing the phone and wondering what to do next. He realised that he was actually quite hungry and as it was now rather late to set out to the Indian restaurant he originally had in mind, he settled for the less congenial surroundings of a nearby small bistro.

Here he had time to eat, observe and to think. He found himself at a small table by the window and was served quite speedily by a young girl with a pretty face, a range of piercings and a short skirt. His spaghetti bolognese was surprisingly good, and as he ate, he was able to survey both the outside world and the clientele, some of whom seemed to be regulars judging from the light-hearted banter with Jude, the little waitress. What was immediately apparent, as Richard began his people watching, was that the world mostly went by as animals to the ark – everyone in pairs. Of course, there were many varieties of pairs, the well-matched and the ill-matched. He concentrated on the latter first. Body language gave away the ill-matched despite attempts – if there were any – at concealment. His attention was caught by a middle-aged couple as they passed, pausing briefly to inspect the menu stuck on the window to the side of the door. But it was already abundantly clear that nothing would satisfy the wife, who rolled ahead with awkward gait, unseeing eyes and a sharp tongue audible even to those inside. When had they last held hands, pondered Richard. When had the short stubby fingers of the little man behind wrapped themselves around those large clenched hands that swung resolutely ahead and cajoled, solicited the body to which they were attached to a private place of seduction? Richard realised with a start that he was actually playing one of Maggie's fantasising games that used to cause them harmless amusement in the early days of their marriage. A seemingly disparate couple had to be selected and a story devised with, of course, a suitably erotic conclusion. Each proposition had been awarded points – the more fanciful the scenario, the higher the score. These recollections caused Richard to become embarrassingly aware of the slight stiffening of his penis. His gaze moved to the curved buttocks of the little waitress, each individually outlined beneath the flimsy, cheap fabric of her shiny, skimpy skirt as she bent towards her customer. The customer, also leaning forwards, displayed a full cleavage, with abundant breasts squashing together to form a deep ravine ripe for exploration. Richard quickly looked away, but his mind was now focused on sex.

It had of course been some time since Richard had had sex. For it was now the beginning of August and Maggie had been gone for nearly a month. Richard was missing his wife and not only for sexual intimacy, but also for the sharing of all other aspects of their life together. The exhibition tomorrow, for example. Maggie would have enjoyed that and he would have benefited not only from her company, but also from her comments and enthusiasm. For Maggie's endearing qualities, which had attracted him to the pretty young schoolgirl in the first place, were her boundless enthusiasm and her readiness to try new things. She was the first girl to brave a pillion ride on his scooter on the rough track at the edge of the field behind the school and one of the first to sport a mini skirt, which occasion he remembered most vividly. Was this the reason why she had jetted off to Australia, he wondered, this insatiable appetite for new experiences, this craving which, when he thought about it more, must surely have been constrained at times as well as expanded on other occasions by her role as wife, mother and teacher? Had she felt more recently that her wings had somehow been clipped? Richard toyed with this possibility.

He then realised that Jude was by his side asking if he would like a dessert. He felt his cheeks reddening and was about to decline a sweet, as Maggie would have done, but changed his mind on whim and ordered an apple pie with both custard and cream. He then continued in his reveries. For the first time since the departure of his wife, he began to contemplate more deeply the possible intricacies of the situation. Apart from being a little sorry that initially he had not been party to Maggie's planning, he had viewed her holiday as a perfectly normal and well-deserved opportunity to travel and savour new experiences after a busy school year. The fact that he would not on this occasion be sharing in these experiences was in a way almost helpful to his own plans at the time. He was guiltily aware that time to complete work projects currently in hand would be personally helpful to him thus encouraging his compliance. So, to put it bluntly, he hadn't really minded. Where exactly was Maggie at this very moment? A glance at his watch and a quick calculation confirmed that she must at this very moment be in bed. Of course, the possibility that she might not be alone never remotely crossed his mind. As to the exact geographical location of his wife, he knew her still to be in the Red Centre and therefore out of contact in terms of mobile and electronic communication. He was unsure as to when this part of Maggie's expedition would end but knew that he would be happy and relieved once again to be in touch.

So Richard paid his bill and found his way back to the flat. As he made himself a cup of coffee he found himself thinking of Martin and his evident sudden departure for Greece. Kate's holiday plans too, he recalled, had been made in some hurry. And if Kate was with a girlfriend, which is what he understood, was Martin's arrival pre-planned, or would his appearance on the scene be an unexpected surprise? Maggie would have fathomed all this out, he felt sure, with her unerring ability to read between the lines. Whatever it was all about, he hoped there was no problem for his daughter.

He suddenly felt very tired and deciding that he was ready for bed opened the door of the spare bedroom to find the bed already made up and some space available in the wardrobe. However, he decided not to bother with unpacking as he had relatively little in his small case anyway and so was soon ready to switch off the bedside light. But he didn't fall asleep straight away. Instead he thought of his wife and the fact that she was geographically as far away from him as she possibly could be. He tried to imagine this Red Centre, this spot in the middle of nowhere that had obviously attracted her in some way. Her last emails from Sydney had indicated her special interest in visiting this place and her delight when she managed to book a trip that seemed likely to meet her requirements. Richard wondered what her intentions were when this particular trip would be over. Australia, he reasoned, is a pretty big continent and there were highly likely to be other attractions on her agenda. But perhaps, after one month, she might decide to come home. What, in fact, was she really anticipating in terms of timescale? This issue had never really been fully discussed between the two of them prior to her departure and her open-ended ticket was clearly intended to keep all options available. Suddenly the alarming thought that she perhaps had a considerably longer timescale in mind struck him forcibly and fearfully, heightening his anxiety. Perhaps Kate would be able to enlighten him as to her mother's plans? But with Kate currently on holiday, he didn't feel like texting her with a query of this sort. As for Tom, he doubted very much whether Tom would be any more acquainted with Maggie's plans than he himself.

Richard woke the next morning in a more positive frame of mind. Having sorted out breakfast by means of a trip to the corner shop for milk and a couple of buns, he arrived at the exhibition in ebullient mood, ready to enjoy his morning. A review of the rooms focusing on gypsies and western literature left him satisfied that his planning for Liverpool was on target. There was a wealth of illustrative material relating to the exaggerated gypsy stereotype as portrayed in literature from the eighteenth century and even more for his own chosen later period. This confirmation that there were no serious omissions to his proposals left him free to wander at leisure to view the photographic exhibits and the musical demonstrations in the theatre illustrating how gypsy migration impacted on the development of western music.

It was only in the train on the way home that Richard's thoughts returned to his wife and family. He looked around him to notice that there were more children travelling than usual and remembered that, of course, it was the school summer holiday. With his project now safely under his belt, perhaps he too would now take some of his allocated holiday days. As the train gathered speed, leaving vehicles on the adjacent of motorway far behind to speed through undulating countryside and local stations, he began to consider the various options. It was not long before an obvious possibility came to mind and he began to reckon just how many days were available before the start of the academic year to make a visit to Australia viable. He realised he should have thought of this earlier at the beginning of the summer break for whilst time was not as yet running out, it was fast disappearing. There was the added complication that Maggie for the moment was not contactable and her next destination unknown so no flight as yet could be booked. Still, he reasoned, it might well be possible to join her for a while.

Richard missed his wife.

Chapter 13

The plane gathered height and Martin finally allowed himself to sink back in his seat. Everything so far seemed to have gone wrong with his plans. Tony's supportive comments, and his willingness to cover a current work commitment, had been instrumental in backing Martin's decision to go to Greece, but neither of the two colleagues could have anticipated the fraught nature of all the travel arrangements. For a start, the plane had been severely delayed, sufficiently so for the free teas, coffees and meal voucher to be made available and in addition Martin was still annoyed with himself for forgetting about his commitment to Richard. Also it had just occurred to him that he had omitted to write down the name of Kate's holiday apartment, although thankfully he had the details of the village. He could, of course, easily find this out by texting on landing, but the element of surprise was high on his agenda. Fundamental to the purpose of his visit was his desire to surprise his lovely girlfriend and to make her a romantic proposal.

Loosening his seat belt as he reached for a sandwich, he began to give this proposition some careful thought. First, he had to locate the girls and then plan some time alone with Kate without, of course, offending Sarah who had invited Kate to join her on holiday in the first place. Supposing he simply arrived at the beach and spotted Kate – on her own would be best – perhaps sunbathing or reading, oblivious of his approach along the shore's edge. Suddenly she would realise there was somebody there, look up and then…And then what exactly? Catching sight of the rather lurid book jacket belonging to the passenger beside him, he wondered whether the whole thing should be even more dramatic. Perhaps he should run the length of the beach, arms, or a cloak, even wings, fanning outwards, a sort of blend of Greek God and Superman, to alight by the distant figure beside a rock. He looked out of the window to contemplate the clouds. Maybe not!

Martin was aware that he had already acted in uncharacteristic fashion and that this in itself would probably intrigue and delight Kate. He only had to tell her that he missed her and loved her and had come to tell her so. There would be a time and a place for his proposal.

More immediately, however, was the need to find her.

The plane touched down in the early hours of the morning with Martin in somewhat dishevelled state. He made his way through heavy swing doors out of the airport, searching in his pocket for the name of the village where the girls were staying. He was rescued by a taxi driver, who studied the name on his crumpled paper, grinned a huge, toothless smile, then drove him as dawn broke through spectacular mountain scenery at high speed to deposit him in what appeared to be the centre of a large village. Here he offloaded his rucksack and paid his fare. Having heard a little of his passenger's story, the taxi driver, knowing that he had not booked any accommodation, recommended the recently renovated taverna behind him; then with a wave and thumbs up, turned the car adroitly around the fountain, shouted cheery greetings to his friends on the seat and was off.

Already the sun was warm on Martin's back. He found himself in a large square, part cobbled and part asphalt, where there was a garage with a small forecourt, a basic supermarket, a couple of shops of some sort and the recently spruced-up taverna. In the middle was an old non-functioning fountain with a stone bench where sat a couple of elderly men. He could make out a church in a slightly elevated position a little further to his right from which direction there was also a tantalising smell of fresh bread.

Martin picked up his rucksack and surveyed the taverna behind him, his every move carefully noted by the locals near the fountain and a young lad repositioning a billboard across the way as he opened up the supermarket. A couple of tourists appeared from the direction of the church carrying bread as they made their way to the supermarket and it occurred to Martin that Kate and Sarah might very well cross the square to visit the bakery each morning. He was not yet ready for any reunion, so strode purposefully towards the taverna, and waited in the bar in the dark interior until a young girl arrived who cheerfully showed him to an available room.

He deposited his belongings, took a long and very welcome shower and, realising that he was extremely hungry, went out to find himself a table near the taverna door in case he needed to make a hasty retreat inside, for he had yet to think out his next move. He enjoyed a lengthy and substantial breakfast, accompanied by several cups of coffee enabling him to while away the time as he observed the various comings and goings. There were only a few other customers at first and just one couple who looked as though they might also be staying, but gradually other tourists began to arrive. The first couple was evidently British with their knee-length shorts, fresh but slightly creased from the suitcase and sporting newly purchased hats. They identified the taverna from some sort of printed sheet, sat down at a table near the front and glanced around from time to time a little uncertainly looking as though they were expecting others to join them. And this was what soon happened. Martin realised then that this disparate group now assembling, about ten to twelve in number, formed the nucleus of a group from 'Select Greek Tours', as advertised on the T-shirt of the young girl who had now just arrived. He was about to be treated to an introduction to the island and more particularly to the locality in which he too found himself. The information upon which he could now eavesdrop might be of use to him in tracking down Kate. He might even be able to get the rep into conversation after her introductory talk.

First, drinks were ordered for the newly arrived holidaymakers consisting of the usual orange juices and ouzos. Martin thought he might as well follow a late breakfast with the latter, so it was in a more relaxed and confident mood that he settled down to hear Amy's information and recommendations. The village or collection of services, local houses and holiday accommodation was, as he had already surmised, not very extensive. 'Select Greek Tours' rentals all seemed to relate to property nearer the beach that was to Martin's left from where the first party members had appeared. There was one main beach in close proximity and a further possibility for swimming involving a twenty-minute walk from behind the church. A path was clearly indicated but involved an initial climb and then eventually an equivalent descent. Sensible footwear was advised. There was a small harbour beyond the beach with a handful of tavernas where local fishermen competed with each other with their 'special prices' for trips to other beaches that were mostly inaccessible by foot. A small island easily visible from beach and harbour was a favourite venue possibly because it offered sandy beaches, in contrast to the local pebbles. But, warned the rep, there was nothing there in the form of any amenities whatsoever so sufficient supplies of water need to be taken, and yes, the local water was drinkable. In fact, the brief introduction sounded pretty similar to others Martin had heard before and he waited happily and patiently in the sunshine while the rep sorted out her lists relating to outings and events for the forthcoming week. Martin made mental note of an evening of traditional dancing on Friday night at the Eleni that might attract Kate and Sarah, assuming he had not found them within the next couple of days. A number of questions were asked, forms filled, credit card details taken and gradually the group dispersed.

'It's possible I've seen them around,' claimed Amy when Martin finally collared her, anchored her with a coffee and recounted his story in part. 'This is a very small resort and there are only a certain number of places to eat at in the evening which is when you see people around. 'Select Greek Tours' is the only company with accommodation here as this is the sort of place that attracts individual travellers and we don't have sole occupancy of most of the places on our books so they could be at any one of our own apartments. There are only a handful of small hotels anyway so they won't be difficult to check out. But yes, a couple of tall blonde girls, quite a striking pair, I rather think I have seen them around.'

Were they the pair at Eric's bar last night, she privately wondered? If so, both girls had been heavily entwined with a couple of Greek dancers. Best not recount that to the charming boyfriend with the disarming smile. Which girl was his anyway?

'I have to get on,' said Amy. 'I have another couple of resorts a few miles down the coast. Both have new arrivals today. Well, good luck in finding your friends. I don't think you'll have too much trouble, even if you can't find out where they are staying. Thanks for the coffee.'

Amy lowered her voice, glancing around. 'By the way, I have to use this taverna because my company dictates it. But the best places to stay are tucked away behind the church, if you don't mind being ten minutes or so from the beach, or down by the harbour. Bye for now. See you around.'

And Amy executed a manoeuvre not unlike that of the taxi driver earlier as balanced precariously on her scooter, helmet and bag of brochures dangling from her handle bars, like him she too was quickly gone.

Martin went back to his room that he personally found perfectly acceptable, if but a little basic, and spread out the map of the resort on his bed. It did appear, unsurprisingly, that most of the action was down by the beach and the harbour. There was a small pocket of development where he now found himself, consisting in the main of older properties, perhaps the hub of the original village, particularly as the church was close by. But there were additional shops and even another bakery marked down by the sea. He was later to discover that bread was delivered once daily to the bakery on the front and that the genuine bakery was sited between his own taverna and the church. As Amy had indicated, there were some apartments in the area around the church, but most focused on the seafront and the harbour. Martin didn't think Sarah worked for 'Select Greek Tours', but this knowledge anyway wouldn't have helped him in his search. If Sarah had been in a position to select her holiday accommodation, where would she have chosen to be? Martin decided he needed to explore the village, so donning cap and sunglasses, he stuffed the map into a pocket, locked his room and went down the stairs.

The heat hit him as he left the taverna. His own room was shaded by an extra additional building protruding from the main building at right angles and he realised he had not as yet appreciated the full strength of the summer sun. He first followed the road down to the sea, passing an occasional gift shop with various postcard stands interspersed with small vacant lots where once there might possibly have been a house, although they really appeared to be simply small parcels of unkempt land. Occasionally there was an animal either tethered to a stump or listlessly lying in the shade of the juxtaposed wall. Nearer the beach were newer properties or old village style houses now renovated and revitalised. Suddenly as the sea came into view the resort became much livelier. The cafés, bars and restaurants were busy and there were more visitors than Martin had expected to see enjoying a lunchtime drink or meal. He eyed the clientele in each restaurant as carefully as he could, thankful for the sunglasses that made this scrutiny so much less obtrusive. He then made his way along the beach to the harbour at the far end. Here again, he surveyed the tavernas attentively. It was a little difficult to linger in such circumstances, as waiters were ready to pounce on indecisive passers-by, hoping to lure them into their own establishments. Martin made his way right to the end of the gently curving harbour and found a concrete seat in the shade of a high wall. It suddenly occurred to him that in his search, he had adopted the wrong technique. If he ever went shopping with Kate, which he avoided if at all possible, when they lost each other as they invariably did, it was always more satisfactory if Martin stood quite still in some reasonably obvious spot to leave Kate to do the finding. Accordingly, he retraced his steps to one of the tavernas, found a seat at a recently vacated table with a most welcome parasol where he ordered a large beer and a Greek salad.

'What I could do with at the moment,' declared Kate, reaching for her rucksack and foraging for the lukewarm water bottle, 'is a large beer and a Greek salad.'

'You had that yesterday and you can have it again tomorrow,' was Sarah's response, as she too reached for her flask. 'Here we have a beach totally to ourselves. You have to pay for that privilege with warm water and a squashed tomato roll, oh and a Greek cheesy thing. I'd forgotten we bought those this morning.' Kate lay back munching, propping her head and shoulders against her bag and drawing up her knees. Both girls viewed the scene before them. It was like an idyllic picture postcard, the small curved crescent of white pebbles, the incredible clarity of the blue green sea and the majestic, protective encirclement of the tall cliffs. Today they had explored a little further from their usual haunts. Finding that a small family group had already laid claim to their usual beach, the one indicated by Amy to her group that same morning which was reached by the path behind the church, they had decided to continue the walk along the cliffs in search of an alternative. They were not disappointed, although the final scramble down to the rocky shore was somewhat tricky. They were hot and sticky upon arrival and revelled in their first plunge into those limpid waters, shrieking and laughing at first and then floating, eyes shut, savouring an immense and profoundly satisfying sense of pleasure. Both girls then turned and swam with slow, measured rhythmic strokes further out into the bay.

'We should have bought some masks,' called Sarah. 'It's brilliant. Just look at this shoal of tiny fish!'

They trod water in amazement, then resumed their swims to return to the beach, shaking out their towels and opening up the rucksacks. And now, having decamped to one side of the beach to enjoy the cool shade afforded by towering cliffs, they were enjoying their picnic.

Sarah turned to contemplate her friend. 'You're thinking of him, aren't you?'

'Yes, I am,' she responded slowly. 'I think about him a lot of the time. You know I do. It's just that it's so lovely here, he would have enjoyed it too. You know me well enough to guess how I feel.'

Kate and Sarah stared out to sea. A sailing boat in the far distance was making leisurely, unworried progress back to harbour. There was now just the slightest of breezes and the small boat way out in the bay appeared to make some modest progress. The girls sat a while in contemplative, companionable silence and then Sarah lay back with her paperback and Kate too stretched out on her towel and closed her eyes.

During the course of the afternoon, the shade advanced to the shore and Sarah turned from her book to look at her watch.

'Time to make tracks I think,' she suggested. 'At least it's a little cooler now, but the sun will strike hot when we leave the beach and it's a bit further back to base than usual. Then we'll have to think where to eat tonight! So many major decisions to make on holiday. Perhaps though we'll give Eric's bar a miss tonight in case we get caught by our two friends again. You can sometimes have too much of a good thing, although I must say they were pretty harmless and quite a laugh. If I ever fancied either of them, I'd go for the one with the curlier hair.'

They both laughed recalling their light-hearted evening in the busy bar with the hopeless music and local wine.

'I'll settle for the one with the better English,' responded Kate.

'That was the same one,' replied Sarah.

'Was it?' queried Kate. 'In which case we'll have to share.'

'And not for the first time!' continued Sarah, both friends chuckling as they remembered their adolescent crushes on the same boy prefect in their school days.

Meanwhile Martin maintained his vigilant but unfruitful watch, whilst enjoying his lunch and the bustling harbour side scene before him, until mid afternoon. He then drifted back towards the beach end of the bay now noticing a small street to his left somewhat hidden earlier by the tables and parasols of two adjoining cafés. It stopped well short of the area of paved seafront and appeared to climb in parallel direction to the road he had followed on the way down. He remembered now noticing it on the plan that he no longer seemed to have in his pocket. This proved a more scenic and intrinsically interesting route to follow and he soon discovered that a small alleyway linked it to the alternative road, which it joined just below the petrol forecourt. A further short distance brought him to the church and a pretty little collection of older properties. This looked promising, the sort of location in which the girls might have chosen to stay had they been given any opportunity. He paused in the shade of a large fig tree to survey the scene, but in the hottest part of the day nothing much moved, and in contrast to the busier beach scene behind him, here there was no sign of any one at all. From where he stood, he could see a dilapidated sign to the side of the church indicating the footpath to the small cove. He began to feel more optimistic. He would follow this path in an attempt to surprise Kate and if unsuccessful, return to base to consider his next move.

After some fifteen minutes or so, Martin stood on the cliff top and scanned the view below. It was indeed a most beautiful beach, nestling between the rocks, with amazingly clear water, the pebbles in the sea clearly visible some considerable way out. There was only a handful of people to be seen lying prone, swimming lazily or pottering around doing nothing very much, but none of them was Kate or Sarah. At this point Martin paused. He had his trunks with him. The water looked incredibly inviting and he was extremely hot. But Kate was not there. He hesitated uncertainly for a few minutes, but finally decided that he would retrace his steps back to the taverna have a shower and rethink.

Drinking his beer as he watched the activities in the square, Martin pondered his next move. What would the girls do this evening? Like him, Martin assumed, they would wish to eat and now that he had fully reconnoitred the village, he was certain they would make their way down to the front. If he positioned himself at the café where the little road leading from the church met the promenade he would have a good view of both routes down to the sea.

Early in the evening, before the sun set, Martin settled himself at his vantage point. The waiters were already out on the promenade, touting for custom and holidaymakers were drifting along, pausing to look at menu boards and to banter good-humouredly. Martin examined the seafront. He could just see the last of the little fishing boats and one larger tour boat tying up in the harbour at the far end but there was no sign of Kate or Sarah. He suddenly wondered whether they might have chosen to eat at a different resort on the island and the thought of this possibility filled him with dismay. The sun was now setting and he looked at his watch with some concern.

He would call Kate from his mobile, just as he had each evening from home.

What happened next was an amazing coincidence that, most fortuitously, proved him to be a true romanticist at heart. It could not have been better planned.

Martin called Kate.

As she answered, she came into view before his very eyes, at which point, he nearly dropped his phone. She and Sarah were approaching down the back street from the church, both negotiating the uneven surface warily in heeled sandals. The two friends were undoubtedly a striking pair as Amy, amongst others, had noted, but Martin had eyes only for Kate. She was wearing a white sundress that complemented her newly acquired tan, her long fair hair loosely tied back. She and Sarah paused by a low wall so that Kate could take her call. Martin could not speak for a moment or two and was even able to see Kate bending her head fractionally to the side as she repeated his name.

'Martin, Martin, can you hear me? Are you there? How're you doing? How's your day been? Where are you now?'

'Look up to your left. No, further up. That's where!' Martin's response was choked. 'And I'm taking the three of us out to dinner!'

Kate's incredulous, upturned face was a picture of amazement and delight.

Chapter 14

The fire now appeared to be out. The three well-wrapped bodies curled beside it had finally succumbed to sleep. The whole camp was awesomely silent beneath an amazing sky, an arching testimony to the unaccountable, the prodigious and the miraculous. But if they woke in the night and strained the ear to listen acutely, they heard the sound of silence, never blatant, never clamorous and never impinging upon any sensibility. Huddled amidst this world of nocturnal activity lay Brad's microcosm, the eleven souls who had chanced upon their intersection. Almost all were asleep, if but a little fitfully. But one was now startlingly, frighteningly awake, wide-eyed, galvanising her senses into comprehending what had happened one dark night, many years ago, so very far away.

Maggie lay in anguish, her thoughts seemingly beyond control, evading and escaping in random fashion, mocking and taunting her, refusing to be ordered and so denying her the comprehension she craved. But, of course, she did understand. She understood only too well that it was Jim's brother who was responsible for the death of their beloved daughter.

One dark night, one man gave one other man the keys of his car: The clock could not be turned back.

Maggie made a conscious effort to breathe slowly and deeply, trying to think clearly. She seemed only able for the moment to focus on the thought of Jim's hands. The same hands that had offered the keys were those she had now come to know well, gnarled with their prominent veins and whispers of sandy hairs on backs and knuckles. These were the hands had explored her own body, at first gently, then more insistently and then finally with an urgency that had guided them both to their lovemaking.

Jim was awake.

'What is it?' he whispered.

Then more urgently, as his hands moved to stroke her cheeks and discovered the silent tears, 'Maggie, Maggie, tell me please! What's the matter? What's wrong?'

At first, she could neither move nor speak and Jim grew increasingly alarmed. Utterly exhausted, she tried to summon sufficient energy to respond. Jim spared her the pain for suddenly, he understood.

'Oh my god!'

They lay side by side, not quite touching.

Feeling nauseous, Maggie indicated that she would make her way to the shack. Jim, reeling from the unwelcome knowledge they now shared, let it be known that he would accompany her, for the little path to the wash area was in total darkness, uneven and fringed with prickly foliage. So, struggling in the dark, they emerged unsteadily but silently from their tent in the thick of the night to visit the shack, both their torches emitting weak pools of light. Jim followed Maggie, ensuring that the beam from his torch also lit the way ahead, longing to have his arm round her, to guide, to help, to comfort, but sick at heart, unsure now of his role and their relationship.

Maggie disappeared into the shack, Jim without comment now holding and balancing the torch at arm's length directing the shaky beam inwards on top of the insubstantial wooden door that gave straight on to the bush. He heard a muted, 'Thanks,' and then a tap turned and there was the sound of running water.

Jim leant back on the wooden frame, as far as the holding of the torch would permit him, exhausted and emotionally drained. He shut his eyes momentarily, replaying again the events of the night. How blind he had been to the cruel twist in his own story, oblivious to Maggie's unbelievable suffering whilst he slept.

He had, of course, often thought back to the night of Gary's accident. This marked the beginning of the disintegration of his own family, but for him and Marlene, the cracks were already there. Perhaps they could all have survived had it not been for Gary's suicide. The period of his brother's imprisonment had been almost unbearable, he acknowledged, and they had all found it very difficult. Gary was desperate, full of remorse, consumed with regret and shame and appalled by the regime of life in prison. Jim and his parents when they visited could see that they were witnessing the self-destruction of a brother and son, but did not know what to do about it. Jim himself visited less and less frequently, trying to convince himself that his increasingly unhappy marriage and the geographical distance of the prison – Gary was relocated for some unknown reason six months or so into his sentence – made visiting more problematic, but knew that in reality he simply couldn't bear to see what was happening to his brother. His father, almost Victorian in outlook, could not cope with the way in which he himself felt branded, categorised on visiting days feeling a slur upon his own impeccable character. Only Jim's mother, who too hated to see what was happening to her son, who also felt desecrated by all the practicalities like queuing at the prison gates and talking behind bars and who too found the journey tedious, kept faithful contact. But she knew then that her son was already lost.

It was she who answered the door to the policeman three years later.

And now Jim, who, in the passing of the years, thought he had found a measure of acceptance and peace, felt agitated, challenged and uneasy. And this appeared to be because he had been fated to find Maggie, a woman, who quite inexplicably, and against all odds, he loved as he had loved no other. And equally inexplicably, still against all odds, he was convinced that she felt similarly. But there was, it now transpired, some earlier and deeply significant connection between them and they had yet to learn of its importance and significance.

Jim's head jerked backwards against the door frame and he opened his eyes upwards. What a night! There were just so many stars! How amazing! The expanse of night sky was simply astonishing. He was dazzled by such a stunning display. He turned quickly sensing a shooting star far to his right and promptly dropped the torch.

Then came a muffled shriek. After a certain amount of grovelling and foraging in the dark, Maggie and Jim found themselves standing together in the now open doorway with one functioning torch between them. Maggie linked arms with Jim, who pulled her closer, switching off the torch as they both turned their faces heavenwards.

'It's unbelievable,' whispered Maggie. 'It's too perfect to be real.'

'Except that it *is* real!' responded Jim softly.

Together they watched the night sky. Jim's arm tentatively encircled Maggie, rubbing her gently as if to warm and comfort her.

'Are you OK?' he murmured.

Maggie did not respond immediately although she moved closer to him. She continued to gaze skywards, mesmerised.

Then she turned towards him and put her arms around him. She pulled him close. He held her tightly. He felt that he could hardly breathe.

'You are not responsible,' was her barely audible comment after a long pause.

After a while, when she shivered in the coldness of the night, they retraced their steps carefully back to camp. From one of the dormant, humped shapes around the fire came a regular, nasal snorting.

'The fire's out!' whispered Maggie.

They moved a little closer.

'Brad will have that going again in no time at all,' said Jim in a hushed voice. 'It looks dead but the embers will still be hot. Look!' And he bent down to retrieve a small twig in the blackened ash near the edge of the stone circle. He stirred gently. At first nothing much seemed to happen, but then there was a sudden glowing orange red. He placed the twig cautiously in the glow and after a second or so, the end flickered with a small vulnerable flame that played its way along the dead wood, changing colour to a yellowish tinge, seemingly gathering strength only suddenly and unexpectedly to wither and die.

'It will revive in no time for an early morning drink,' added Jim in a low voice.

The anticipation of morning could already be felt in the night sky: There could now only be a few hours before the planned departure for the Uluru sunrise. Both Maggie and Jim now craved sleep. However, both secretly feared that this would cruelly elude them.

'Shall we sleep out here?' whispered Jim.

Maggie hesitated before replying. She was now exhausted and what she really wanted was a well-sprung bed in a curtained room with clean, sweet smelling sheets and the luxury of clean clothes. Perhaps these would ensure the certainty of a deep and dreamless sleep, sweet oblivion, a still mind. However, failing this, perhaps she would be able to open her tired eyes to the stars and find some measure of peace.

So as quietly as possible, Maggie and Jim retrieved their sleeping bags and extra blankets and settled themselves beneath the splendour of the night sky.

'This sky is just so vast,' thought Maggie, as she lay wide-eyed on her back. 'Everything in this country is on such a huge and overwhelming scale.' And she thought back to the flight and how she had peered through the small window of the plane and seen a huge expanse of emptiness and then later the dusty roads that stretched unendingly into the hazy distance. She thought of the magnitude of the giant, red rock and the immensity of the sky above. It was almost too much to bear. Her thoughts returned to her walk round the base of the monolith and she recalled the eagerness of the ants she had observed and the patterning of their industrious line in the dust. Looking upwards she observed the pattern of the stars and glancing to one side, the dark formation of the semi-circle of tents. Werner had been fascinated by the patterning of the branches in the red river gums, she remembered, and by the dance of shadow on bark. So Maggie, almost in a state of semi-consciousness, found comfort in her search for form and drifted in and out of sleep.

Jim barely slept at all. There was simply too much on his mind. It was true that he was not responsible for his brother's actions, but what, he reflected, were his responsibilities now? Beside him was a woman, half-asleep, for whom, nevertheless, he felt himself accountable. Jim was a man of reason, logical mind and clarity of thought. He was not given to impetuous decisions. Yet sleeping restlessly beside him was this woman, a married woman whom he had known for barely a week. Unknowingly and previously, their paths had once crossed. Now they were once again entwined. But to what end? Jim wished he knew.

Eventually he too fell into uncomfortable and intermittent sleep, waking with a start when he sensed movement close by. It was Brad, poking at the fire to stir it once again into life to provide his party with a hot drink prior to witnessing the long anticipated rising of the sun. He carefully balanced the big, battered, metal container between the three large, raised stones and gradually his group stirred, groping around in the dark and piercing cold to assemble round the fire, warming their hands around large steaming mugs of tea and coffee. There was little conversation at that time in the morning and as everyone felt sleepy, Maggie and Jim's extreme fatigue went unnoticed. Most slept in the 4WD during the drive to the starting point where Brad goaded them into action for a short walk of some half an hour along a well-defined stony path to his chosen location.

'I wake up now,' came the voice of Henriette as she overtook Luke to catch up with Maggie who was carefully following in Jim's tracks. 'You are sleeping outside last night? You are seeing many moving stars? Is it more cold than in the tent?' The two women linked arms and continued together until Brad indicated that they had arrived at their destination. They were at a point where paths crossed, clear of trees and vegetation to one side. All eyes strained in the darkness towards the east, bodies tensing in readiness for the promised spectacle, Mike preoccupied with the necessary preparations for capturing the moment on camera. They were all ready, waiting. Conversation once again ceased. Maggie was now close beside Jim, whose arm was around her waist.

And then it happened, with first of all a tantalising moment of lightening in the sky that seemed to hover in time and space, and then what had been promised arose slowly, dramatically, with majesty in full unremitting splendour. Each frame, each horizontal segment of the dazzling sphere lingered as if for a fraction of a second and then developed, swelling and expanding until the circle was complete and resplendent. The rising of the sun breathed its life-blood and the world was once again ablaze with colour and revivified as the hearts of the observers were quickened and reanimated. There was an audible gasp of admiration from the group in the clearing with a 'Bravo, bravo!' from Henriette and much hugging and embracing. Jim drew Maggie closer, turning her shoulder towards him and lowering his face to hers. The kiss they shared was tender and forgiving. It was a new day.

Chapter 15

When the two girls paused by the wall for Kate to open her bag, Sarah eyed the seafront trying to decide which restaurant looked the most promising for their evening meal. She glanced casually to the far left, where the blue painted café with the wide terrace commanded a fine view of the sweep of the bay.

'How's your day been? Where are you now? Can you hear me? Are you home now?' she heard her friend saying, raising her voice in order to hear above the noises of the street.

Sarah, suddenly alert, fixed her gaze on the café where a young fair-haired man, also on a mobile, leant perilously forward on the wooden rail. Surely it was Martin! She could not take her eyes off him; his physique, the way he moved, was uncannily like him. But Martin was in London and Kate was at that very moment talking to him on her phone.

Delighted comprehension dawned on both girls at exactly the same moment.

'Martin!' shrieked Kate at the top of her voice.

The young man at the café then appeared to be executing some sort of tribal war dance as he swung round on the spot, waving his long arms in the air.

'Martin!' she yelled again, as at one point he seemed to be seriously at risk of catapulting forwards over the balcony.

Full marks, Martin, thought Sarah privately and delightedly. And well done me!

Kate was fortunate not to break an ankle as she ran full pelt down the rough unevenly paved street in her inappropriate footwear to reach the promenade. Martin meanwhile descended the steps from the terrace to sprint along the front, much to the amusement of those out strolling at a much more leisurely pace. He swung his girlfriend round with many hugs and kisses, and greeted Sarah likewise when she caught up with them. With arms round both girls, Martin guided them along the front. There would be opportunities later for him to be alone with Kate, but tonight was to be a celebration for the three of them.

'The evening's on me,' said Martin, 'but you two know your way around. Which bar? Which restaurant?'

'Well,' declared Sarah, 'if this is to be on Martin, I certainly intend to make the most of it. The Oasis is my suggestion – if that suits you, Kate.'

'Then maybe the restaurant right by the harbour's edge,' added Kate, her eyes shining, hardly able to believe what was happening.

'OK with you, Martin?' asked Sarah.

'Everything is more than OK by me,' laughed Martin as he squeezed Kate's hand tightly.

The silvery path of the moon stretched into inky darkness as the three of them sat by the harbour late into the night.

It was a perfect evening.

Finally, arm in arm, they strolled unsteadily back along the seafront, Kate and Martin escorting a tipsy Sarah uphill to her apartment.

The pair made their way to the taverna, where they lay together, clothes and bedding discarded. A little rivulet of perspiration formed between Kate's breasts, which Martin gently explored with his tongue before clambering on to her. Their hot sticky bodies eventually disentangled and Martin lent over to reach the bottle of water on the floor. They both drank from it, gulping greedily, and then, with Kate reclining on her back, Martin proceeded to trickle water into her belly button, tracing the flow with his finger as it pooled on her skin and found its way in the crease of her waist to the damp sheet below. It was still so hot despite the small fan. Martin now directed the fan to follow the route of the tiny stream. This was cool and refreshing to Kate's skin and she laughed tantalisingly as she encouraged him to direct more rivulets to those other softer and secret parts of her aching body. The bottle was discarded with some urgency as Martin's leg straddled Kate to claim her as his own.

The next day dawned with blue brilliance as it was bound to do. Sarah had thoughtfully announced that she would visit the island's capital town by the local bus and heroically managed to catch it, despite feeling somewhat fragile. Kate and Martin ate a late breakfast overlooking the square, drinking copious amounts of black coffee and eating surprisingly large amounts of fresh bread, tempted by the inviting aroma from the nearby bakery. Martin was pondering his next move. He needed the perfect location. Kate enthused over the beach she had discovered with Sarah. It sounded idyllic, but Martin was searching for a new location, their own discovery, a place for themselves for a day.

'What's the best way to discover a perfect beach?' he asked, leaning back balancing on the back two legs of his chair and stretching his long legs before him.

'Maybe the map for starters,' suggested Kate. 'Then foot, bike, car or boat.'

Martin contemplated these possibilities.

'Only a little bit of foot,' he said. 'It's just too damned hot to walk far. As for car, I'm pretty sure there's no rental place here. Bike then – if they are available? Boat?'

Kate considered the options. Boat appealed most. There is, she thought, always something very satisfying about travelling by boat.

'I could get the map,' offered Martin allowing the front legs of his white plastic chair to hit the ground. There was a cracking sound. Martin rose and examined the chair legs. 'No big deal,' he commented. 'Was probably already cracked.'

'How many times have you been told not to do that,' commented Kate, but with unconvincing concern. Martin went off to get his map.

Several little inlets and coves, clearly inaccessible by road or path, looked inviting, promising isolation and privacy. Down on the harbour front they pottered amongst fishing gear, tarpaulins and coils of rope to check out the possibility of hiring a boat or persuading a fisherman to ferry them to one of their chosen locations. Typically, there seemed a dearth of little boats at that particular time. However, they understood from one swarthy youngster with a shock of curly black hair offloading cans of Coke, that there might be the possibility of a man with a boat in about half an hour. Half an hour became an hour which they passed in delightful indolence beneath a parasol with a couple of large beers and then they noticed a small boat enter the harbour to be hailed by their dark-haired friend. After much gesticulation and nodding in their direction, they were beckoned to the harbour side. The elder man leapt adroitly from the boat making way for the younger who began untying ropes indicating that Kate and Martin should board.

'Hang on a minute,' requested Martin, 'you don't know where we want to go yet,' and he began fumbling with his map. 'We're after a scenic beach that we will have to ourselves for the rest of the day. Look, what about this one?' and he indicated one they had earmarked earlier.

'No, no,' replied the young Greek shaking his head. 'No, you no want that one. You want small island.'

'I don't think we do,' replied Martin decisively. 'Tour boats go to that one.' He had remembered Amy's pep talk. 'We'll have it to ourselves for an hour or two and then the whole of Greece will arrive with the tour boat, the music and the barbecue. We want to be by ourselves. Just the two of us.' He emphasised his point again, this time hoping to clarify his request with added gestures. 'Small beach. Small beach. Two people. Just two. Special beach. Special beach for my girlfriend.' And he put his arm around Kate, squeezing her close whilst looking earnestly at the young fisherman and nodding his head for added emphasis.

'Not that one island. Other one, very small. No see on map. Very good island. This small island we go. You will like island. I promise you will like island.'

Kate grinned at Martin who shrugged his shoulders.

'I don't care where we go,' she said happily. 'Anywhere sounds good to me. And anyway, it's quite obvious that our guide has already made his decision. Let's go.'

The faces of the three of them relaxed into big smiles as the little boat left the harbour setting off in the opposite direction from yesterday's beach. At first, they kept fairly close to the shore, passing cove after cove seemingly unreachable other than by sea. Then rounding some rocks, they turned seawards, the water becoming a little choppier and cooler, thought Kate, as she trailed her hand in the water. She felt absurdly happy, still unable quite to believe that Martin had joined her on impulse and deeply grateful also to her discreet and loyal friend. She too knew that today would be a special day.

'Now you see it!' called the young lad above the noise of his motor, gesticulating wildly with his right hand. At first sight, their island appeared little more than a lump of rock rising splendidly from the deep blue of the sea, but as they drew closer, Kate and Martin could see that there was more to it than first met the eye. Dramatically perched at the height of the crag were the whitewashed remains of a tiny chapel. As they approached they made out vegetation of some sort and a few gnarled bent trees. There was even the possible vestige of age old terracing. Strange to think that such a small islet might once have been inhabited.

'We go round,' explained their guide.

To the west were the remains of a little landing stage.

'You have plenty water?' queried Yannis. Martin assured him that they had come well provided. 'Then you take this,' added the young man, delving beneath one of the wooden seats. He handed a plastic carrier bag to Kate. 'I come at half past four,' he informed them. Then he was off with a smile and a wave, blowing a kiss to Kate. 'I love you, I love you,' he called dramatically, bowing low as he steered the little boat away.

This was, of course, to be echoed by Martin, but not just then, not until they had explored their island.

The two of them watched the boat disappear and turned to grin at each other. They left their bags near the landing stage, noting reassuringly that its decrepit state and the small pebbly beach would no attraction for bigger boats, and followed an overgrown but easily visible path that led directly upwards in order to have a better view of the lie of the land. It was from this vantage point that they spotted the perfect location for a swim. There was no sandy beach, which was rather to be expected, but instead, veering slightly to the right, was an inlet almost entirely enclosed by smooth blue grey rock, where the water was deep, clear and inviting. Just occasionally the swell of the sea sent a modest surge into the pool.

'You go on down,' said Martin. 'I'll nip back for the bags.'

Kate had barely made her way down to a flattened area of rock, slightly shaded by a jutting out ledge and a sparse almost horizontally growing tree, when Martin bounded down to join her.

Hot bodies, one tanned and one glaringly white, hit the water, which initially felt cold and caused both of them to surface with gasps and shrieks. They were both drawn to the narrow opening connecting with the sea, swimming out into the open with happy abandonment, and then returning, Kate first to continue floating in their beautiful pool, and Martin following with a strong rhythmic crawl. He grabbed Kate from behind, strong hands grasping firm breasts, pulling her to him so that they were both treading water in tandem, Kate spluttering and laughing from the sudden attack.

'Let's have sex in the sea,' urged Martin, further encircling Kate's slippery body as he pressed himself to her.

'Let go, you brute,' yelled his beloved. 'I'm out of my depth. It's not possible. Not with you slithering around!'

Then followed more frantic splashing and further splutters as they fought the swell of the sea and each other in an entanglement of arms and legs.

'You can't,' shrieked Kate as she emerged from another unanticipated ducking. 'It won't work! You're just flopping around like a bit of seaweed.'

'I would hope more than a bit of seaweed,' retorted Martin, punishing her by squeezing her nipples tightly. But, possibly owing to the depth of the water and the occasional surge of the sea, sex was indeed quite tricky, and amidst much giggling and struggling, they abandoned the attempt, concluding their antics with a happy kiss.

'Oh well,' concluded Martin, 'owing to the slight on my manhood, there would appear to be nothing much else to do other than to eat our picnic.'

'What's in here?' was Kate's response as she opened the carrier bag that Yannis had given them.

'I'd forgotten we had that,' said Martin, leaning to look as he handed over a bottle of water whilst biting into a sandwich.

'It's a bottle of the local wine. Fancy him giving us that! How did he come to have it in the boat anyway? Are we supposed to be buying it?'

Martin examined the label.

'Actually, it's quite a reasonable one. I think it's what we had last night.'

'You're right,' agreed Kate, taking it from him. 'Would you like some? It's rather warm, but it is a red. We could put it in the sea for a bit. Or do you think we ought to save it for the boat back and share it with Yannis? There's still something in the bag. What do you think it is?'

'Some of those sweet Greek squashy pastries,' said Martin, peering in. 'Very squashy, squashy pastries.'

'That's really nice of him,' said Kate, 'although I'm not sure I like them very much. They are incredibly sugary. How did he have that ready for us?'

'Are they a bit stale?' asked Martin. 'Do you think he's had them in his boat for a long time?'

He dug his finger into one of the sweet meats and scooped out honey and flaky pastry to stuff in his mouth. 'Superb,' was his verdict. He delved in with his finger and offered some to Kate.

'Delicious,' was her comment.

'So what should we do with these goodies?' questioned Martin.

'We treat them as a lovely and much appreciated gift,' was her response. 'I'm not sure that I've room for them now, but we could enjoy them as a sort of afternoon treat and toast our day on our perfect island.'

'Nice one,' said Martin, 'but as for our island, we've hardly explored it as yet. I know it's a bit hot, but we could surely manage to climb up to the chapel. Some clothes would be a good idea for starters.'

So, suitably clad and with sun hat and cap, they followed a winding path, which soon treated them to a panoramic view of the whole island. It really did begin to look as though it had once been inhabited and even farmed in a modest way.

'People could never have been self-sufficient here, surely,' reasoned Kate.

'Doesn't seem that likely,' agreed Martin, 'but maybe there was only the chapel and literally one or two dwellings. There'd be masses of fish and the mainland isn't far. Perhaps a handful of people lived here for only part of the year.'

In the course of their ascent, they came upon what could have been the overgrown remains of a couple of very simple houses. There was little more than the outline of rough stone buildings. The chapel, however, was surprisingly in remarkably good condition. There was still a roof and once they had pushed open the solid wooden door, and their eyes had become accustomed to the dim interior, they could even make out the remnants of wall paintings.

'What a gem,' declared Kate in tones of admiration. 'Look, fresh flowers! Someone has been here very recently. Candles too! And what is this bowl thing for? This place must be used. It's magic.'

So Martin had another opportunity to seize his moment: There were even matches on a shelf to light the candles. He took Kate in his arms and in a remote chapel high up on a tiny island rising from the depth of the deep blue sea he uttered the words that had come from the mouth of a young Greek boatman some hours earlier. He followed his statement with a question that sang in Kate's ears as the sweetest of melodies.

Later, as they leant up against the warm stones of the chapel wall looking out to sea, Martin took from his pack the red wine and the squashed sweetmeats. They raised the bottle to toast their future and ate the simple food of the gods.

Chapter 16

Martin opened a bottle of wine. He and Kate, just back from Greece, had been joined unexpectedly by Tom.

'You're lucky to find us home,' said Kate when she received Tom's call. 'This time last week we were still in Greece. But yes, of course, seeing as you're in London, come on over.'

Kate, now lay back on the Turkish rug, her head propped up on a well-aimed cushion from her brother who lay sprawling on the couch. Martin was examining the label on the bottle.

'Your dad left this one when he stayed over just as I shot off to claim you back. Very good of him, especially considering the mess I'd left the place in. South Eastern Australia. 'Plum and cherry characters on the nose with a hint of spice. Good with pasta and meat.' Which leads me to an important question. What are we cooking tonight?' he asked, turning towards Kate.

'Seeing as we have my brother here, who'll probably claim to be famished, we might as well go round the corner to the pasta place,' replied Kate. 'But we'll get there reasonably early as it is sometimes a bit crowded on a Saturday night. Have we any nibbly things to have with our wine? And anyway, you haven't finished telling us what you are up to,' she added looking towards Tom. 'Didn't you have any hint of these redundancies?'

'Sure, big hints,' responded her brother. 'Everyone's known it's been on the cards for a while. It's the chaps with the families who've taken it to heart, but the company's pretty decent. There's the parent company for those who'd relocate to the UK – and a number of the guys are Brits anyway. Natural wastage and those who got out earlier make it no big deal really.'

'So what about you?' continued his sister.

'All good,' replied Tom, deftly throwing a handful of peanuts into his mouth. 'I've not been there a huge number of years, but the pay-off's not at all bad. In fact, there's actually an opportunity for me back here, not that I'm interested,' he hastened to add, sensing that Kate was about to question him further.

'So what's the plan then?' asked Martin.

'A bit of a change,' replied Tom. 'I had something sort of lined up with Kip – internet security, e-crime, whatever. It's still on the cards, but postponed now for a bit. And yes, this wine is a good one.' He sniffed his glass appreciatively.

'Well, now you are here,' continued Martin. 'Not that we aren't always delighted to have you, but are you intending to be with us for this weekend, this coming week or, alarming thought, have you an extended period in mind?'

Kate giggled. 'You are the perfect host, my dear love! Let me try to get some further information out of my big brother. Enlighten us further,' she persisted. 'When did you personally know you were to be made redundant, when did you decide to come here and how long will you be in London?'

'Two days ago, yesterday evening and for the weekend,' was the prompt reply. Kate and Martin slowly digested this information.

'So,' mused Martin, 'you only officially knew you were to lose your job on Thursday. Yesterday, Friday, you decided to come here and tomorrow you're off again.'

'That's about it,' said Tom.

'Are we going to be given any details concerning these speedy decisions?' continued Kate.

So Tom elaborated. He had decided to 'do his own thing', namely to abandon his current lifestyle in favour of travelling the world, reasonably confident that he had sufficient resources to make this possible and prepared to take the risk of a career break at this stage in his life. He had contacted Kip that same Thursday evening, now that the project they had previously had in mind was on hold, to see if he would be prepared to backpack around the world with him, but Kip, though sorely tempted, could not match Tom's impetuosity. He still wanted more time to research their other option. However, an equally impulsive unattached young man from the adjoining department whom as yet Tom knew only vaguely, and with whom he found himself in conversation over an extended Friday lunchtime, apparently jumped at the opportunity. So Tom was back in London to deal with a few practicalities and to bid his farewells. He had rung his father upon arrival at Heathrow arranging to see him on the Sunday and then spend some time with Kip, returning to Paris to finalise his plans with Miles.

'Well,' said Martin and not without a trace of admiration, 'I must say you don't lose much time once your mind is made up.'

'And neither did you!' Kate, her glowing face wreathed in smiles, directed the warmest of loving looks towards her partner. Martin basked in his unaccustomed role of conquering hero, as Tom glanced enquiringly from one to the other.

However, Tom had to wait for his enlightenment until the three of them had finally been found a table at the local restaurant. He had already guessed that Martin and his sister had their own story to tell. Like Richard, he had been a little surprised to hear that Kate was off on a holiday with a former school friend, but had read no significance into the proposed holiday. It now seemed that Kate had accompanied her friend a little reluctantly – the true purpose of the holiday remaining undisclosed – and that it hadn't taken Martin very long to realise that he missed her and couldn't do without her. So the tale was recounted in the main and then both Kate and Martin hesitated. They had decided to surprise family and friends with an engagement ring, which hadn't as yet materialised, since they had not yet had the opportunity to check out any jewellers. But they were too happy to keep their secret to themselves, which resulted in Tom ordering of a bottle of sparkling white and much clinking of glasses. Tom was genuinely delighted for his sister and pleased to think that Martin would become part of the family, for although dissimilar in many ways, the two men enjoyed an easy understanding and mutually appreciative relationship.

'You won't have been able to contact Mum as yet,' commented Tom after offering his congratulations, 'but what about Dad? He didn't say anything to me on the phone.'

'No,' admitted Kate with some hesitation. 'I suppose we would have liked to share our news with all our parents at the same time, so perhaps we should have held off any announcement until that became possible. Anyway, we'll certainly tell Dad now and then Mum when we can.'

'We could all drive up tomorrow morning,' suggested Martin. 'Unless you're already sorted out with a train ticket.'

'Sounds a good idea to me,' agreed Kate. 'We haven't seen him for a while so we can check out how he's getting on without Mum.' A sudden thought struck her. 'You could well meet up with Mum in Australia,' she declared, turning to her brother, 'or is that part of your plan anyway?'

It had indeed crossed Tom's mind fleetingly that he was likely at some point in his travels to find himself in the same continent as his mother. But further than that, he had not thought.

'It might be possible,' he accepted. 'I suppose it all depends how long she's away and where Miles and I get to. It's been what now? Over a month? I've no idea what she's planning. Has anyone? Do you think Dad has any idea?'

'I think she might have been planning long term,' volunteered Martin, trying to recollect what had actually been said on that summer day in the garden.

'I don't like her being so out of touch,' confided the daughter. 'In the early days we had lots of texts and long newsy emails. I understand totally that she can't contact from where she is now, but I look forward to having some more news in due course. She'd be so excited to know of our engagement and I'd love to know what she's up to. Anyway, Tom, what do you think about us all going to see Dad tomorrow?'

'Seems a good idea,' agreed Tom, 'providing my soon to be acquired brother-in-law can put up with me in the back of the car.'

'He could try!' acknowledged Martin.

'We'll have to give a ring on the way up the motorway,' said Kate, now thinking of the practicalities of the visit. 'And suggest we take him out for a pub meal, because although he's expecting you, Tom, he won't know we're coming too.'

'I expect it would have been a pub meal anyway,' said Tom, 'But, yes, we ought to let him know. Can't spring too many surprises on the chap tomorrow.'

Back at the flat, Kate disappeared into the kitchen to make some coffee.

'So what will happen with Danielle now?' asked Martin.

'Michelle.'

'Sorry,' said Martin, adding a little wryly, 'sometimes difficult to keep up.'

Tom grinned, then shrugged. 'There's never been anything serious in it for either of us, but we've had some good times. I've decided to stop searching for the perfect woman for now. Neither Miles nor I have programmed women into our immediate plans although we probably won't mind if we come by one or two on the way. Anyway,' he added as Kate reappeared with the coffee, 'You've laid claim to the perfect girl and they don't grow on trees, you know.'

Richard was quick to answer the door, even as Kate fumbled in her bag for her key.

'Good to see you all,' was his cheerful greeting as he welcomed them. 'Come on in. You've made good time since your phone call. This is the earliest I could have expected you. Motorway not too busy then?'

'Perfectly reasonable journey,' confirmed the prospective son-in-law, with a strong firm handshake. Tom bounded energetically into the house making for the living room almost as if in expectation of seeing his mother.

'It's strange to come and find that Mum's not here,' commented Kate, echoing Tom's first thoughts. Everything about her parents' home was both just as it was before Maggie's departure yet at the same time different. 'The feminine touch,' thought Kate. 'No fresh flowers, too many old newspapers lying around, bathroom adequately clean but no fresh fragrances.' Yet Maggie's scent still lingered in their bedroom, Kate discovered, as she glanced in at the open door.

'Completed the inspection?' asked her father, as she came downstairs again. 'How many marks do I get?'

'Full marks I'm sure,' she replied, giving Richard a hug and a kiss. 'Although possibly not for the sideboard,' she added, tracing a wavy line on the dusty surface with her finger.

'So what's your special news?' asked the father turning to the son, when they were all settled with a coffee in the living room. 'I gather there's some particular reason for your trip home. Did you say there were some big changes at work?'

So Tom outlined the recent events affecting his company and acquainted his father with his future plans. Richard was not overly impressed. 'I hope you've really thought this through,' he commented finally. 'It's a good company you're working for with opportunities both in the UK and in France. You're doing well there. You have a good salary, pleasant working conditions, excellent prospects.' Richard was clearly not well pleased by Tom's decision.

'But I'm bored, Dad. I agree with all you say, but I want something different for a while,' remonstrated Tom, 'And I'm in a fortunate enough position to be able do something about it. I want to travel. See things, have new experiences.

This in itself could open up all sorts of new possibilities for me. Surely you can see that?'

'Sometimes I wonder what's got into all my family,' said Richard heavily and they all knew that he was no longer referring to his son, but that he had his wife very much in mind.

'Come on, Dad!' comforted Kate, placing an arm around him. 'Mum and Tom both want a bit of time out, a well-deserved holiday for Mum and a change in direction for Tom. You know you enjoy a fresh challenge yourself! Haven't you been delving into your gypsies recently when your head would normally be buried in medieval documents? How are your gypsies anyway and did you have a successful time in London? Martin was very sorry to abandon you to our not so tidy flat and thanks for the excellent wine you left us. We enjoyed it very much. We had something special to celebrate last night which we'll tell you all about when we get back from our lunch.'

So Kate was able to lighten the atmosphere, just as her mother would have done. It occurred to Martin, in conversation with Richard as they walked back from the pub, that perhaps he should have requested permission from his future father-in-law for his daughter's hand. Did anyone still do that, he wondered, or did the fact that he and Kate had been living together for some half a dozen years render that superfluous? He was able to compromise by elaborating a little on the Greek holiday so that the announcement they made later was not entirely unexpected. Richard, like Tom, was delighted and like Kate only sorry that Maggie was not there to share in the news.

'We must get this news to your mother,' declared Richard. 'I've been wondering seriously about getting out to Australia myself whilst there's still an opportunity before the start of the next academic year. I've barely taken any of my allocation to date. Trouble is, I can't make contact at the moment and I've no idea when this Red Centre part of her trip ends, nor whether her intention is to return to Sydney or to continue travelling.

The three young people exchanged glances. Why had no one thought of this suggestion before? There was no reason at all why he should not plan a short visit to Australia. Their parents could have some point together, their father would feel reassured and Maggie could continue with her grand tour if she so wished.

'Have you searched for flights?' asked Kate.

'I'm waiting to see where to,' explained Richard. 'What I ought to do now is to email my plan so that your mother picks it up when she next has internet access. Then she could book us somewhere for a couple of weeks or so depending where she happens to be at the time.' Or come back with me, was his secret thought.

'I probably could catch up with her at some time,' mused Tom, 'especially if she does prolong this trip of hers. Perhaps we could explore a particular location together.'

'There's no reason why you and I shouldn't have a holiday in Australia at some time,' added Martin, turning to Kate. 'You'll have a ring to show her in due course. She'll certainly want to share in the news of our engagement, if but a bit belatedly. Come to think of it, if she's not back towards the end of the year, we could get out there for a dose of winter sunshine.'

'And why not?' thought Kate.

With the possibility of a family Christmas on the beach, the rest of the afternoon passed happily. Tom bade his father a perfectly amicable farewell and Richard wished his son good luck in his travels. Kate and Martin drove home contentedly, for if Maggie was not yet ready to return, the family was now prepared to visit.

It appeared to be a very simple solution.

Chapter 17

They returned to the camp in high spirits and preparations for breakfast were soon in full swing. Mike and Luke applied themselves energetically to the fire as Jo, Jim and Maggie began to cut up generous hunks of bread. Henriette took control of the sausages whilst Brad cracked eggs beside her and plates, mugs and cutlery were speedily and noisily assembled. It was as if the sunrise had inspired and reinvigorated them. They were all in a visibly relaxed mood and the atmosphere was one of happy conviviality.

Brad looked up from the task in hand to observe his group, aware that they had now experienced the highlights of what he had to offer. The magic of Uluru never failed. This shared experience in the Red Centre would be with them for the rest of their lives.

'See what you do now! You are breaking them. You are not attending properly to your eggs.'

'Sorry, Henriette. You can have two eggs to compensate.'

'I am having two eggs already,' pouted Henriette. 'You make us get up so early and you are making us very, very hungry. Now I am starving!'

'Looks as though you'll pull through,' commented Luke as he made his way to the log, eyeing her plastic plate which bent dangerously under the weight of her food.

Brad was interested to note this comment. At the beginning of the trip, he had had reservations about the integration of young Luke into the expedition. He seemed a particularly gauche and awkward youth whose independent travels so far had not resulted in the usual growth of self-confidence or ability to socialise that might have been expected. The two older women, perhaps playing the maternal role, had initially helped him to feel valued and in so doing had enabled an awkward young man to develop and to find his way. Brad wondered whether Luke himself would come to recognise this in the future when looking back upon this period of his life. He could become a skilful zoologist or botanist, mused the leader, who was aware of the detailed notebook Luke kept relating to the varying habitats and wildlife he observed within the various areas they had so far explored. There would be the opportunity, Brad hoped, to introduce him to the botanical gardens in Alice Springs before they all finally dispersed. He remembered too the conversation they had had in the dried up riverbed relating to creeks and waterholes and how Luke had contrasted this landscape with the open woodland of hard stony ground with the mulga trees and spinifex. Brad had then told him of the fresh water claypans that could appear after the rains, attracting small animals to drink such as the marsupial mouse and sand goanna and how these animals searched for higher ground when the rain flooded their burrows.

'Always on the move,' commented Luke, 'Not much permanence. A fragile existence. A bit like me really.'

The two men sat quietly.

'The fragile habitat's the norm here,' continued Brad. 'In the morning in the dunes you can trace a myriad of intermingling tracks in the sand and the spinifex plains, the low areas between the dunes, are home to more species, the tarkawara, mutingka, lungkata and muluny-mulunypa.'

'Sounds like poetry.'

'You're right there. Poetry and stories. Imagination runs riot here. Anything could happen. And, of course, it's a landscape of respect. That's how the whole thing works and how it has evolved through history.'

And Luke had shut his eyes and leant back on the rock.

Brad now balanced his own plate in his hands and made his way to join the others in the circle, squeezing himself into a space between Luke and Henriette, who was enthusiastically devouring her eggs, bacon and sausages.

'How are you going to cope with croissant and coffee when you get back home?' questioned Beck, amused by the young girl's appetite.

'I am never having croissant and coffee for my breakfast. Only foreigners think the French are eating this.'

'So what do you have then?'

'I am eating cornflakes and I have an orange juice, or sometimes it is hot chocolate. Sometimes I am not very hungry and I am not eating breakfast at all.'

'Have another sausage in readiness for the frugal time ahead,' offered Beck, spearing one from her own plate.'

'Why are we talking about going home?' said Dee. 'We're only just over halfway through this trip – there's more to come.'

'But we may have had the best bits,' commented her husband. 'We've seen the sunrise and the sunset. They surely will have been the highlights, whatever else happens.'

'You have seen the sun rise once at Uluru. You have seen the sun set once at Uluru,' interrupted Jo. 'It will rise and set every day for the rest of your life, whether you see it or not. And it will always be different.'

Quite a profound thought for breakfast, pondered Maggie, glancing at Jim and wondering what he was thinking. He returned her glance with a smile. Had they really had the best bits, he secretly wondered. What was to become of this trip for the two of them?

'Dee's right,' said their leader. 'There's more to come. And before you get too comfortable around this fire, you need to remember that we're striking camp today and moving on. I give you one hour, so we need to get going. The basic equipment, including tents, gets left here for the next group, so its sleeping bags, blankets and personal luggage into the trailer and then a big clean-up – cooking area, washing shack and the fire. Don't leave any personal items here, for there's no way we're coming back. Then we'll be travelling for a bit passing through Aboriginal territory and although I agree, you've witnessed the splendour of the rising and setting sun in the Red Centre, I can promise you more treats in store. We erect our own tents tonight and of course,' turning to Henriette, 'I've promised you an en suite with a bucket and string.'

'I think I am looking for the train to Paris.'

So began the clean-up operation, with the group working well as a team under Brad's guidance.

They set off mid morning and drove for some time without seeing another vehicle. The cold of the night as usual quickly developed into a sunny day of cobalt blue sky contrasting with the dusty red road ahead of them, desert sandhill country. Maggie sat beside Jim, trying yet again to make sense of the outback and the recent events to which this scenery had been the backdrop.

How had it all started, this Australia thing?

She recalled, from what seemed like a long time ago, her farewell from school and her summer birthday celebration amongst family and friends in her sunny garden. She remembered the secret planning of her special retirement trip and how it seemed to go slightly wrong when first announced, as Kate handed her the knife and she cut her cake. There was that uncomfortable, mercifully brief, period of confusion and discomfort and then the tedious long-haul flight and her arrival at fascinating, vibrant Sydney. Overcoming her fear at the time of her assault she continued her travels to find herself here, at the very centre of this great continent.

She gazed ahead, as if transfixed. The road had no end to it and led ever onwards into infinity. The red earth, the deep blue of the arcing sky by day and the velvet, sweeping blackness of the sky by night with its never-ending multitude of stars were too vast for comprehension. Here, everything was magnified and she felt exhausted by the intensity of her own emotions.

It had started with the rock and the small fissure or cave where present and past had become inextricably jumbled, for this was where she had watched the industrious ants and thoughts of her family had come to mind. Although she would never recover from the loss of her little girl, she was able then to smile and acknowledge the happy memories.

The 4WD jolted along, so that the passengers bumped against each other and Maggie was very conscious of Jim's sleeping frame lurching beside her. She stole a sideways glance. His eyes were closed although she did not think he was asleep.

She stared ahead to relive once more the telling of his story. She had felt physically sick when its inevitable cruel outcome slowly began to dawn, but now regretted her moment of revulsion towards the man in whose arms she had so recently lain. Yet it was the very thought of this intercourse, of the connection of their two bodies, that was at that moment simply too much to bear. It was as though the sex between them had become sullied, sordid, a betrayal. Then he had dropped the torch at the shack.

It was not Jim's fault.

Then the sun had risen.

She turned compassionately to study his face once more.

What was it she felt for this man, whom she had known for so short a time?

And what about Richard?

Jim opened his eyes and rested his hand on his companion's thigh. He too had grappled with thoughts concerning the strange chance of their meeting and the brevity and intensity of their relationship. Even if he felt exonerated from blame in respect of the actions of his brother, he could not rid himself of feelings of guilt where Maggie was concerned.

He loved Maggie.

But what did she feel for him?

And what about Richard?

A sudden swerve jarred all travellers into consciousness. The speck on the horizon, visible for some time, a vehicle similar to their own creating a swirl of dust in its path now approached. Both drivers maintained both their speed and central positions on the dirt track until the last possible moment, when they swerved abruptly amidst much tooting of horns, shrieking of passengers and amicable waving.

'Why are you driving like this?' remonstrated Henriette. 'Long time we see him coming and you stay in the middle.'

'So you prefer me to keep to the left?'

Again, another lurching of the 4WD, swaying of the trailer and cries of occupants as Brad turned his vehicle into the bumpier unevenness of the left-hand side.

'OK for you now?'

'No! I am not liking this either. You go back now please. Middle is much better.'

Again, bodies bumped into each other and Jim took the opportunity to advance his arm across Maggie's lap.

The journey continued and time passed.

'Now see where we're coming to,' said their driver.

There seemed to be some sort of settlement ahead and all peered curiously, craning necks, as dwellings of some sort began to be discernible in the dust and heat haze ahead. Eventually they slowed down as the first of the Aboriginal shacks came into view, a flimsy wooden single-storey construction with a tin roof and verandah. In front were the vestiges of discarded consumerism, a rusting old car on its side, a broken television, some old mattresses and what looked like a pile of old clothing. There were a couple of plastic chairs on the verandah and further old mattresses on which sat a couple of women. Children played amongst the rubbish where the blackened remains of a fire could be seen. The occupants of the 4WD fell silent. Compelled to view the scene before them, they none-the-less felt some embarrassment at their intrusion into the lives of others. No heads, apart from those of a couple of small children, turned in their direction. A little further on, a woman of indeterminate age sat near the roadside. She was swarthy and black with a tangled mass of tousled hair, dark but with streaks of orange. She crouched on her haunches, her gnarled left hand clutching her chin. Her face was broad and full, eyes sunken and squinting. Her nose was wide, expanding and full and her cheeks had the hardness of shiny conkers. She was wearing what appeared to be a full and long skirt of tweed like fabric with an oversize, loose, multi-coloured, baggy blouse. She remained, unmoving, as their vehicle passed. Maggie was hypnotised.

Suddenly, she became aware that their leader was speaking.

'So when administrators offered decent housing, it related to what officialdom considered appropriate, which of course did not equate with the needs of the Aboriginal community. Visible possessions are just not important. It remains a problem.'

That was what one kept hearing, remembered Maggie. She also recalled how Brad had explained that eye contact would be thought inappropriate. But the children are quite gorgeous, she thought. How sad to be unable to exchange a smile.

At a point where a lesser, undefined track met their road was a larger building which Brad explained was the one shop – a supermarket that stocked a wide range of basic necessities from food items to household products and clothing. Here he stopped briefly for those who wished to stock up with canned drinks or any other goods. Maggie scanned the shelves with interest. Enough to survive on, she concluded, but all rather drab, although she noted a reasonable supply of items for babies and children. Strange, she thought, to travel to a remote settlement the other side of the world and find recognisable makes of disposable nappies for sale. A young woman worked the till, displaying little interest in them or their purchases. They were few others in the supermarket at that time, although there were more women squatting outside to the front of the building. Little else was happening – a couple of lads disinterestedly kicking a Coke tin between them and three or four dogs scrapping together – as they returned to the 4WD to continue their route. Apart from the adjacent petrol station, there was nothing of note and the community was soon behind them.

The waterhole that they reached after some further four or so hours was certainly lush by contrast. It had the appearance of a small lake edged with quite high rocks and even boasted a sort of beach of mud and gravel. Brad confirmed the hole safe for swimming and some of the hardier members of the party were soon in the water. But not for long, for the water was surprisingly cold and there was in addition work to be done as it was necessary to set up camp before evening. Jo and Beck proved adept at this task as did Mike, happily recalling former scouting days. Being small and basic, the tents were easy to erect and even Henriette felt capable of the task. As expected, the washing arrangements left her much to desire, but all was functional and reasonably discreet.

'But already I think of my long, hot shower when we return to Alice,' she commented.

Talk of returning to Alice was a focus of the conversation later round the fire, as the chicken joints began to bubble in the pot. They discovered that they all had accommodation arranged for a further night there so the idea of a final last evening meal at a restaurant was mooted and welcomed. After that, Jo and Beck would return to Sydney for work, Mike and Dee were to visit distant relatives in Brisbane, whilst Werner and Eric planned to visit Adelaide.

'And what about you, Brad?' asked Dee. 'Have you another trip planned or do you get some time off?'

Henriette found herself listening with particular attention.

'I'm between trips for a while. My next one starts in about ten days or so. Although I've a small place in Alice, the family has a cattle ranch further north which my brother now virtually manages. I might have myself a week or so up there.' He moved forward to stir the pot, and sensed, but did not see, the young French girl's eyes upon him. He felt redness upon his neck and face, which could not be totally accounted for by the intensity of the campfire.

'And what about you, Henriette?' asked Luke.

'Oh I am not knowing for the present,' she replied in some confusion.

'Well,' volunteered Brad after a moment's pause, 'I'm going to persuade Luke to hang on for a further day so I can take him round the botanical gardens. You'd enjoy that too. Why don't you stay on for a day or so, and join us?'

That, for Henriette seemed to be a satisfactory start to what she hoped might be a further stage in their relationship. Once Luke was on his way, she could consider her next move.

'Nobody asked us what our plans were,' said Jim much later that night, after darkness enveloped the camp and they cuddled together in their small tent.

'Too polite, I think. Perhaps they feel uncomfortable at the thought of us two oldies together. We're neither of us the type to have a holiday romance and the idea of a relationship, if indeed any of them have been bothered or interested to consider the matter, must probably appear almost obscene.'

'But,' very gently, 'what are our plans?'

There was a long silence.

Finally, slowly and haltingly, she replied, 'It's a strange feeling I have here – as though disassociated from everything I have formerly known and understood. Here we are cut off from everything but somehow we seem to have been destined to meet by some strange and amazing coincidence. Rationally, I know that the return to Alice Springs will bring an end to our relationship. But for now, I don't know.'

It seemed to Jim that the pounding of his own heart must surely awaken the whole camp.

'Perhaps we could continue together for just a little longer?'

Their arms were now tightly around each other. 'We could extend our holiday. We could go anywhere.'

He waited. There was no response, but he felt the tensing of her body and then its relaxation and softening.

'Is there anywhere else you would like to go?' he coaxed gently.

'What were your original plans?'

'Flexible, but I think I might have gone on to see the Great Barrier Reef. A visit to this country would somehow be incomplete without that experience.'

Maggie thought of the great, wide, open ocean and the majesty of the reef with the beauty and abundance of its priceless treasures. And she thought about sharing all this with the man beside her, with whom she would also share her body before the night was over.

The idea of the reef was delightful.

Chapter 18

The party dining at the Emu were in lively mood. They were eleven in number, seated at their own long wooden table in prime position overlooking the street, a scene typical of activities centred on Alice, since many of the trips into the outback ended in this way with the farewell dinner. As often, the group was mixed in terms of sex and age range, but bore the familiar mark of individuals brought together in a shared experience characterised by a particular sense of bonhomie. As the evening progressed and more alcohol was consumed, the inevitable toasts were proposed.

On this occasion, it was Brad to whom the glasses were raised. The ten participants were fully aware of their indebtedness to the enthusiasm and expertise of this young, bronzed Australian leaning back on his chair with a cheerful grin. He had witnessed such occasions many times before, but for him, each celebration was unique. However, despite adamant assurances to the contrary and much serious exchange of contact addresses, he knew that few of them would ever meet again. After many years leading such expeditions, this was not, in his view, a matter of regret. On the contrary, it was, in his opinion, cause for celebration that a group of people previously unknown to each other, now at the parting of their ways, could converge in such harmony. Throughout the trip he had been concerned, as always, only with the well-being of the individuals with whom he had been entrusted and had delighted in their pleasures and achievements. He would like to think he would remember them all, but realistically he knew that, in time, some faces would fade, simply because over the course of the years he met so many. On the other hand, those now round the table would possibly remember him more readily, not because he was a great guy in any sense, but simply because for them, there had been only one trip and one leader.

But for now, he could relax, for all had been safely and successfully accomplished. Looking round, he saw Dee in animated conversation with Luke, discussing the last day at the waterhole that had offered them the opportunity of a morning's walk with an Aboriginal guide. They had scrambled over rough earth to stony ground where they had been fascinated by the rock art and over a lunchtime picnic listened to stories of the journeys of Ancestral Beings. Their guide had produced seed-grinding tools and described the way of life of his father and forefathers since time immemorial. Werner had questioned him further about Aboriginal paintings and was now anxious to view some of the art displayed in shops in the Mall before the next day's flight. Their guide had explained that many Aboriginal artists supplied a diversity of art to shops and galleries run by white men in Alice and that Werner would be able to see a range of paintings on bark and paper; also carvings and didgeridoos. He expressed the hope that this situation would change over the years, but currently the white man was still necessary if the art was to reach outlets further afield. Werner had been intrigued by the paintings he had seen at Uluru and their associated stories. He had peered closely at the central circle of interwoven dots, his close gaze spiralling ever outwards to spy the python with her eggs and the poisonous snake sidling in from the bottom of the painting. His gaze followed the paw prints of he knew not what and the more readily identifiable wallaby tracks from the top. He sought out the human footprints and the spears and had then stood back in admiration and contemplation. 'They say so much, these paintings! I want my work to speak as clearly.'

Brad, who had been interested to watch Werner at work with his sketchbook during the course of the last few days, and like Jim and Maggie thought the young man to be quite talented, faced him squarely.

'But so does your art. Those red gums of yours tell their own tale.'

Werner made no reply, but secretly he was deeply encouraged by Brad's openly honest approval of his work. He was pleased too that Jim had also been impressed and had actually requested two sketches that he had insisted on purchasing. Werner somehow felt that the appreciation of his friends was worth even more to him than his success locally last year in exhibiting at a couple of not insignificant exhibitions. He began to believe that Eric's overt admiration was not misplaced. He began to believe in himself.

Eric meanwhile had turned towards Mike, who appeared to be recounting some exploit that required much waving of hands. The young German had remained much of a foil to Werner, quick to praise his friend and protective of all his endeavours, but he too had also had his day – notably during the exploration of the creek with his impromptu and expertly executed gymnastic display. It had won him a round of applause from the group and subsequently encouraged him to practise his daily exercise routine in front of his tent before breakfast, when it then became Werner's turn to admire the efforts of his friend.

It fell to Mike to give the final farewell speech. Although they would all be in Alice that night, they were in different motels and apartments, so this really was the last goodbye. In actual fact, since there is little more to Alice than Todd Mall, some paths were bound to cross the next morning, and indeed Jim and Maggie in fact found themselves breakfasting in a café with Beck and Jo whilst whiling away the hours before their afternoon flights.

'So you're off to Cairns then?' commented Jo.

'That seems to be the plan,' replied Jim, 'but we'll probably move on a little further up the coast. The general idea is to see something of the reef.'

But the Australian women were no fools. They, like the others in the party, had witnessed the developing friendship between these two, and knew that the exploration of the reef, impressive and rewarding as it may well prove, was not the main focus for the extension of the trip. They kept their thoughts to themselves, however, and set about giving some practical advice about various locations and how to visit the reef.

'It's a vast area, hundreds of islands and goodness only knows how many individual reefs.'

'What you want to watch out for,' added Beck, 'are trips in the smaller boats to the lesser-known islands or sand cays. Then you won't find yourselves moored up to pontoons alongside numerous other boats with masses of divers and snorkellers.'

'Get yourselves into the rain forest too, masses of interesting flora and fauna, quite enough to keep our Luke happy for the rest of his life.'

Coincidentally, as his name was mentioned, Luke together with Brad and Henriette came into view at the far end of the Mall. However, the threesome seemed intent on their mission and carried on walking without noticing the group at the café.

'Looks like the botanic garden expedition is under way,' commented Beck.

'And we must get on our way too,' added Maggie. 'We have packing to do before we're off. But thanks for the invitation to Sydney. We may well look you up.'

But privately, Maggie and Jim were both aware that they probably wouldn't.

And so Maggie and Jim bade farewell to the Red Centre. Their flight to Cairns left on time and the two travellers peered through the window for a last viewing of a landscape that had played such a significant role in both their lives. How amazing, thought Maggie, to have lived as we have done so entirely in the present, and be totally unaware of what might happen the following day, or even the same night.

Formalities were quickly completed at the airport, where they picked up a hire car and headed out of town. After only a short while they decided to stop at an inexpensive motel for they both suddenly felt inordinately tired. They climbed the stairs to their modest room and both fell into a deep sleep as soon as their heads touched the pillows. Despite the rather thin mattress, to the two weary travellers it felt like heaven.

It was also heavenly to wake up the next morning. Both felt incredibly refreshed, the sky was an azure blue, breakfast beckoned and the day lay ahead of them. They felt the warmth of the Australian sun permeate into their backs as they ate their bacon, eggs, sausages and hash browns on the terrace and discussed their plans for the day. They decided to continue north, up the coast, leaving Cairns behind them, so left in good spirits to enjoy a leisurely drive, finally stopping at a small resort, some several hours later.

'This is lovely!' commented Maggie. 'Just look at that beach!'

To their right was a curve of pristine sand edged by palms and green foliage. There was a small, wooden jetty, with not much happening, and the outline of an island was just visible on the horizon. The resort road was flanked to the water's side by tough but springy green grass that showed evidence of regular watering and to the left by a collection of various properties, a few cafés and an indifferent looking small hotel. At the far side of the horseshoe, beyond a dried up river mouth, there appeared to be cabins and possibly a campsite. But it was the beach that was king.

And so, in the late afternoon, installed in a small self-catering apartment overlooking the beach, with ice cubes in the making and provisions acquired from the nearby supermarket, Maggie and Jim sat on the verandah, with an as yet insufficiently cool bottle of wine on the rickety table between them.

As Jim took Maggie in his arms that night, the years once again rolled away and bodies that were no longer smooth and firm felt almost young. The waves broke rhythmically on the shore close by.

The following morning, after an early morning swim, they were once again sitting on their verandah. Out to sea a low line of cloud edged the horizon and behind them, the coastal fringe gave way to a dense rainforest interior, almost as though the two of them were caught in a narrow, albeit inviting, strand in between. For some reason she could not explain, Maggie began to feel slightly uneasy. She was aware, but guiltily resentful of the fact, that her family now deserved some news of her whereabouts and situation. The isolation of the Red Centre had insulated her from thoughts of making contact and she had been able to delude herself that she had had no choice, whereas in reality a problem had been lifted from her shoulders. But now there were decisions to be made.

She went into the cabin to find her mobile.

Jim followed her, carrying the breakfast plates. 'What are you after?' he asked, as she searched through her rucksack.

'My phone. I can't think where I put it. I was wondering whether I'd get a signal here in Queensland.'

'When did you have it last?' queried Jim, kneeling to help.

Maggie thought back to her last texts.

'Not at all in the outback, obviously,' she said. 'Can my last text really have been from Sydney? I suppose it must have been.'

'Have you tried all the pockets in your rucksack?'

Together they searched Maggie's rucksack and then the case she had left at the motel in Alice whilst on the Red Centre trip.

'I rather think I had it in camp, initially not realising I wouldn't be able to use it. There was so much scrabbling around there in tents in the dark that I suppose I could have lost it.'

She went through the both the rucksack and case once again.

'Well it doesn't seem to be here,' concluded Jim. 'But no worries, as they say in these parts. We'll find somewhere to make a call. Sorry I haven't a mobile to offer you.'

Later in the day, at a phone box in a small pedestrian area of the resort, Maggie's attempt to contact home was unsuccessful. Presumably, Richard was out and they had no answerphone. Kate's number for some reason seemed unobtainable.

'OK then,' said Jim. 'It's an internet café we need. Tomorrow, we'll investigate both an internet café and possible trips to the Barrier Reef.'

Jim felt torn by Maggie's evident concern to contact home and the fear he nursed inwardly that external influences would now begin to play a significant role in their future plans.

They returned to the beach in the late afternoon. The day was cooling so they abandoned plans to swim once more and walked hand in hand back from the jetty to the furthermost side of the bay, crossing the now sandy river mouth with its small pool of rather stagnant water.

'Look at this!'

They stopped to read a wooden notice on the beach.

'Crocodiles! Surely you don't get crocodiles on a beach!'

'Salties!' commented Maggie, recalling her Manly friend and his stories. 'I suppose when the river is in full flow, some of them might make their way down here.' She turned back to eye the scrub, twisted roots and rough grass bordering the beach, scrutinising the undergrowth for signs of movement. 'Not the right season, I suppose. Strange country. Full of surprises!'

They continued their walk, clambering upwards when the beach ended to follow a small and rocky path that bordered the sea. Here the vegetation became thicker and eventually more difficult to penetrate. The evening too was drawing on and they had lost the warmth of the sun. Eventually they decided to retrace their steps along the beach back to the cabin and then later set out to find a place to eat in the resort.

There were quite a few possibilities but after investigating a number of menus, they settled on what appeared to be a fairly nondescript beachfront restaurant that offered the possibility of eating kangaroo, which neither of them had as yet tasted, and was well patronised, an encouraging sign, they both felt. Now wearing their jackets, they opted to eat outside and were soon giving their orders to a cheerful young Australian lad. Again, as Maggie had noticed and appreciated early on in her travels, this youth seemed genuinely interested in the arrival of another couple of tourists and cheerfully enquired as to where they were staying and their holiday plans. Jim mentioned the possibility of a trip out to the reef and the waiter was speedily forthcoming about the options available.

'Masses of trips out there, but take your time, if you're able, to check out what suits you best. The tourist info up on the left there will have masses of details, but watch out for the varying sizes of boats on the tours and make sure yours offers the option of a glass-bottomed boat. Lots of places around here offer a trip, so shop around and get what you want.'

Required by another customer, he turned from their table, but another diner sitting in close proximity, overhearing the conversation, manoeuvred his chair round in the rather restricted space, to face them and continue the conversation.

'We've just done it,' he volunteered, indicating a teenage boy opposite, presumably his son. 'Yes, they do offer trips from here, but it's worth going up the coast a bit. The next significant place you come to – can't think of its name at the moment, but you can't miss it – runs a great trip. Smallish boat – the only one anchoring at a small cay. Takes a while to get out there, but a fantastic day out. Just brilliant! Quite unbelievable! Corals have been growing on the reef for more than twenty-five million years they say! Now get your head around that. That's old that is. Very old. Some age, I'd say. What do you think to that?' And he turned to his son for confirmation. But his son was busy with his steak, and gestured to his father to get on with his.

'They say about thirty species of whales, dolphins and porpoises have been recorded in the Great Barrier Reef and six – or was it seven – species of sea turtles come to breed. I think it was about five thousand species of mollusc that have been recorded – or have I got that wrong?' He turned again to the boy. But then the waiter arrived with their meals and they were saved further facts and figures, fascinating though they might be.

'Thanks for the info,' said Jim, as he picked up his knife and fork and started to tackle his kangaroo.

They enjoyed both their meal and the sense of good fortune. Later, as Jim was settling their bill, Maggie glanced upwards to see an enormous bat hanging motionless in the branches above them. 'Look, even the bats here are larger than life.'

Jim, behind her, examined the tree. 'There's another one. See there?' And his hands on her shoulders pulled her closer, turning her slightly to one side. He dropped his hands to encircle her waist as she leant her head on to his shoulder. She was conscious only of the thick velvety blackness of the motionless bats amongst the dark leaves and the excitement she always felt at the proximity of Jim's body. Every physical sensation seemed magnified. It was as though they were young lovers. She recalled his touch as they surveyed the canyon in the early days of the outback venture and the tingling of her body on that occasion. How could this be happening to two elderly retirees? But Maggie found it difficult to recognise this description of either of them.

She shivered involuntarily and Jim, assuming she was feeling chilly, further enveloped her within his arms, gently rubbing her sides. Together they turned to make their way back along the beachfront.

Chapter 19

Next morning, as soon as they woke, they knew it had to be their day for exploring the reef. The sky was azure blue and the wind had dropped. They breakfasted speedily and packed the car ready to drive further up the coast, as had been recommended the previous night. Thoughts of emails slipped easily and effortlessly from their minds, with the result that Maggie remained blissfully ignorant of the increasingly pressing communications awaiting her.

Their good fortune continued as they located the jetty where there was a board displaying the daily timetable. It appeared that they had not long to wait before the start of the trip, which at a quick glance around was certainly not over subscribed. They sat on a seat near the end of the jetty and watched a little family on the beach for it was clear that they too had booked the reef trip and the children, aged about ten and twelve, were already very excited.

Soon they were on board, seated in the basic but adequate lounge, listening to a commentary on the programme of activities for the day. It soon became evident that they were being treated to the same discourse as their friend of the previous night, and they exchanged amused glances as facts and dates were detailed. 'According to the Great Barrier Reef Marine Park Authority,' drawled a cheerful Australian voice, 'corals have been growing in the region for as long as twenty-five million years.' More vast and incomprehensible facts and figures, mused Maggie.

Initially, the idea of a dive appealed strongly to them both, but further information suggested that this was perhaps not appropriate for novices, so they settled for snorkelling and possible short trips in the glass-bottomed boat. In carefree and happy mood, they made their way up on deck to enjoy the view of the receding coastline and the glimpse of the occasional whale, which caused much interest on board amongst their fellow passengers.

When eventually the tiny sandy cay was sighted and anchor dropped, the passengers busied themselves with collecting wetsuits and diving gear. Amidst the melee Maggie and Jim, finally attired in their wetsuits after wrestling with obstinate zips, grinned happily at each other.

'Let's go!'

Jim was first down the ladder and trod water some yards from the boat as he waited for Maggie. They adjusted their masks and were off, a little tentatively at first, as it was some time since either of them had snorkelled.

They entered another world. Both had been avid readers of their guidebooks and had listened with great interest to descriptions of the reef from their travelling companions, but they were emphatic in agreement later of their lack of preparedness for the sheer beauty of the Barrier Reef which was beyond any expectation. Maggie surfaced first, spluttering in her haste to pull off her mask to shout to Jim.

'This is unbelievable!'

'Fantastic!'

'Did you see those greenish yellow fish? The ones with those startling bands of white with the sort of yellow green tail?'

'What was that big rather sombre darkish-looking one lurking on the bottom?

'Where?'

'Over there!'

They pulled their masks on again and were quick to swim off through the green-blue, milky opalescence of the reef shallows. The intensity of the colours of the huge variety of corals surprised Maggie for, despite what she had been told, she had somehow expected the underwater sea scene to be more muted. She was also taken aback by the varying depth and temperature of the swirling sea. At times her stomach almost grazed the rocky corals and waving fronds of anemones. Then suddenly she might find herself at the edge of a cliff face, swimming over a narrow chasm with its bed of sand. She was amazed too by the indifference of the fish that swam around close to her, nuzzling, even brushing against her wetsuit. Huge shoals of tiny fish would suddenly turn in direction, apparently at whim but perfectly in tune. Cleaner fish nibbled at the gills of larger fish as some fish of the deepest of blues glided by, streamlined and resplendent. Others, broad and flat in shape, lurked nearer the bottom, whilst, in contrast to the orange, yellows and reds, some wore a camouflage of patterned shades of blue. The whole reef was alive with patterns. Within this patterning, thought Maggie, as she observed anemone fish sheltering in waving fronds of anemones, was an interdependence, such as Brad had described when talking about the fragility of the landscape of central Australia.

She surfaced, spluttering to clear her mask of water and looked round for Jim. The small sandy cay was close, so she waded awkwardly ashore for a brief rest and was soon spotted by Jim who made his equally laborious way out of the water to join her. They sat side by side on the sand to compare notes.

'I saw a gorgeous little one with a nose just like a hedgehog. What could it be?'

'I can identify very few, if any,' confided Jim, 'but I don't mind at all. It's quite enough just to see them. There seem to be a myriad of small orange yellow ones. And as for the plant life, it's all so colourful. Did you see those tightly packed yellow plants that look like minute chrysanthemums? And what about those pale, slate green flat fronds tinged with purple? And a branching orange most delicate plant that reminds me of the tracery of Jack Frost on my window pane as a kid?'

'Come on! Let's get back in!'

It was another day that neither of them ever forgot.

Although lunch was available on board, Maggie and Jim were too entranced to eat. The rest of the available time was given to indulging in the magic of the world beneath the sea.

Finally as the boat blew its hooter to call all passengers aboard, they climbed the ladder, rid themselves of their wetsuits and found a couple of seats on the deck. The return journey passed pleasantly and unremarkably, the passengers laid back in cheerful mood.

Back at the cabin after their most memorable day, Maggie and Jim realised they felt both tired and hungry. Jim took the car the short distance to the small supermarket and returned, just as Maggie had finished sorting out their swimwear and towels, with a pizza, chips and fruit which they ate happily on the verandah, balancing plates on their knees. The evening was cooling and they soon turned in to bed, with aching limbs, but happy hearts.

It was another couple of days before Maggie thought of her family at all. She was sitting on the verandah with a book in her hand and a can of beer balanced on the balustrade.

'Oh my god!' The book slipped from her hand. 'I meant to contact the family when we arrived here! How awful to realise that I totally forgot about them. I can't believe how I could do that!'

Hearing her voice, Jim emerged from within the cabin.

'What happened? Why didn't I get round to it? We were going to email them!'

Jim bent down to retrieve the book from the floor and sat down heavily on the chair opposite.

'Yes, we were.' He thought back to their arrival at the resort. 'We went off to the reef, didn't we? And then, I suppose, it went out of our minds. I am sorry. I should have thought of it too. I suppose the reef was so extraordinarily mind blowing and then we had a couple of lazy days here, not bothering to think about anything in particular.'

Maggie was quiet for a few minutes. 'I feel really awful to think that I could forget them all so completely. It makes me feel horribly guilty, as though I'm an evil mother.'

Jim leant forward to pat her knee. 'Come on, it's not as though they aren't all adults with lives of their own. Mothers are allowed to have lives of their own too you know.'

'Of course they are. But they don't forget their children – or their husbands,' she added quietly.

They were both silent. Maggie contemplated the situation in which she now found herself. How could she so totally forget Richard? How could she be so disloyal to a husband who had always looked after her so well? How was it that she was now with Jim? What about love?'

Jim felt as though his body had been given a severe blow from which he struggled desperately for breath. He both understood and shared in Maggie's dilemma. Best deal with the practicalities first.

'Let's get going then. We'll go back down the coast seeing as we don't know what happens further up and find somewhere to email.' He pushed himself up from his chair and offered a hand to Maggie. 'Later, we need to talk,' he added gently, meeting her eye as she stood.

She understood perfectly.

There was little conversation as they drove, as they were both keeping a lookout for a likely place from which they could email. They did not have too far to travel before they saw a likely café and Maggie finally found herself seated in front of a screen with a rather worn-out keyboard.

'I'll be pottering around outside,' said Jim. 'Come and join me when you're ready.'

Maggie sat quietly to collect her thoughts. She would email the children first and Richard, of whom she felt so especially guiltily uncomfortable, last, this being a communication that would demand more careful consideration.

She logged on. Her machine seemed a little slow to respond, but finally she was connected. A number of emails awaited her attention – the usual advertisements and unsolicited mail and a few other undemanding communications. What she had not expected was to find five messages awaiting her from the family. There were two each from Richard and Kate and one from Tom. She looked closely at the dates. A couple from Richard and Kate related to way back on her trip and she opened them first. They were remarkably similar in content, assuming she would not receive them until some time had elapsed and her Red Centre trip was over, but nevertheless wishing her well, informing her of a few everyday happenings at home and sending love. She opened Kate's second email, recalling as she did so her daughter's holiday in Greece and her own inward concerns as to the underlying reasons for the sudden decision. However, she was pleased and relieved to hear that Kate seemed in good form, and that all was well with regard to her relationship with Martin, who in fact appeared to have joined the two girls for the last week of their holiday. Kate continued to explain that she had some particular news to share with her mother and that she and Martin were now contemplating a holiday in Australia at Christmas, assuming Maggie was still there, to catch up properly with all that had been happening to them both. Maggie allowed herself an inward guess as to Kate's special news and felt a motherly pang that she was not immediately available for her daughter. So Kate was planning to visit at Christmas! Maggie allowed her thoughts to move forward to December, unable to visualise her own personal circumstances that far ahead. Still, in some way or other, it would be good to see them then.

Next she opened Tom's email. Prepared for unpredictability as far as her son was concerned, she was nevertheless surprised to hear of his redundancy. She was even more taken aback to read of his possible arrival in the near future in Australia. Where and how did he think he was going to meet her? She read the email again more carefully and reached the conclusion that Tom's plans as yet were a little undecided. Knowing her son, surmised his mother, if a world trip was in the offing, he was more than likely to loiter somewhere inviting en route. He would inevitably become side-tracked. She could imagine him emailing a change of plan from Thailand, for example, or some other exotic location that might cause him to linger. Yes, as in the case of her daughter, she would have time to prepare for a visit from her son, should it actually materialise.

Richard's second email was a long one, uncharacteristically, for he was not a letter writer, although any paper he authored was meticulously and painstakingly crafted, with an enviable fluency and command of language. Maggie paused, leaning back in her chair, to think of her husband. She could picture him so clearly writing this email. He would be in his study, the downstairs room overlooking the garden, the additional room that had persuaded them to buy their house in the first place when he was initially appointed to the college. Here he had room for his computer, his books and somewhere to house all his notes and paperwork. He had been delighted at this prospect, for him the overriding feature of the house, for the London flat was cramped in comparison. Fortunately, Maggie, who had done her homework before making an appointment with the agent, had already ascertained that its position was also suitable for the local schools and the requirements of children – she was pregnant with Tom at the time. It was not a pretentious house, nor even a particularly characterful one, being very like its neighbours along the lane, but it met their requirements. And Maggie did not want to search any further. Her pregnancy tired her and this house offered so much that had been missing in London. Also, it was quite unlike their previous home where every space reminded them of Tina. There the entrance hall had really been too tight for the buggy, which meant stepping over it every time they needed the stairs. The small, front room had been given over to Tina, although she had slept in it very little, still being at the stage where Maggie could not contemplate her being in another room at night. Nevertheless, a great deal of baby apparatus was stored there, which was why Richard had lost his study. The house itself was a terraced, Victorian building, unmodified, full of nooks and crannies and rather hard to keep warm. This house was new, freshly decorated and with efficient central heating. Moreover, they could just about afford it, given the difference in house prices between London and Central England.

So there he would be, with the slatted blinds shielding the computer from the afternoon sun half caught in a pile of books on the desk – she would have jerked those blinds free had she entered the room – and probably a dirty coffee mug to one side. His desk was his pride and joy, purchased when an aunt left them a small legacy, a regency reproduction with the smoothest sliding drawers and handles that had so attracted Kate as a small child. However, now his personal affairs spread far beyond the confines of his desk and drawers. Stacks of books were in piles on the floor, but these were systematically filed and Richard could usually be relied upon to locate with ease any required text or paper. Maggie recalled that prior to her departure, Richard had begun to research a new literary project relating to gypsy culture and she found herself wondering how that was progressing. And how was he himself getting on without her? How much did he miss her, she wondered? He would not have had an affair in her absence – of this she felt uncomfortably certain. How much pain and suffering would her actions cause, were he ever to discover her act of disloyalty? Whatever happened, he must never find out. He did not deserve this.

She became aware that the young man at the counter was observing her. Clearly she had been sitting back in somewhat of a daze in her contemplative mood. She shook her head slightly, as if to gather her wits together, and began to read his message.

Richard asked first how she was enjoying the trip and referred to her time in the outback, hoping all went well for that venture. He added that he had felt some discomfort at the thought of being unable to make any contact and said he was looking forward to hearing from her in due course. He mentioned the house and garden and their display of roses and said he had had contact with the family, including her parents who were also hoping to have news of her soon. They were well, he wrote, although her mother was having increasing difficulties with her mobility and the practice nurse had suggested some items and gadgets that might alleviate the problem to some extent. Here Maggie felt a further stab of pain, for she was aware that she had given very little thought to the comfort of her parents either since leaving Sydney. He had seen his friend Roger in London and stayed at Kate and Martin's although the two of them were away in Greece at the time. More recently, Kate and Martin, together with Tom, had driven up for a surprise visit a few days ago and they had all had an enjoyable meal at the Horse and Groom. Martin and Kate seemed very happy after their holiday and Tom was his usual self. She was not to worry, but Tom had been made redundant – although offered a most attractive alternative proposition in Richard's opinion. However, being Tom, he was going to indulge in a bit of travelling – just like his lovely Maggie. Here Maggie, chastened, glanced downwards before resuming the reading of her email. He added – somewhat wryly his wife could imagine – that independent travel seemed to be the flavour of the month and no longer the monopoly of the young. He then continued to say that he would therefore like to suggest joining her as soon as possible for a couple of weeks together as he would love to see her and still had the opportunity to do so before term began. Hopefully, she would pick up this email shortly and could let him know where she would be. He would fall in happily with any plan of hers and would book a flight as soon as he heard from her.

Then followed various closing comments that Maggie barely read. She looked up stunned. Again she was aware of the young man's gaze. Her reactions were puzzling him. She continued to sit for a few moments, feeling as though she was caught in a net from which there was no means of escape, as she swum desperately in ever-decreasing circles. How was she to respond to Richard? Whatever her course of action, it was clear that one of two men whom she held dear would be caused great distress and heartache. What was she to do?

She needed to talk with Jim. She needed some time to think. She picked up her printout and left. The young man's eyes followed her as she departed.

She couldn't see Jim at first, expecting him to be where she had left him – sitting in the shade on the low wall to the side of the café – so began to walk to the far right, along the pavement, where it looked as though there were some seats amongst the palm trees. However, carefully studying the beach as she walked, she soon spied him down on the sand, sitting close to the sea, arms encircling his bent legs and head bowed forward. He was wearing the long-sleeved khaki-coloured shirt with sleeves rolled up and rather crumpled long shorts that she remembered him wearing on their first meeting. His hat was pulled low on his head. He looked vulnerable. He glanced round to see whether Maggie had completed her messaging, but missed seeing her. He turned again to stare seawards. She couldn't help thinking that he had the air of one defeated.

Maggie, whose compassion had focused only a short while ago upon Richard, now felt the deepest commiseration for the figure on the beach. How was it possible to be merciful to them both? Her behaviour had been inexcusable and had damaged them all.

There was a seat behind her and she sat down heavily, dully and disheartened. Just then Jim turned again, this time standing to scrutinise the seafront. He saw Maggie sitting despondently and with some anxiety and trepidation made his way to join her.

'All right?'

'Not really.'

There was a pause. He waited for her to continue.

'They all seem to be coming to Australia.'

Again, he waited.

Maggie, who had been staring disconsolately towards the sea, moved to face him squarely. With head lifted and shoulders back she composed herself to be less dramatic and to enlighten Jim about her communications. She managed a wry smile as she spoke.

'They miss me, but they seem fine. Kate and Martin are planning on coming out at Christmas time with what Kate describes as 'special news'. My instinct leads me to believe that this is news of an engagement, and that would be good. Tom's lost his job but that's no worry to him. He's setting off pretty imminently on his travels and plans to include Australia in his itinerary.'

Maggie contemplated the waves.

'And Richard?'

'Perhaps you'd better read this.'

He hesitated.

'No, it's OK. Please.'

He read it once. Then he read it again. Then he handed it back to Maggie. Both watched the breaking of the waves on the sand. The water surged and massed, and then exploded to break on the shore, forming translucent bubbles as if of soap that lived but briefly, then to shrink and pop.

'Have you replied yet?' he asked hesitatingly.

'No. I just don't know what to say.'

She sat quietly.

'You see, I'm not sure whether I want Richard to come just now. It sounds dreadfully disloyal and callous to say that, but…'

Her voice trailed off.

'I'm so sorry,' whispered Jim. 'All this is my fault. I can't help my feelings for you.'

'Well,' said Maggie, determined to recover her composure and trying to lighten the atmosphere, 'my mother would have said we were old enough to know better. In fact, that's a saying I often employed for Tom who could sometimes be a pain to his sister.'

Grateful for her last comment, Jim tried to consider what best to do next. But before he could speak, Maggie repeated his earlier comment.

'We need to talk,' she said.

He was relieved.

'Do you want to talk here? Or would you prefer to go back? Obviously you need to think how you wish to respond to Richard's communication, but what about the children. Did you reply to them?'

'I meant to, but forgot after I read Richard's. I suppose I could do those now and then I think I'd prefer to go back to think things through. On second thoughts, I'm not in the mood for replying to Kate and Tom straight away. Let's go home now, and then we'll have to come back here tomorrow. That's another day gone, I know, and these messages were all sent a while ago, but one more day can hardly matter too much and I need to get this right.'

And Jim was content with that response. But what he had noticed particularly was her expression 'going home'. I may still be in with a chance, was what he dared to allow himself to think. But the inward voice nagged him, prompting him to query whether his hope for being in with a chance was in the best interests of either of them.

Chapter 20

Richard had still heard nothing from his wife. He sat at his desk to see if there was any message, but of the considerable number of new emails none was from her. He leant back thoughtfully with his hand on his chin to trying to work out the timing of recent events. It was now mid August. The outback expedition must surely be over and he really should have had some news by now. He half stood in order to open the blinds a little further, sat back at the computer and then, changing his mind, made his way through to the kitchen to put the kettle on. He took his mug of coffee back to the living room, where he stood a while in front of the patio doors looking out into the garden. He was beginning to be anxious. Maggie would certainly make contact when she could, he reasoned, and there could be many explanations of why so far she had not. Possibly the expedition had been extended in some way. Maybe she had joined another group and was still in a remote, isolated area. He would surely have heard somehow had something of significance gone wrong but perhaps there had been a minor problem of some kind. If she had found herself in hospital, or something of that sort, he would surely have been informed.

He returned to his study with his mug in his hand. Perhaps he would give Kate a ring just in case she had some news. Martin answered the phone. Kate was literally at the front door, on her way to the Saturday market, but came to the phone in response to Martin's call.

'No, I've had no recent news either,' she replied. 'I sent an email after we got back from being with you last Sunday, but it might not always be easy for her to pick them up. We'd have heard if anything had gone amiss. She did warn us that she would be out of contact for a while. When did you last email?'

'A day or so after your visit. I said I would like to come out to join her for a couple of weeks before term starts, but time is going by. Already, there's barely two weeks left now this month and my preliminary enquiries about flights – and these are to Sydney which might not even be relevant – indicated that some are fully booked anyway. I wish now that I had thought of this before. It almost looks as though it will be too late this summer to get out there.'

Why on earth *didn't* you think of it before, was Kate's private thought, but she did not say this to her father.

'Don't worry about her Dad. I'm sure she's OK and we'll hear soon. You could still make your couple of weeks if we hear from her in a few days, which I'm sure we will. Anyway, how are you doing? Anything of interest planned?'

'Tom's still up here, but over at Kip's for the time being. Doesn't seem to have taken him long to sort out his travelling arrangements. Won't be long now before he's off, although whether he'll actually make Australia for a while is anyone's guess. No not much planned here. Mowing the lawn, I suppose and rescuing Mum's hanging baskets if they're not too far gone. Your watering last weekend helped, but they don't look their best.'

Father and daughter ended their conversation.

Kate turned to Martin.

'Dad's worried like I am.'

'Relax. She's on holiday!'

'It's all right for you. It's not your Mum.'

Martin moved over to the door. He put his arms round Kate. 'Sorry. I didn't mean to upset you. I genuinely believe there's nothing wrong, which you will undoubtedly come to realise very speedily. And as for her not being my mum, she soon will be, sort of, and anyway, as you know, I also have her well-being at heart.'

Kate smiled, reassured. Martin trapped her even more tightly in his arms, pulling her towards the couch. 'Are you sure you really want to go to the market at this very moment?'

'Yes I am,' she responded, giggling. 'Let go, you brute. If I don't get in some shopping, you will be sorry. None of your favourite Italian cheese! You could of course come with me. On second thoughts, forget it. I'll go on my own rather than listen to your pathetic excuses.'

She planted a quick kiss on his cheek, wriggled free, and was soon heard slamming the front door.

Richard too was off to do some shopping and took the car to the nearest supermarket. He was not long gone, but it was time enough for a distressing and most significantly inconvenient event to take place.

Opening the front door, he didn't, of course, immediately notice the broken window over the kitchen sink at the back of the house. But he did notice a trail of papers in the hall from his study to the living room. He then became aware of further disturbance and his heart sank as he realised that someone had broken in.

It didn't occur to him to shout out in case anyone was still around. Instead he pounded his way through the hall and made straight for his study. His worst fear was realised. His computer had gone! He groaned inwardly to himself. Papers were strewn around the room and he thought of his current work and research and the hours of irretrievable effort that had gone into it. He dropped to the floor and scrabbled his way through dislodged books and scattered files. To his enormous relief, it looked as though whoever had been interested in his computer had not been equally attracted to his project. Although there would be much sorting out to do, perhaps all was not lost. He felt angry and found himself muttering to himself and clenching his fists as he rescued various objects from where they had been scattered. It then occurred to him that the rest of the house required investigation. Where else had this wretched housebreaker been? He went first into the living room, where he expected to see that the television had also disappeared. This room too had been disturbed. Clearly the thief or thieves had come over the fields for there was mud everywhere. Fortunately, at a quick glance, nothing appeared to be broken, and the television, much to his surprise was still in its place. Too old a model for you, he muttered. However, in the kitchen, where he saw where entry had been made – the window was broken and the fanlight above it wide open – their recently purchased radio was missing and the back door was ajar. The escape route, he assumed, and then groaned inwardly remembering how he had left the key beside the door, rather than putting it back on the hook in the boiler cupboard. Then he remembered. It was he who had left the fanlight open! How could he have been so stupid! What about the bedrooms? He ran quickly upstairs, treading the now-soiled stair carpet, to discover that all the doors were open and drawers were pulled from the furniture. Clothes and personal possessions were randomly discarded and his anger increased at this attack upon the privacy of his family. A number of trinkets and ornaments were discarded on beds and floors and he approached Maggie's dressing table in alarm and concern. The drawer had been wrenched, but appeared to have stuck halfway. All mixed up together were a knot of necklaces and bangles and some empty jewellery boxes, one of which he recognised as being that containing the bracelet he had given his wife on her twenty-first birthday. What else was missing? How would he know? Was the ring his own mother left to Maggie still there?

The thought that he ought to notify the police came suddenly to mind.

The officer who listened to his distressed account remained matter of fact and, to Richard's mind, somewhat unconcerned, but details were noted and he was alerted to the fact that 'someone would be round.' He was also advised for the time being to leave things as they were. He went back into the living room, itching to be able to begin the clear up. He needed a bit of a hand.

He thought of Judy and Karl down the lane. Karl was at work, but Judy appeared very quickly in response to his call and did what anyone would do in such circumstances. She went into the kitchen and, careful not to disturb anything, she found the teapot and made some tea.

Two policemen duly appeared and turned out to be both efficient and sympathetic, although quick to point out his indiscretion in leaving a downstairs window open, a fact he already deeply regretted. He was advised to make a list of everything missing and take some time and care over this for the purposes of insurance.

'You'd be surprised,' commented the younger of the two policemen,' what people remember ages after. One woman didn't realise the cash she left ready in a kitchen drawer to pay the window cleaner and gardener was missing until they came round again. She also had a stack of euros on the sideboard that she clean forgot about until she was packing for her holiday.'

'It's my wife's jewellery that concerns me,' said Richard. 'I'd find it difficult to remember what she actually possesses, and she's away at the moment.'

'Would Kate know?' volunteered Judy. But Richard wasn't sure that she would.

'Do you think you'll get them?' questioned Richard.

'Sorry, but I have to say that it's rather unlikely,' said the more senior of the two. 'This has all the indications of an opportunist burglary by amateurs. The likelihood is that they're two or three lads together, probably only about fourteen or fifteen years old. They're likely to be well away by now, gloating over their goodies. It certainly looks a bit like a spur of the moment kid's job to me. Not a professional one. They've left fingerprints for starters and even a respectable footprint in the back garden. But those are unlikely to be of much help unless they've got a record. Sorry, but that's the truth.'

'Is anything likely to turn up? I'm certainly worried about all the stuff I have on my computer, let alone the damned inconvenience of now being without one.'

'Kids usually get rid of stuff amongst themselves. It's the professionals who are more likely to use the pawnshops – more often car boot sales for the lesser stuff. These youngsters, if youngsters they are, had a heavy bit of equipment to carry – that computer of yours. We don't really know whether they had any transport available, but judging by the mud, it looks as though they came over the fields and my guess is anyway, as I've said, that they are kids. There's quite a line of houses here fronting this road. If that's the route they took back it's possible someone saw them. They may dump stuff. Sometimes that happens.'

The police left and then followed the laborious and distressing procedure of clearing up. Judy enlisted Karl's help too and that of another friend, and together they set to work, removing mud and cleaning carpets whilst Richard struggled with sorting out all the items that had been thrown around so haphazardly. His feelings towards the perpetrators were extremely vicious. Whilst I'm here on my hands and knees, he thought, clenching his jaw, some kids somewhere are having a great laugh at my expense. It was reassuring, however, to begin to suspect that in reality not too much of monetary value appeared to have been taken. His computer and the possible loss of some of Maggie's jewellery were the items that worried him most. He sat back on his heels contemplating the latter. Perhaps, as had been suggested, he should phone Kate asking if she could remind him of any special pieces? Or should he try to acquire the information from Maggie herself? The problem here was twofold – one, the apparent difficulty of making any contact at the present time and, secondly, his concern not to worry her unduly about a situation currently beyond her control.

He was being called.

'Come on, Richard, a break now. We're doing pretty well here. What about you?'

'Getting there, I suppose.'

Over coffee, he started to voice his concerns to his friends, but was interrupted by the phone. By chance it was Kate. He hesitated at first as to whether to involve his daughter at all, but after one or two pleasantries, explained briefly what had happened and made his request for information about the jewellery.

'I'm so sorry about what has happened and grateful to think you have friends with you, but you're probably OK where Mum's jewellery is concerned. She only keeps the non-valuable things in the drawer. Hopefully your burglars didn't touch the drawer under the divan. At the back is that wooden box that Grandma used to have. Anything that's of value is likely to be there. Go and have a look while I hang on.'

It was just as Kate said. Richard was enormously relieved.

'You'll be pleased to know that the bangle you made her with those particularly brightly-coloured beads when you were about five is there too!' They both laughed.

'Isn't Tom still with you?' she continued.

'He's with Kip at the moment.'

'Give him a ring, Dad. He'll come and help with the rest of the clearing up. I'm only sorry that it's really difficult for me to come straight up just at this time.'

'Don't worry. It's getting sorted. There's no need for me to bother Tom.'

So Richard didn't ring his son, but his daughter did. And Tom appeared on the doorstep early the next morning, ringing the bell because he couldn't locate his key and, much to his father's surprise, proved to be practical, useful and also very good company. Tom tackled the stairs, which Judy and the others had not quite got round to the previous evening and set about a temporary repair to the window.

'They moved the garden bench to reach the fanlight,' said Tom as he stood on the steps, hammer in hand to board up the window, 'and then aimed for the fastener. Presumably they couldn't quite reach it, so smashed the glass below. With that brick down there,' he added nodding over his shoulder.

'Obviously I regret leaving the small window open, but I don't see how it is visible from the lane.'

'We'll walk down to the pub when I've fixed this,' said his son, 'and see what's on view from the front.'

Turning right out of the drive, they paused by the far end of the property looking backwards towards the house.

'You can see the back of the house because of the slight bend in the road,' commented Tom, 'and also, this bit of replacement beech hedge of yours is still on the thin side.'

Richard was forced to agree.

Father and son enjoyed a second pub lunch together in the course of a week and lingered in the pub garden over their beers. Now that his burglary ceased to demand his full attention, Richard turned the conversation to his concern for Maggie. Tom was of the opinion of his sister. 'You'd get to know bad news,' he reassured his father. 'She's probably having a great holiday and lost track of time, or is in some place where communication is difficult. Anyway, aren't you about to get out there?'

'If I don't know where she is, I can hardly make arrangements to meet up with her.'

Tom acknowledged that this was so.

'I'm sure you'll hear soon. Why don't you try emailing again?'

'Without my computer!' was the reply.

'Email from Karl's, or go into college.'

However, it was not necessary for Richard to take up either of these suggestions, for they had not long returned home before they received a phone call from the police station.

'Well, you are in luck!' the officer informed him. 'Hard to credit, but your computer is here with us and seemingly undamaged.'

'That's great news. Where was it?'

'Found in the bus shelter in Bennetts Road, sitting on the bench!'

'In the bus shelter!' exclaimed Richard incredulously.

'Apparently, the woman opposite found it. She said she thought she had vaguely registered something there some hours previously, but had thought nothing of it. However, later on, when she was doing some gardening in the front, she went over to investigate. When we talked with her, she thought perhaps she had seen some kids mucking about earlier. They hung around for a while and then made off. As you are probably aware, there's not much of a bus service to your village on a Saturday.'

'Are you telling me that a couple of kids found my window open, decided to take what they could and then made off to catch a non-existent bus home with their heavier than anticipated load!'

'No, sir, what I'm saying is that your computer is here at the station and you might like to come and pick it up.'

'What about the radio?'

'That would be pushing your luck too far!'

Later in the evening, father and son sat chatting together companionably in the living room.

Why has it taken me so long to feel comfortably relaxed in the company of my son, thought Richard. He realised Tom was speaking.

'So what are you going to do now, Dad?'

'Well, I'll contact Mum again tonight,' replied his father. 'I won't say anything about our burglary as all seems reasonably sorted now and it would only worry her. As for going out to Australia, I certainly want that window properly fixed before I leave the house, but more significantly the days are passing somewhat speedily and the start of term looms ever nearer. I could kick myself now for not joining Mum earlier on. Much as I miss her, I'm almost resigning myself to planning a Christmas trip although part of me can hardly believe she'll still be out there then. And what about you,

Tom? I assume you're not going back to Kip's tonight, but what are your plans for tomorrow? And when is your flight?'

'No. I said my farewell before I came over yesterday. I'll base myself here tomorrow, if you'll put up with me, and then have a week or so down in London with Kate and Martin. My flight's in a fortnight's time.'

'And where's that to?'

'Bangkok. I fancy seeing something of Thailand.'

'Do you think you'll see Mum at some point?'

'Maybe. I'll see how things go. Perhaps we'll all get together out there at the end of the year.'

'Possibly,' agreed Richard, privately thinking that the end of the year seemed a very long time ahead.

When Tom went up to bed, Richard sat a long time at his desk. Finally, he sent another email to Maggie. In it, he spoke of his love for her and concern for her safety. He confessed to missing her, but for her own sake, tried to refer positively to her holiday, expressing the wish that she was enjoying all the experiences the country had to offer and then went on to discuss plans for his own proposed visit. He didn't want to disappoint her if she was looking forward to this, but after much soul-searching, finally suggested that it might be better if his trip was postponed until Christmas.

Then he also went to bed, but the last couple of days had been too eventful for sleep to come easily. He thought of Maggie, of course, wondering quite where she was, and of Tom for whose company he had found himself unaccustomedly appreciative. He thought of Kate in London, of his potential son-in-law and his future inclusion within the family and what that new relationship would bring for them all.

And he thought of the dead daughter, who would never know any of this.

Chapter 21

They said little to each other during the short drive back along the coast. As Jim turned into the resort he slowed down in the parking bays in front of the supermarket.

'Neither of us had much in the way of lunch. I know you've a lot on your mind and we've some talking to do, but although you will probably say you're not hungry, I'll pick up a few things while we are here.' Maggie nodded. Before her unseeing eyes the life of the beach continued. Children climbed and shouted from the slides and swings on the well-mown green grassed area between the beach and the stores, and although there were now few swimmers in the sea, there were still many people sitting on the sand or walking along the shoreline.

Jim emerged with his purchases, but disappeared into the bottle shop before rejoining her in the car.

Back at the cabin, Jim installed Maggie on the verandah, returning shortly with cups of tea for them both.

It was Maggie who spoke first.

'I need more time. How can I best do this?'

'In what way, more time?' hazarded Jim uncertainly.

'I don't know how I feel able to say this,' she continued, hesitatingly, 'but I find myself guiltily wishing for more time before I meet up with Richard again. In other words, if it is really necessary to spell it out, I don't wish my husband to come just now. How awful does that sound to you?'

Jim did not reply. He got up from his chair opposite, moved round to her side of the table between them, squeezed her shoulders tightly, bending to kiss the nape of her neck, and went inside. He returned promptly with two large brandies in plastic beakers.

She smiled wanly. Jim pulled his chair beside hers and motioned her to have a drink.

'Apart from the occasional white lie that everyone tells from time to time, I have never deceived Richard and I strongly believe that he has never deceived me. But I think I am going to have to tell some sort of untruth to prevent him coming out here. I can't simply not reply to his email because he will worry that something had gone dreadfully wrong, and anyway, that would entail not replying to the children either. I don't have it in me to pretend I got their messages, but not his.' She sipped her brandy, gazing out to sea. 'I could say that I've booked some other trip that's just about to start. Perhaps I could suggest he comes later – say around Christmas if that's what Kate's planning. Maybe Tom would meet up too.' She sat quietly in reflection. 'Another thing that crosses my mind is that term must begin fairly soon. I could use this as a reason for suggesting that the visit is postponed. It's hardly worth coming out here for much less than a couple of weeks.'

So the two of them sat on their verandah where they remained for a long while as darkness fell around them and the strange nocturnal sounds of an alien country were set in motion. At some point, Jim disappeared inside to return with supper – a couple of omelettes with crusty bread and some melon.

The temperature fell and, clearing their plates, they withdrew inside where Jim switched on the rather old-fashioned standard lamp with its dated, fringed shade and pulled up the two comfortable rather shabby armchairs.

He knew that, even if they had until Christmas, at some point the situation inevitably would have to change and that he would then lose her. Neither of them would ever be able to sustain a casual affair.

As if reading his thoughts she turned towards him.

'I think we both know that this can't last forever, but I just can't bring myself to let go yet, even though it won't make things any easier later.'

Jim's big tanned hand moved to cover Maggie's, resting on the arm of her chair. He remained silent. If there was a chance that their relationship might continue for a while, even if the eventual outcome was as they both anticipated, he knew he would acquiesce wholeheartedly.

'Is it very cruel of me to want just a little more time with you? Will you think any less of me? I know that I am being most selfishly disloyal.'

Jim's face crumpled and would not keep its shape. She felt the wetness on his cheeks as he half fell from his chair to bury his head in her lap. Then, regaining composure, he cupped her face in his hands and kissed each cheek in turn. Finally, he raised himself from this somewhat awkward position with a creaking of the knees that caused them both to smile.

After that, conversation flowed more easily and they sat late into the night over numerous coffees as Maggie considered how best to respond to her emails. Resolved in her decision, however, she could not, unsurprisingly, rid herself of her sense of guilt, which would have to remain buried deep for the next few months, and she was certainly under no illusions as to the gravity of the planned deception. It was indeed no blessing to have been gifted with the capacity to love two men at once.

And so the lie was fashioned. Replying to her children would be relatively straightforward so she decided she would do this first. Richard was to be put off with one or two very plausible excuses. It was quite likely anyway that by the time contact was made, there would be little of the summer holiday left. It might therefore be better to postpone a visit until a later date. Additionally, Maggie would point out that she had planned a further trip that was a little awkward to cancel at short notice. In view of the comments too of both the children, perhaps a Christmas visit could be planned which would give everyone more time to make travel arrangements.

Before going to bed, they each had another brandy. Both woke in the early hours, reluctant to move or speak, unsure as to the wakefulness of the other.

They breakfasted indoors and, too early to immediately make their way to the café, went for an early morning walk along the beach, a little subdued, but resolute in the decisions of the previous evening.

Back facing her computer, with the same youth regarding her with interest from the counter, Maggie remained determinedly focused. On this occasion, Jim sat with her in front of the screen as she reopened Kate's second email to remind herself of its contents. She responded in positive vein, supportive of a Christmas visit from her daughter and boyfriend, commenting on the clearly successful Greek holiday and the fact that Martin was able to join her. As to the 'special' news her daughter wished to share with her, Maggie said she would allow herself to guess, but for the present, would keep her thoughts to herself. Tom she replied to similarly, wishing him well on his travels, hoping in due course they would meet up in Australia. Then it was Richard's turn.

'I'll wait down on the beach,' said Jim.

Poised and ready to type in her well-rehearsed reply, she visibly jumped when alerted to a new email which, before even attempting to open, she somehow she knew to be from Richard. So she abandoned her premeditated reply and opened the newly received message, composed that night when Richard sat late at his desk after his son had been helping him put to rights the effects of the burglary. She was immediately taken aback by the contents. So it was Richard who now proposed the postponement of the trip! It was indeed ironic to have spent a long evening with her lover planning, quite unnecessarily it now transpired, the means of deceiving her husband. At first, she found herself unreasonably resenting the fact that Richard had effectively been allowed to cancel first. Then her better nature intervened and she reread the communication more closely. There was no doubt that he genuinely regretted the change of plan and also clear, that were she upset by this, he would come anyway, if only for a ridiculously short time. His love and concern were most apparent and it was clear that he was missing her. He hoped she would understand that a visit towards the end of the year was both more sensible and viable.

Maggie squared her shoulders as if to as if to strengthen her resolve and after some time in careful deliberation, composed a thoughtfully calculated response which, she hoped, was tinged with sufficient degree of regret, whilst acknowledging his logical analysis. His email was signed 'with all my love'. Here Maggie paused once more, before bending back to her task and writing the same. Then she sat back to reread her message. After some further contemplation, she added a postscript to the effect that her next planned trip would probably mean no internet access for a while, adding that she also seemed to have mislaid her mobile and asking him to let Kate and Tom know. Finally, after once again looking up with unseeing eyes, seemingly lost in thought, she leant forward with pursed lips, and with a positive click of the mouse, she sent her letter.

Jim was not actually on the beach this time, but sitting on the low wall nearby. He turned as she approached. For a moment, he wondered whether she had been shaken in her resolve, for something in her expression suggested she might have changed her mind. However, he was quickly reassured as she lowered herself beside him and outlined what had happened. She took his hand and squeezed it, turning with a smile to face him and pulling him to his feet.

'So, with all this wonderful time ahead, what are we going to do with it?'

'Jump over the moon together, as far as I'm concerned,' was his happy response, 'but we could start with a coffee at that café over there. Actually, I could do with another breakfast altogether. I'm starving. What about you?'

The young girl who served them was amused to see the pair of them tuck into breakfast as though they had already spent a couple of hours windsurfing, like the couple of tanned, athletic lads at the next table.

'Let's move on from here,' proposed Jim. 'This has been the reef part of our tour, so what else is it we want to see?'

'We could go further north, but I'm not sure when rain and monsoons begin to arrive.'

'Not yet, I wouldn't have thought,' was his reply, 'but if it's a taste of the tropics you want, we don't need to travel much further from here to explore the rainforest.'

There was for them both the sense of a weight lifted from shoulders. Time would inevitably catch up with them, but for the present they had only themselves to think of and no major decisions to make, beyond the planning of their holiday schedule. They left the café to feel the already hot sun on their backs. It was going to be a gloriously sunny day.

Once again, they found themselves playing the role of tourists, and back at the cabin on the verandah they gave further serious thought to their next move.

'Why don't we leave tomorrow, when perhaps we'll have a bit more energy?' suggested Maggie, conscious of the rather sleepless night. 'But for the sake of a change of scenery now and something a bit different from our usual beach, go up to the jetty where the reef trip started and take a boat out to one of those small nearby islands? Then, this evening, we can plan exactly where we want to go tomorrow, even book up somewhere to see something of the tropical rainforest?'

'Good idea. Come on then. Let's get going. The morning's half gone already and it's going to be such a beautiful day!'

The short drive to the jetty took them past flawless, idyllic bays where majestic forests swept down almost to the shore. En route, they viewed the inland scenery with heightened interest for there was something about that interior that was both fascinating and a little intimidating. Once at the jetty, they bought tickets for a trip to a small, relatively close island that apparently boasted nothing in the way of a resort and little in the way of facilities – a modest shack serving drinks and light refreshments was apparently available, but little else, just the beaches, so they were informed.

It was not long before they were on their way in a small craft with a jovial crew and a handful of passengers, making speedily for the island ahead, and looking behind them to the panoramic view of the thickness of trees hugging the beaches that they had passed earlier.

As for the island itself, they discovered on landing that it boasted a series of small mostly interconnected bays and coves of the sort that any tourist would die for. There was just sufficient sense of isolation and remoteness to suggest adventurous exploration off the beaten track and just that welcome degree of comfort for those who desired it. And Maggie and Jim did indeed desire it – in the form of a couple of sunbeds, where not so young – and young too – travellers could stretch out, protected from sand and sharp shells, able to read without getting a crick in the neck. They dragged the sunbeds beneath some tall palms.

'Bliss,' sighed Maggie as she put her book to one side, turning on to her front and inviting the warmth of the sun to seep deep into bones. It was not long before they were both asleep.

She was first to stir, and finding they were in danger of now being in full sun, woke Jim gently to suggest they relocate and then swim. The water was warm, clear and translucent and although here were no stones or rocks, there were numerous shoals of small, darting fish clearly visible. They then pottered along the shoreline, following a rough footpath to the next tiny beach, before retracing their steps to delve into their rucksacks for a late afternoon snack and welcome lukewarm bottles of water.

That night, they returned to the beachfront restaurant where they had eaten the night before their exploration of the Barrier Reef. The same young lad was working there and greeted them like old acquaintances as they settled themselves at an outside table. 'Perhaps,' commented Maggie, acknowledging the lad's welcome, 'the same bats are here too!' Both peered upwards. 'There are even more this time! The tree is full of them!'

'So did you get to the reef?' enquired their young friend, returning with a couple of menus.

'We did indeed,' replied Jim, 'and we followed your recommendation to the letter. An excellent trip, so thanks for that suggestion.'

'Here much longer?'

'Moving on tomorrow to explore the rainforest.'

They sat contentedly together with a renewed sense of ease and an assumed mutual consent to look forwards rather than back. It was now quite dark with the lights from the terrace and the pavement illuminating the thickly leafed tree that afforded a home to the impassive bats. The night air was softly warm, without the cooling breeze of their previous visit.

With their meal came a scribbled address from their waiter friend. 'Mango Tree Lodge. Only about two hours drive from here on the highway. It's very much in the rainforest and the very last bit is a bit bumpy without a 4WD. Just in case you haven't yet got a place to stay. I'm pretty sure you'd like it.'

'Thanks,' said Jim. 'Your last bit of advice sorted us out well, so perhaps we'll trust you again!'

After their meal, they strolled hand in hand back along the beach, close to the water's edge, dodging the occasional adventurous breaking wave, finally discarding their shoes to tread the cold firm sand beneath a sky of thick velvet. Although there were nowhere near as many stars as they had witnessed in the Red Centre, the display above was decidedly impressive. They paused to look seawards and skywards as ripples of water teased their toes, swirling round their feet sucking and dislodging the sand and inviting them forwards. Jim's arm pulled Maggie close as they stood side by side, remembering Brad's comments about the cosmos.

'What was it he said?' asked Maggie. 'As few as tens of millions to more than a million million?

'Stars in a galaxy?'

'Yes, but he said trillions and quintillions even. How can anyone get their head round that?'

They gazed upwards, silently.

'Do you think we might see a shooting star?' she continued.

They scanned the heavens with roving, hopeful eye.

'Not quite a full moon, but you can still see the man. You can certainly make out eyes and a nose. Quite a magical idea, don't you think? I would really like it to be true.'

He squeezed her closer in agreement and turned her gently to face him.

They slept deeply after that night and awoke, as a child awakes, alert and fresh for the adventures of a new day.

They bade farewell to their seaside location and soon found themselves driving further north, through the world heritage areas where reef and rainforest came together in breathtaking splendour.

Mango Tree Lodge was a little elusive, the last few kilometres, as they had been warned, quite taxing on both navigation and steering. As they left the coast, the road, initially surfaced, ploughed into the depths of a forest of amazingly tall trees. Very little sunlight penetrated, but where it did were pools of dancing light. The atmosphere was humid and there was a pungent, strange smell of vegetation and the echoing raucous calls of unfamiliar birds. The road became narrower and unsurfaced, but it was clearly well used and certainly manageable in their small car, provided Jim kept a watchful eye on dried-up deep ruts and occasional rocks and boulders.

The lodge was of wooden construction with an upper externally reached balcony, or walkway, supported by strong knotted poles that linked the half dozen rooms available.

'You could have this room at the end,' suggested Irene, who had come out to greet them as they came to an abrupt halt on the uneven approach to her home. 'We've only one other couple at the moment and they're at the far end, but we have a little family arriving tomorrow. You'll feel more private up here. As you can see, the balcony is shared, but you've each got a table and a couple of chairs.'

She showed them into their room, which looked most comfortably equipped.

'It's delightful,' said Maggie appreciatively. 'I'm sure it will suit us very well.'

'As for meals,' she continued, 'breakfast is included and eaten down there, usually outside.' Here she gestured to an adjoining annexe on the left. That part of the house is where we live – that's just my husband and me and our son Jeremy who is often around and sometimes one or two of the lads who work in the forest. Our eldest took himself off to Adelaide, so we don't get to see him that often. Evening meal, you can join us if you wish – just let me know in advance. And now I think you might welcome a nice cup of tea – make you feel at home! Our family came out from little old England when I was a kid, but we get back from time to time to see a few of the old folks who are still around and I sure know how much you all still like your cuppa.'

With that, she was gone, leaving Maggie and Jim to unload the car, freshen up and settle themselves in the wicker chairs on the balcony.

Irene returned with tea, homemade biscuits and numerous pamphlets and leaflets about the local area and rainforest in general.

'There's an interesting forest walk you could do on your own this afternoon if you wish,' she suggested, thumbing through the brochures to find the relevant details. 'It's effectively the route you've just come up from the coast, but you won't see anything of the road from the path. There's a small shack at the coast road that sells a very limited range of pretty basic stuff, if you're after any necessities, but you won't see much else. Some of the trees and plants along the way are marked with numbers relating to information on this sheet, but much of it has got a bit overgrown. You may possibly see our endangered cassowary, although that's more likely up here early in the morning. Treat them with respect. They can be nasty, but we have visitors who come especially for a sighting. Sometimes they're lucky and sometimes they aren't. Anyway, I'll leave you to your tea now and we'll see you at supper if you wish.'

The invitation for the evening meal was accepted, the most welcome tea drunk and the leaflet examined as they enjoyed their biscuits and the view from the balcony.

There was no doubt that Irene's suggested forest path was amazing.

'Everything about this country is on such a huge scale,' marvelled Maggie, craning her neck upward to view trees that were perhaps even some two hundred feet high. They towered high above everything else, the tops of other trees forming a dense canopy, so thick that only diffused light penetrated, hardly reaching the forest floor at all. Everywhere was a medley of lush growth, struggling for survival, pushing, jostling, twisting and twining. Plants grew on other plants, suffocating and strangling others in the fight for light and the means of survival. Roots were strangely visible, distorted and tortuous and there was much evidence of decay and enormous grotesquely-shaped fungi. Progress was inevitably slow, as there was so much to see and marvel over. In addition, it was quite stiflingly hot and they paused frequently to drink from their bottles. When they retraced their steps, it was as if they had never trodden the path before as they continued to be utterly absorbed in this new and different world, finding more and more strange plants to astonish them. And everywhere was the background accompaniment of bird sound and possibly that of small hidden as yet unknown creatures of the rainforest.

Over a communal supper that night they marvelled with the other guests over such spectacular scenery, finally climbing the steps back to their room beneath the huge expanse of a starlit sky.

Chapter 22

Before Tom left, he and his father took a final walk round the garden, primarily to admire their workmanship relating to their temporary repair of the window.

'Not a bad job for the time being,' concluded Tom. 'But you'll have to get it properly fixed.'

'And remember to shut it when I go out,' added Richard. 'Your mother would certainly have checked on that.'

'Well, she's not to know!'

'By the way,' continued his father, 'I did send a message last night to Mum, saying it seemed more sensible now to wait until I can get out there for a bit longer. I just hope that's OK with her, that is, when she finally gets to receive it. It still worries me a little that none of us have heard any news for a while.'

'Oh come on, Dad, we've been through all this before! She warned us herself that this would happen. Relax, she's fine. We keep telling you you'd soon know if things had gone wrong. You may well get a response quite quickly to your last message when she's back in civilization once more. No good getting in a stew. Her plan is to be away a while, at least, it was at the start, so you'll have to get used to being without news from time to time. It's not always so easy when you're away somewhere. Sure I won't be expecting to send regular updates home when I'm travelling! Although, of course,' he added, forestalling the likely response from his father, 'I've never been that great at keeping in touch!'

'Well, I have to agree with that! Still, I'd like a word from you from time to time, so bear that in mind. On a different note, do you think you will get round to seeing her?'

'Certainly on the cards. But it's Thailand first. Miles has a mate out there who is running some sort of bar, or something, on a beach somewhere. We may hang around for a while. Not impossible to think we might be drifting down under come Christmas, but then again, you might want some time just with Mum yourself if you make it around then.'

What stopped you from going earlier was his actual thought, but one he kept to himself. That's the older generation for you, he mused. So much dithering they miss the boat.

'What about this Miles then?' continued Richard. 'Was he a college friend?'

'No, a work colleague. I don't really know him that well, but when this redundancy thing blew up we got chatting and found we seemed to be on the same wavelength. We'll soon find that out. Well,' looking at his watch, 'I'd better be making tracks soon. Said I'd be round at Kate's place late afternoon.'

'Time for a quick coffee then before I run you to the station. And thanks again for your help and company these couple of days.'

As the train sped towards London, Tom found himself thinking about his father more compassionately than usual. He had found him to be older, more vulnerable and less sure of himself than the distant figure he remembered. He too had been aware of the slightly uncomfortable nature of the relationship between them particularly during his adolescence, conscious of the contrasting closeness of bonds that some of his friends had eventually forged with their fathers. Kip, for example, shared his enthusiasm for football with his dad and, as a teenager, had never been averse to kicking a ball around with him in the local park. Sport undoubtedly helped in this respect, he reflected. But even Stuart and his Dad, who had certainly never shared a similar passion, had had many a drink together at a time when Tom had been quite cautious in even admitting to his father that he was already a regular frequenter of pubs.

'You were always so damned pigheaded,' was Kate's sisterly comment, when after a convivial evening meal cooked by Martin – and a number of beers, which had given rise to the topic in the first place – Tom voiced his feelings concerning his relationship with his father during his growing years.

'Was I any more obstinate than any other teenager?' questioned Tom with an element of genuine surprise.

'As stubborn as the proverbial mule, I should say,' was the reply. 'And if you boys are sticking to beers, I'll switch to wine now, assuming we've got some in the fridge.' Martin duly returned with a bottle in hand.

Tom ran his finger round the top of his glass. 'I'm not sure that it was totally my fault,' he continued after a short pause. 'Dad was always wrapped up in his own thing. He never seemed to have time for us.'

'Rubbish!' retorted his sister. You have either genuinely forgotten, or at some point chosen to forget. What about those endless sandcastles he built year after year down in Devon and all the stuff he sorted out in the garden for us to play on? As soon as you complained that the swing was too sissy, there was that playhouse thing in the tree. You made that together you remember, with much banging away and hitting of nails and that knotted rope that dangled from it?'

'Yes, but that was when we were really young,' he volunteered defensively after another pause. 'I'm meaning when we were older. Perhaps Dad was just better with girls, or maybe you really were the favourite.'

'Have another beer to help you recover from possible sibling rivalry,' offered Martin, pushing a further can in Tom's direction.

'Come to think of it,' continued Tom, in pursuance of his current trend of thought, 'maybe I was always a disappointment to them. Did you know there was a baby who died?' he questioned Martin, turning to face him from his sprawled out position on the rug. 'A girl. Tina. She was killed in an accident. I suppose you'd never quite get over something like that. Then they had me, soon after. Perhaps I didn't match up. Perhaps I was a poor replacement.'

'I knew there was a child who died,' commented Martin quietly.

The three of them were silent.

'You can't possibly believe that,' said Kate 'And you know it. It must have been desperate for them. All credit to them that they got on with their lives, produced the two of us and gave us both a great childhood. You were a trial as an adolescent, that's all. Worse than most. Just fortunate you've turned out OK, relatively speaking. More importantly though, you seem now to have recovered your relationship with Dad from what you've been saying about the last few days at home with him. Be grateful for that, and for the fact that perhaps you've grown up at last. A late developer, it would seem, but perfectly loveable nonetheless.'

With that, Kate raised herself from floor to couch, planted a kiss on her brother's head and in a few words and simple gesture lightened the tension, as Maggie would have done.

On the evening prior to Tom's departure, the three were again together in the flat when they received Maggie's messages.

'So she's fine, just as I said she would be,' commented Tom to his sister, moving aside so that she too could check her emails.

'Well, I must say she seems to be having a good time,' commented Kate. 'Looks as though the decision to delay the trip has turned out to be a mutual sort of arrangement. Anyway, I'm pleased to have heard from her. Now we'll all have to think quite seriously about Christmas. I don't think we'll be able to keep the news of our engagement till then so perhaps we'll have to let her know by email when her next trip is over. I wonder where she's going exactly, and do you think this is with a group again?'

Then Richard rang.

'So you've heard too, Dad? Yes, we've just received her messages. So you needn't feel too bad about not going, as it doesn't look as though things would have worked out very easily, does it? Did she tell you exactly where she is?'

Father and daughter chatted for a while, and not without a degree of relief, before the phone was handed over to Tom so that his father could wish him well on his travels.

To celebrate Tom's imminent departure and the fact that they had now heard from Australia, the three of them went out to eat at an Indian restaurant. Tom was in cheerful mood, full of youthful optimism and vastly over ordered for them all in his contagious enthusiasm.

'We'll have some of this,' he exclaimed, 'the Goanese – it's seafood in a coconut-based sauce of pureed garlic, ginger, chillies and pepper – a hot one! And the lamb jhalfrazi, hot and spicy with green chillies.'

'Fine,' said Kate, relieving him of the menu, 'but we'll have something a bit milder as well.'

The order was eventually given and three young people with hearty appetites, a happy sense of bonhomie and excited anticipation for each of their futures enjoyed eating together and indulging in lively reminiscences, hazarding progressively wilder and more extravagant guesses as to that which yet lay before them.

However, they felt a little less positive about their night out some several hours later, when each of them began to feel decidedly less certain that the hot prawn dish had been a welcome addition to their meal.

Tom sat at Heathrow in the early hours of the following morning, feeling that this was not an auspicious start to his travels. Miles just hoped his friend would not throw up on the flight and Martin struggled into work, but came home early. But it was Kate who undeservedly suffered most, since she had eaten far less than the other two, for she was the one who was most violently sick. She ate nothing at all for three days and did not eat again at an Indian restaurant for a very long time.

She did not know it then, of course, but the days of eating out at restaurants of any kind at all in the immediate years ahead were, in any case, soon to be most tragically curtailed.

Richard too, unusually for him, was also eating out that night. Judy and Karl were having a few friends round for a meal and had persuaded him to join them and, now that he had heard from his wife, he felt more in the mood for company. Conversation revolved around families and their usual activities, but Richard's burglary was still very much the local gossip.

'I can't believe you got your computer back in one piece!' exclaimed Judy. 'And it was found in the bus shelter, of all places!'

'It was my neighbour, Heather Murray, who spotted it,' added Judy's friend, Wyn. 'She said she saw a few kids mucking around when she was weeding her front border, but thought nothing much of it as they looked pretty harmless. They seemed to be having somewhat of a disagreement, but no rough stuff, no fighting or anything. Anyway, one of them ran off and then the other two left shortly afterwards, but in the opposite direction. It was only when they'd disappeared she realised something quite bulky was on the bench, went over to find your computer in a dustbin liner and called out to Alan to bring it back over. I suppose the kids realised it would be a rather heavy and awkward item to carry around.'

'Lucky for you they didn't chuck a few bricks at it, just for kicks,' added Karl.

'I was fortunate there,' agreed Richard. 'And thanks to these people here,' nodding in the direction of his hosts, 'the house was soon put back to rights. Tom arrived to help too, and fixed the window temporarily.'

'So what have you got lined up for yourself now?' asked Judy. 'I gather Tom is off to see the world.'

'Another one off on a year out!' interrupted her husband.

'Not quite the student gap year for Tom,' continued Judy. 'Remember, Tom's been away working in France for a good few years now. And he did a fair amount of travelling before that, didn't he?'

'He did,' agreed Richard, 'but a lot of it was in Europe.'

'Why don't we bugger off too?' persisted Karl.

'Because of work, dear, the thing that brings our money in. You remember? Let me clear these plates away and bring the puddings.'

But travel was still the agenda and Wyn continued the conversation by asking for news of Maggie. Richard described her ventures, as far as he knew them, and talked of the family's plans to visit at the end of the year. Then Wyn's husband recounted incidents relating to their New Zealand trip, a whirlwind of a tour, as he described it. They had seen both islands over a twelve-day period, travelling by both coach and train, with some very early starts from their hotels for a great deal of sight-seeing. It struck Richard that this couple had seen much and absorbed little and he privately thought to himself how Maggie, by contrast, would be making every effort to capitalise on her experiences. How he wished she were there beside him around the table in the company of mutual friends. They needed more time together, he reflected, opportunities for normal everyday activities that could so easily be squeezed out of daily life. For the first time in his career he found himself considering the blatantly obvious, that he was now at that stage of life where all this could become feasible. He began to think about the possibility of his own retirement.

Chapter 23

Life in London settled back into a more normal routine. At work, Martin was pleased to be offered unexpected promotion and, although this was hardly the motivating factor regarding the purchase of an engagement ring, was spurred into action on this front. Together they scoured the jewellers for something to Kate's liking. This took a couple of weekends, as his bride to be, now recovered from the unfortunate effects of that Indian meal, indulged her prerogative of frequently changing her mind, finally abandoning the more traditional high street retailers for a ring she saw in an antique shop in Covent Garden. The single topaz adorned a broad band of gold and to Kate it was priceless perfection.

'It sort of goes with the yellowish tangerine streaky bits in your hair,' claimed Martin.

'You refer, of course, to the beautiful blonde highlights in my shiny golden locks,' he was duly informed. 'We'll have to let Mum know our news somehow,' she continued. 'And I'd love to show her my ring.' She lovingly caressed the ring, the stone now gracing the finger of her left hand. 'It may be that we'll have to resort to email to give her our news, although I'd much rather speak with her. An email doesn't somehow seem right.' She gently prised the ring from her finger and handed it back so that Martin could complete his purchase.

'And no,' confirmed Martin, 'you can't wear it now. There has to be a fitting moment for its presentation.'

The perfect moment presented itself later that same evening with the two of them together and alone in their flat.

'So what sort of wedding do we fancy?' asked Kate, disentangling herself from his arms and propping herself up against the pillows.

'Just the two of us – no one else there,' was the reply, his long frame sprawled on the bed, as he pulled her back into his arms. 'On top of a mountain, beneath the sea, in a snow cave in the Arctic, Southend Pier – anywhere. I don't care.'

'Well, well, we have become quite the romantic,' she teased, extricating herself once again, now drawing his head on to her lap. 'Quite happy with small and low-key,' she continued, 'but close family's a must – and some friends of course. Thinking of friends, we must see something of Sarah soon. After all, she did set this all up.'

'Set this up! I thought I set this up! Didn't I come all the way to that Greek island to propose?'

A lovely and knowing smile lit up her radiant face. 'So you did, lover boy! Still, I want to show Sarah my ring. What about meeting up in town some time, or inviting her over here? And I want Dad to be able to admire it too!'

However, it so happened that the showing off of the ring took place in Essex the very next Saturday as a result of a phone call from Sarah herself.

'Jen would love to make contact again,' she explained. 'Matt's away on a works thing in Amsterdam and she would love us to go down. It's easier than her coming up because of Callum, who must be about one now or perhaps getting on for two.'

'Perhaps as Matt's not there, I'll let you two go off together so you can enjoy your girlie lunch.'

So the two of them duly met up and talked non-stop on the train to Rayleigh arriving at Jen and Matt's little maisonette in time for coffee. Jen was delighted to see them both and very happy for Kate with news of her engagement. The ring was much admired, but conversation very disjointed as a result of the presence of the youngest member of the group.

'With luck we'll have a bit of a breather over lunch,' the increasingly harassed young mum explained hopefully, clearing a space on the floor which was littered with toys and removing their empty coffee mugs beyond her son's reach.

Kate watched Jen's little lad with the renewed attention which her recently acquired status now demanded. It did indeed appear that an enormous range of material requirements were necessary, from the clearly obvious toys and also from the amount of equipment in the small room where they all found themselves when it became evident that a nappy change was highly necessary. There seemed to be special mats, bags and boxes for all eventualities. However, this did not make the task straightforward for the little chap squirmed and fought his way through the whole procedure. Sarah's valiant attempt to distract by waving cotton wool before his eyes badly misfired, as this was grabbed and thrust first in the air and then rather dangerously towards his not-yet clean bottom.

'Quite a performance!' commented Kate, laughing at his antics, whist Jen grappled to restrain her son.

'Gotcha!' she exclaimed finally in triumph, bending low over him and planting several hearty kisses on his tummy, which he fought off as best he could, laughing and dribbling. He then crawled off speedily with a strange almost crablike sideways gait with his mother in hot pursuit ready to clear the path ahead from any potential hazards.

'No wonder you've not put on any weight!' commented Sarah, picking up the now half unrolled pack of cotton wool, securing the nappy sack and putting the room to rights as best she could.

Delightful as Callum was, all three were grateful when, as Jen had predicted, the baby was put to bed for his lunchtime sleep, but not until he had been fed, which proved another battleground, with much food landing in various places.

'He's beginning to feed himself,' explained Jen, adroitly fielding three plastic spoons at once. As each one was gleefully and tauntingly dropped, so another appeared to take its place. But this did necessitate a fair amount of bending on Jen's part.

'Is it all right to scrape food up from the floor and put it back on the spoon?' asked Kate, anxiously.

'That's nothing to the handfuls of dirt he puts in his mouth in the garden,' replied his mother. 'Fortunately, the latest thinking is that we take cleanliness too seriously in this country and the lack of any experience in dealing with germs is not helpful to the child. Now that's one theory I really do believe in!'

Jen kicked the debris to one side to allow for a bit of space for their own lunch and the three girls welcomed the opportunity to talk without interruption over Jen's lasagne.

Kate and Sarah gave news of their recent holiday together without giving too much away about its real purpose. However, Jen was very taken with the idea of Martin's romantic gesture in pursuit of his girlfriend.

'You couldn't have found a better way to make a man pop the question!' she laughed, without realising the full significance of her comment. Like Kate's mother, she had not appreciated this aspect of Martin's character and in retrospect it would seem probable that Martin had even been unaware of it himself. The other two exchanged conspiratorial smiles.

'And what about you, Sarah,' continued Jen. 'Have you a man at the moment?'

'Not quite yet,' replied her friend. 'But next time we meet, I fully anticipate otherwise.'

She proceeded to tell Jen, as she had told Kate on the way down, of the most recent appointment in her office. 'Trouble is, he's my line manager, so I need to tread carefully. But so far it seems to be going to plan. We're expanding more into long-haul now and going to be checking out Kerala soon. He has particularly asked me to be part of a very small team to go out there and has now suggested an informal get together at the local wine bar to give us the opportunity to get to know each other a bit before the trip. So far, couldn't be better!'

Both girls laughed and wished her well.

'What about your plans now?' asked Kate of Jen.

'I would quite like one day to get back into work,' she ventured. 'But it doesn't seem that practical at the present time. Matt's work is now going to take him away on occasions – not a lot, but enough to make life a bit tricky were I working. Childcare is so expensive and although my parents would help out in any emergency, they don't live near enough to make more support feasible – even assuming that's what my mum would want anyway. She is always very occupied with her own activities and doing a lot of short courses which she really enjoys.' Then, turning to Kate, 'I gather your mother is away in Australia at the moment. What exactly is she doing there?'

However, Kate was denied the opportunity to discuss Maggie's project or anything else relating to her family as Callum was heard vociferously announcing that he was now well awake, full of energy and ready to tackle the rest of he day.

'We'll go to the local park' said Jen. 'It's nearby and not bad. Anyway, I'll have to try to tire him out to have any hope of getting him to bed at a reasonable time tonight.'

So armed with a bag of stale bread, the three friends set off to the nearby park, fed ducks, pushed swings and conversed erratically. When the time came to leave, Callum waved them off with great gusto, clutching his soggy chocolate digestive to his wet T-shirt, to be scooped into Jen's arms when it became clear that he wanted to follow them down the road.

'God, she's always on the go!' commented Sarah, casting a last backward glance at Jen, who was trying to wave with a wriggling protesting child in her arms. They turned the corner and were finally out of sight.

'Yes, but he's quite a sweet little chap,' was Kate's reply, trying to imagine the possible role Martin might play in such a scene. She concluded he might be not unlike Matt, who by all accounts very much enjoyed playing with his baby son but was not so forthcoming where getting up at night was concerned. 'Though,' their friend had reminded them when topic this had been raised, 'he does have to get up for work each morning. And he's the one paying the mortgage!'

Paying the mortgage was the theme Martin continued when he met her at the station.

'This is a nice surprise!' said Kate as she spotted him at the barrier. 'I hadn't expected you'd meet me here.'

'You tell me how you found Jen and then I'll say what I've been up to. Let's start with a coffee.'

Kate recounted the day's activities, describing the baby in some detail and then asked Martin how he had been occupied.

'This promotion, that I wasn't particularly looking out for, but seems to have come my way, is going to mean we'll be quite a bit better off. Since I've been at a bit of a loose end today, I found myself idly, then a bit more curiously, looking into estate agents' windows. Perhaps we should now begin to think whether we ought to buy rather than rent, even go for a bigger place. The agents will be shut now, but I've picked up some stuff and we could look in a few windows on our way home.'

This was somewhat of a surprise to Kate as she was perfectly satisfied with the flat, and they had never really thought along these lines before. She glanced at the brochures on the table.

'But these places are a bit of a way out!' was her first reaction.

'I think it's got to be if we are thinking of purchasing,' he replied. 'Obviously, it's only the vaguest of thoughts at the moment but if we are going to be a boring old married couple, perhaps we should think about the sort of things boring old couples do, like buying a house, mowing the grass and visiting the local tip.'

'Well, well, I can't believe this can be the same dashing, handsome bloke from whom I received the most romantic of proposals. So this is what my ring is all about!'

Kate thought of their present flat and its close proximity to everything they enjoyed doing, then of Jen's rather unprepossessing maisonette in its drab location. For a moment she hesitated, but her thoughts then turned to Callum, the extra bedroom and the kitchen door that led into a small patch of garden with a red plastic toy car.

'Good thinking! We'll mull it over!'

And with this, they made their way home, the brochures now stuffed into Kate's bag.

Richard's concerns were of a different nature. Thankful to have heard news of his wife and relieved of the necessity to make plans for a long-haul flight, he now thought he might take himself down to the Cotswolds. With his gypsies neatly filed and catalogued ready to be delivered in due course to a probably less than enthusiastic audience, he was now on the trail of some interesting beasts in the form of mythical wood carvings that he hoped to find in a village churchyard. This would also give him an opportunity to have another look round Gloucester Cathedral, in particular, the high altar where he was also on the look out for a well-loved garden bird – or at least a certain story associated with his favourite robin. In addition, he thought ought to drop in on his in-laws who would be pleased to have news of their daughter.

He decided to make his wife's parents his first port of call, phoning from his mobile when he drew near to their village. Unusually, his father-in-law answered the call, something he normally left to his wife since he had become rather hard of hearing. However, having finally ascertained the purpose of the call, David sounded delighted at the thought of a visit from his son-in-law, and said he would go to put the kettle on straight away. Richard stopped briefly at the crossroads to pick up a packet of biscuits and a box of chocolates before pulling up in front of the bungalow where Maggie's parents had moved when her father retired from his practice in Croydon. They chose this part of the world having spent many holidays in the area in years gone by and although they had found the winters harsher on occasions than they had realised as summer visitors, by and large, it had been a good move.

David greeted him at the door and took Richard through to the living room where Betty was seated in the chair by the sun lounge. He bent down to give her a kiss.

'I won't get up, Richard, bit on the stiff side these days, but, my, it's good to see you! We've been thinking about you a lot and hoping you're not too lonely on your own. How's our Maggie doing then? We haven't had much in the way of postcards. She's doing all right over there, is she? What a long way to go on her own!'

Richard was secretly a little alarmed to witness Betty's lack of mobility, and collaring David in the kitchen, where he went to offer a hand with the coffee and biscuits, tried to find out how life was treating them both.

'Old age,' said David prosaically. 'Comes to us all.'

'So pleased our Kate is going to marry that young man of hers,' continued Betty as Richard carried the tray back. 'Nice to think we have a wedding to look forward to.'

'She's told you her news then?' asked Richard. 'Maggie doesn't even know they're engaged yet. It's been quite difficult to keep in regular touch because she's been in such remote areas. So if you get to hear from her somehow, perhaps you'd better keep that to yourselves to give Kate and Martin a chance to tell her first.'

They chatted happily for a while until Richard, glancing surreptitiously at his watch, decided it was time to leave as he didn't want them to begin wondering what to do about lunch.

'I have to be off now,' he said. 'I'm on the hunt for a manticore.'

But his father-in-law was on the ball. He knew his churches.

'You've not so far to go then,' he said. 'Wonderful wood carvings.'

'That's the one that's half man and half lion, isn't it?' added Betty, who appeared to be equally well versed in the mythical creatures.

'Look out for the leopard too,' she continued, 'but he's quite a sweetie in comparison. Not at all fierce looking. The sort of leopard you could keep in a basket in the corner of the living room.'

Richard said his goodbye and went off to find an amiable, although as it transpired not easily visible, leopard. He pottered around the very attractive church and found a pub for a quick bite before driving on to Gloucester.

The cathedral was one he and Maggie had visited a couple of times with the children. He remembered how Maggie had maintained Tom's flagging interest on one occasion when the torrential rain outside suggested the wisdom of a lengthier visit than had originally been anticipated by challenging their young son to find an image of football players on the stained glass window. But now Richard made his way to the high altar simply because he had recently been intrigued by a tale relating to a robin and an eighteenth century woman who had been granted permission to keep these friendly garden birds in the cathedral. This was because she was convinced that the soul of her dead daughter had been transferred into a robin, so in return for her upkeep of the altar, she was permitted a golden bird cage with matching seed and water troughs and curtain. He hadn't known this story on that very wet day many years ago. Kate and Tom would have enjoyed it.

The drive home found him reflecting how very much seemed to have happened since his wife's departure. Had the last couple of months really been so much more eventful than normal, he wondered, or had it just appeared so? Certainly engagements, redundancies and burglaries were not every day occurrences, but it had been a more emotional period too. Not only had it been a question of missing Maggie, but he also seemed to have rediscovered a relationship with his son. Now other considerations were playing on his mind. Today, for example, had left him delightfully contented as a result of a pleasant day out, but also concerned for Betty's well-being, having been made aware of the deterioration in her health.

And he was now also contemplating a significant change in lifestyle for himself.

Chapter 24

Maggie and Jim spent a couple of weeks at Mango Tree Lodge, fascinated by the breathtaking tropical forest, awed and astonished by its diversity and antiquity. Their delight and enjoyment added to their heightened sense of well-being and physical pleasure so that days of delight and enchantment led to mutually pleasurable nights. These were their halcyon days and they surprised even themselves.

'I'm not sure that pensioners are supposed to indulge in such lovemaking,' said Maggie, retrieving her crumpled nightdress from the floor. 'The younger generation would find it quite obscene. All the wrinkled and flabby flesh!'

'I can't imagine to which of us you are referring,' was the laughing response, as Jim adjusted her pillow and lay back in contentment.

Maggie shut her eyes and thought about relationships of other older friends. Jane had met Tim after Alec had died. Ann had found Terry on an internet site and their subsequent wedding had been a most joyous occasion, the sparkle in their eyes, when she next met them, suggesting that the relationship was deeply gratifying to both, emotionally and physically. Perhaps her own generation had been permitted to age a little more slowly than the previous one, she concluded, thinking particularly of her parents. For herself, there had of course been the sexual revolution of the sixties; although now, in retrospect, she sometimes wondered whether she had blinked at the wrong moment and a hugely significant social change had passed by as though it were a full bus at a request stop. Yet, unknowingly, she must once have caught the taste of freedom, when in those far-off days at a festival she had held a flower between her teeth. It was as though that flower had become a perfect garden rose, picked in the fragile light of early morning. She and Jim were aware that they no longer had the firm, ripe bodies of their youth, but their sex was still spontaneous, fulfilling, and above all, so *comfortable*.

She smiled at the thought of comfortable sex as she pushed the sheet away with her feet and drew back the curtains, so that the morning sun flooded into their room.

Over breakfast on the balcony, whilst Jim gave his attention to the guidebook, she studied his face more closely. His fair skin, now more freckled, was well tanned although his nose had not lost its tendency to peel and his sandy hair was tousled, probably uncombed, but then there was not much of it anyway. His ears protruded possibly slightly more than she had noticed previously and were a little red rimmed, perhaps because he regularly omitted to apply sun cream. His neck was wrinkled, though not as much as her own, she thought, and reddish rather than brown and light hairs were visible on his chest where the buttons of his shirt remained undone. Hunched over the book, his frame was hidden behind the table, but he was not of large physique, although was he now carrying just a little extra weight, she wondered? His long legs, sticking out at right angles, were on the thin side, with various moles and blotches, and his feet encased in his now shabby sandals showed evidence of patches of hard skin. But despite all this, in her view, he did not appear elderly at all. He looked at ease in his body, relatively active and fit, ready for the pleasures and challenges ahead.

She buttered another toast and considered her own appearance. She felt comfortable in shirt and shorts, the type of clothes in which she had been virtually living since her arrival. This consequent ease, as in the case of her companion, extended to her body and general sense of comfort. She had long abandoned using make-up, although at home rarely left the house without it. Her hair, she felt, was probably somewhat of a mess, since it had received less attention than usual and the steamy humidity of the rainforest was an enemy in this respect. She would need a hair appointment somewhere in due course, she thought, as her roots were now beginning to show through, but found it hard to consider this a high priority. As to her well-tanned body, she was still quite slim and felt fit as a result of all the recent swimming and walking. In herself she felt young, so she dared to hope that she appeared reasonably so.

Moreover, she continued in her reasoning, there are certain advantages one brings to an affair in later years. The vicissitudes of life itself are an immense preparation. Experience in the act of love itself is also advantageous. She suddenly realised that Jim was speaking.

'We'll have to go for this,' said Jim enthusiastically, looking up and handing her the book. 'Then we'd know something about bush tucker.'

So they went on a walk with Les, who told stories of swags and camps and early exploration of the rainforest. He showed them scorpions and ants, describing the way in which the Aboriginals delved into the green ants' nest for bush medicine to cure problems with the sinus, and the possible use of this knowledge for current medical purposes. He found them a nest, a huge, massive, apparently loosely assembled nest on the ground and invited their guesses as to which creature it belonged. It turned out to be a communal nest for the small scrub hen, its eggs a valued source of food. 'Life is fragile here too,' he explained, describing how this bird together with its close relative, the scrub turkey, was now a protected species. He showed them buttresses of gigantic roots, where a fire could be lit and food cooked, with the flavour enhanced from the gum leaves of an adjacent eucalypt. They hiked further to a source of water where overhanging vegetation fringed soft sandy banks for Les to talk of finding mussels and fishing for eels. Always they were reminded of the antiquity of the land and the giants that inhabited it. 'See here, these cycads,' he said. 'Each metre represents a hundred years of growth. So who saw this fella, I wonder!' They looked up. And they wondered.

It was not only the antiquity and diversity of this landscape that struck them, but also its dangers. 'See here,' gesticulated their guide. 'Now this real beauty, the giant stinging tree, these big heart-shaped leaves. It's sure got an awesome reputation. It's got these fine hairs on its leaves that go right into your flesh. You'll feel that sting maybe up to six months. Those tribal folk knew their landscape and understood nature. It's all about respect, respect for the land.' This they had heard before.

Towards the end of their time at Mango Tree Lodge – and they did get to see a cassowary on the very last morning – they contemplated their next move.

'I gather it gets pretty humid these parts come November,' reasoned Jim.

'Perhaps we could go back to the coast for a bit as yet,' suggested Maggie. 'Maybe not exactly the same location, but somewhere not far-off.'

As a result of this suggestion, they left the lodge, waved off cheerfully by Irene, and followed a route that took them first through sugar cane plantations and then to a beach where an estuary invaded the sea with its muddy tangled-root mangroves.

'I'd hardly describe this as a caravan,' said Maggie, surveying the capacious mobile home at the edge of the site. 'Seems quite luxurious to me.'

This was the start of another week of contented living, in which they spent much time on the beach, reading, talking and recalling the highlights of their recent experience in the rainforest.

Into the second week, however, and independently of each other, both found themselves in a more pensive mood. Maggie was first to voice this new awareness which had given rise to the first slight hint of tension between them.

'What is it?' she asked.

Jim shifted his position on the long cushioned seat, below the large picture window that gave a view of the mangrove swamp, thinking how attuned each of them had become to the sensitivity of the other.

'It must now be some thirty-three years since Gary's suicide. It was just that I registered the date yesterday with that calendar up in the kitchenette. Usually, I have that date very much in my mind, but this year I was surprised to see that it had almost escaped my notice.'

He patted the space between them, inviting her closer. 'Even though I made off to America soon afterwards, I couldn't escape remembering the date. And when I returned some ten years later, just in time to see my mother before she died, I realised how she had clung on to his memory. She told me in just about the last conversation I had with her how she always visited the cemetery on this particular anniversary and requested that I should continue this tradition when my father was no longer in a position to do so. Of course, this time came sooner than she might have expected, as he only survived a further six months. But the thing was, I somehow never felt able to do exactly as she asked. You see, Gary's birthday happened to fall a short while before this wretched other anniversary, so that first year I duly made my way to the cemetery on the anniversary of his birth rather than his death, just hoping they would all understand. Gary would have done, my father too probably, but sometimes I feel less sure about my mother and there's something not too good about denying someone a dying request. Anyway, this is what I have done ever since, apart from a couple of years when I was far away at the time, and then this year, when I'm afraid to admit that I forgot the birthday date totally but appear, rather belatedly, to have remembered the other. It's not as though I spend my life feeling miserable about Gary. Of course, a life ruined in such a way is incredibly sad and I'm deeply sorry that it was so but it was all a long time ago. Life goes on. Time doesn't heal, but it does pass and things change.'

He turned towards Maggie to continue, 'And now that our lives are bound together by some amazing twist of fate, I hope you have it in your heart to view our mutual tragedy similarly.'

She sat beside him quietly, his hand on her knee. She remembered how, what now seemed like a very long time ago, she had sat dreamily contemplating the cave and first felt the pressure of that hand upon hers. The moment was so clear in her mind that she sensed again the herbal fragrances of the warm, magical air and felt the dry, red crumbly earth in her hands. Despite the magnitude of the revelations between them that were yet to come, Maggie recognised that this had been her moment of salvation. Tina's short life was a cause of celebration. 'The fact that our paths should ever have crossed is a coincidence beyond belief. But as regards the intertwining of our tragedies, I think I fully came to terms with my own that day at Uluru. The connection we were later to discover was a tremendous shock. But what happened to our two families simply happened, that's all. Sadly that's how it is. Yes, there are things both of us could have done or not done, but neither disaster was our fault. We cannot alter what is past. And,' she added, 'you're right, the memory of the most unbearable events is tempered with time. You mustn't torment yourself with thoughts of a birth day or a death day, but simply remember Gary when and as you wish.'

Thus the tension between them was relieved for the time being, but they did not make love that night. Both feigned sleep and Maggie began to wonder whether, after all, it was time for her to return home.

In the morning, any opportunity to discuss her thoughts with Jim quickly evaporated with an early morning visit from the camp warden.

'How're you two doin?' he drawled cheerfully. He had dropped by, he informed them, to tell them, having forgotten to mention it the previous night, that there was an organised excursion to a crocodile farm that day, to be followed later by a river trip to see 'them fellas.'

'We'd like to, wouldn't we?' asked Jim, turning to Maggie, who, in cowardly fashion, felt some relief at the thought of postponing the voicing of her current concerns.

Some hour or so later, they gathered at the camp entrance with a group of about a dozen others to board a minibus to take them to the crocodile farm. They assembled first in what appeared to be a greenhouse where the babies were reared. Small animals are always so appealing, thought Maggie, and this applied in full measure to the crocodiles. The babies, only inches long, were most endearing and appeared totally unthreatening. 'But don't touch these fellas,' warned their guide. 'Even these littluns can leave you with a bit out of your finger.' He took them through the life story of a croc, recounting a few of the well-documented stories of unlucky encounters with these aggressive reptiles. They usually involved some poor, unlucky, unsuspecting soul, minding his own business on the river bank, pounced on without warning by an opportunist crocodile with an amazing turn of speed and agility, and then dragged underwater as bubbles rose to the surface. Some of the stories referred to the dazed incredulous expression of the unfortunate being before he or she was pulled under. The tales were graphic in their telling and Maggie shuddered.

Out in the enclosures where the adults were to be found, nothing much at first appeared to be happening. In fact, there seemed to be rather a lack of crocodiles. Then the group began to spy them, so well camouflaged against the rocks that they had originally thought the enclosures to be empty. But none of the reptiles moved. Only an occasional flickering of an eye could be seen. Just then, a member of their party screamed as a grinning keeper prodded a particularly large beast with a long probe causing the creature to round on him with jaws open. But the keeper was enjoying his well-rehearsed routine and grinned at the alarmed tourist as he threw large chunks of meat to his charge.

The evening part of the expedition, after lunch and an afternoon drive to the appointed riverside location, proved great fun, if but a little lacking in large beasts. 'Look out for the reds of their eyes,' instructed the guide. Calls of 'Red eyes! Red eyes!' had them all lurching from one side of the small craft to the other, worrying the youngest member aboard as to the possibility of capsizing. Although they could hardly describe the boat trip as the most daring of ventures, a good time was had by all and the spirit aboard was decidedly convivial.

'Look,' said Maggie as they scrambled from their small craft at the water's edge. Her companions directed their eyes to the notice board she was indicating, just beside the small wooden raft that served for climbing aboard.

'Beware of crocodiles. Do not approach the bank.'

They all beat a hasty retreat.

'But that's where we were told to get on!' exclaimed Maggie.

Jim shrugged and grinned. He had enjoyed the evening and additionally struck up a lively conversation with the passenger to his left, who had just spent some time in Darwin.

It was late when they returned to camp and Maggie did not find an opportunity to broach once more the subject of their future together until the next evening after supper. They were again seated on the long cushioned bench with the caravan patio window open to the night sky and the no longer discernible estuary.

'Jim' she began, a little haltingly, 'we need to talk about our future together.'

'You mean,' he replied, uncertainly, 'where we might like to go next?'

'Jim, we've had a great time together, but none of it has been real. I mean, it's been holiday all the way along. Not real life. We haven't experienced everyday living together.'

Jim had feared this conversation. He tried to forestall it.

'We could try to resolve this,' he suggested after some hesitation. 'It's difficult to know quite what you mean by real life. Neither of us has a real life, if what you mean is the

233

experience of living together whilst in employment. I've been retired for a sufficient length of time to understand that real life for me is to a large extent what I choose it to be. No longer governed by the workday routine. So holiday is in effect real life. You have come more recently to this stage and have not yet, perhaps, come to appreciate what it means.'

Here he paused for a while, but Maggie made no response.

'We could try something different, if you want,' he hazarded. 'We could return to Sydney. We could go back to the UK together. I have my flat in London. We could go anywhere, come to that.'

Anywhere, anywhere, he pleaded inwardly and frantically. Just so that we can last together until Christmas!

There was a long pause.

'I'm sorry, so sorry. But I now know I just can't do this. I have a home and a family.'

She found she could not stop the tears, and Jim held her close, squeezing her tightly so that she could not see that he was crying too. They remained closely entwined as the nearby-distorted shapes of the mangrove trees disappeared into the thickening darkness of night and the first stars appeared in the night sky.

Eventually, they moved apart slightly to face each other. Jim placed gentle hands to her cheeks and drew her close for a compassionate and loving kiss, as he had done before at the magical setting of the sun.

'But what about you Jim?' she sniffed, having to some extent regained her composure. She had a family and he did not.

'You mean what shall I do now?'

I shall wail and shout and bawl and bellow, was what came into his mind. I shall raise a ululation that, like a Mexican wave, will have no ending. I shall bay at the moon and roar like a lion. I shall exhaust myself totally, then curl up into a ball in a dark place for an endless hibernation.

'Yes. What are you going to do?'

'I'm not sure yet,' was what he actually said. 'Presumably we've got just a few more days together. You'll need some time to sort out travel arrangements and flights. I might stay on for a bit, not here, but somewhere different. Up north, possibly. I really don't know. I can't quite think for the moment.'

Tears again welled up in her eyes. He put his arm around her and cuddled her close. 'But you mustn't worry about me. Maybe I haven't got family around, but I've many good friends, plans and projects in mind. Rest assured, I'll make a good life for myself.' Here he paused for a while. 'But I won't forget you. I shall always think of you.'

'Oh don't please. This is too painful.'

Maggie continued to dab at her eyes, sniffing miserably.

'Come on, Maggie. It's not so bad. We've had a good time. We've been soulmates for a while. What we've had between us, no one can take away. It will always be with us. It should be enough.' He hoped he spoke with the conviction he could not feel, while she too made every effort to be convinced.

Much later, feeling considerably calmer and more philosophical, and after they had even managed to raise a couple of glasses to toast the future, Jim moved into the bedroom where he could be heard rummaging through various possessions.

'Maybe it's time to give you this,' he said, placing a package into her hands. 'As you can see, I've not got round to wrapping it elegantly, but I'd like you to have it now.'

Maggie was both surprised and moved and could feel her heart racing. She accepted her package gracefully and smilingly. Then she started to unwrap it slowly, savouring each moment, unable to guess what it could be and prolonging the moment of discovery. She thought she could feel a picture frame beneath the final layer of thin paper. Then the last sheet of crumpled tissue fell to one side. It was a picture, but for the moment, it was upside down. Slowly, slowly, she turned it, first looking up at Jim and then bending forwards, cradling the picture on her lap. She raised her face upwards, her eyes shining.

'Jim, this is perfect!' she exclaimed in amazement.

The sketch showed the intricate dance of light and shade on the leaves and branches of a red river gum.

'Our day at the creek! How amazing! Dear Werner! He really is a gifted artist, don't you think. You must have requested this of him. How can I thank you for this! I shall treasure it always, and every time I look at it will think of you and all that you have meant and will continue to mean to me.'

She laid the picture carefully to one side, then jumped up to kiss him, encircling him with her arms. The gift resulted in a few more tears, but more of happiness than sadness.

'Just a moment.' Jim disappeared into the bedroom again.

He returned with another package of similar size, but even more roughly packed than the first. This time he opened it himself.

'Gracious me! It's the twin to the other! It's the same tree, but do you see, it's from the other side. Look at the shape of this branch here! It's virtually a mirror image. Ah, but not quite! See here! Artistic licence I suppose. They really are lovely.'

'So,' said Jim, 'One for each of us.'

He refilled their glasses.

'Here's to Werner.'

'And to the creek!'

'And Uluru!'

'And all our group!'

'And us once more!'

As for the arrangements that would now need to be made for their parting, they could wait a short while.

However, these were abruptly and cruelly taken out of their hands when Martin fell off a friend's ladder.

The ambulance arrived quite quickly, but he was pronounced dead on arrival at hospital.

Chapter 25

A few early autumn leaves lay stuck to the wet grass, for there had been heavy rain overnight. Maggie and Richard were both awake. Already their curtains were drawn back and a grey sky was lightening. Richard climbed back into bed and passed a cup of tea to his wife.

Maggie propped herself up with the pillows. Her whole body ached with overwhelming weariness and despair.

It was now a month since the funeral and a month plus a few days since she had lain so unsuspectingly beside Jim. As she sipped her tea, it occurred to her that she had not once thought of her other life in Australia since touching down in Heathrow. It was as though some supercharged programme that forced her to function out of utmost necessity had driven her; but now that they had survived the immediate practicalities of this unbearable family tragedy, the programme had ended. Yet in reality of course, it had only just started.

It was possible that there were the slightest of sounds from Kate's room and both Maggie and Richard stiffened, turning their heads involuntarily to try to ascertain whether their daughter was also awake. Kate had not returned to either the flat or her job since Martin's death. The parents could not console the daughter and this upset Maggie especially as a mother, for it was heartbreaking to be unable to offer any solace.

She resorted to devious means. The doctor had prescribed medication to ease Kate's pain and this she had rejected. But this had been surreptitiously included in a homemade soup that Kate had been persuaded to eat.

'I don't think it was her,' said Richard. They both lay back again and Maggie allowed her aching eyes to close. Richard looked across at his wife. Whatever eventual homecoming he had had in mind for her, this was not it. She, who had been so strong for all of them, now seemed frail, dejected, vulnerable, as they all were. From Maggie, the family derived their strength. They needed her. He must protect her and support her. Somehow they would pull through all of this. He examined her face more closely and thought it possible that she had fallen back to sleep. The tan already seemed less apparent, as though it was now almost indecent or inappropriate to reside there and sadness had made its sketches at the puckering to the corners of eyes and mouth edges. Her lips looked cracked, her skin dry and her hair more grey than he seemed to remember. Perhaps, if he could get up very carefully without waking her and open the bedroom door without the slightest noise, he could come back with toast and coffee.

Maggie heard the soft opening and closing of the bedroom door and guessed what he was up to. This homecoming was not of her choosing either, but it had happened and could not now be changed. Events had overtaken her in such a rush of confusion and emotion that she literally had not had time to think. But now, as she lay in bed awaiting the delivery of breakfast that she felt sure was on its way, she thought back to when she first heard the news.

Richard's email that simply said, 'Phone immediately. There is some news,' filled her unreasonably with frantic alarm. It was as though a sixth sense alerted her to the fact that there was something seriously wrong. She spoke with Richard and later, hopelessly unsatisfactorily, with an incoherent Kate.

Jim sorted out everything. He insisted on accompanying her to Sydney.

'You will at least let me know you arrive safely,' he begged.

'No communication. I'm sorry. No. Please don't try to get in touch.'

'Just one message. Just to let me know how you find things. Just so I know you are all right.'

'And where would it stop? No. I'm sorry. No. It can't be. You accepted this too.'

But this sounded so cruel, and Maggie yearned to soften the blow.

'I shall never forget you. I shall think of you especially at sunrise and sunset. I feel that I owe you a great debt, and from the depths of my heart, I wish you well. But we will not meet again.'

Parting is not sweet sorrow, she thought. It is hell.

She remembered little of her flight. She did nothing. She ate nothing. She saw nothing, although she vaguely recalled a film on a screen in front of her. But if there were words, she did not hear them.

Finally she arrived at Heathrow, and found herself in her husband's arms. Then somehow, she rediscovered her old self, or if not her old self, a semblance of the same with which she would have to make do in the circumstances. She could not find the right words for Kate, but she found some words at least that of necessity had to suffice for the time being. She contacted people. She made arrangements. Others said that she 'kept going'. And that is what she did. Maggie kept going.

But now, it seemed, there was nothing else to do. Tom, who had flown straight back from Thailand, had by this time returned. There was no reason why he should not. Martin's parents and family had lives that had still to be lived. Her own parents, grieving for a granddaughter as they had for a daughter, had been driven back home and Kate's friends, including the faithful Sarah who had taken extended leave in support of her friend, had jobs and lives to resume.

What was to become of their daughter?

Maggie heard their bedroom door open gently and a smell of coffee announced Richard's return. She managed a wan smile to thank him – her husband for whom she had had no personal time since arriving home.

'I would have said I wasn't particularly hungry,' she said, 'but I must say, I think I could do with some toast. I'd rather forgotten what large chunky doorsteps you always cut.'

Richard settled himself back in bed.

'It seems an awfully long time since I was last here,' she continued, dropping crumbs on to the sheet. 'And somehow, we're going to have to try to get back to normal, whatever that means for our poor dear Kate. But I can only think all the time how unbearable it must be planning for a wedding that turns nightmarishly into a funeral.' Her lower lip trembled.

They both paused and Maggie put her plate to one side.

'I won't be in at the college this week. What can we best do that might help our Kate? We could try to take her out somewhere – leave the house – get a bit of fresh air – a change of scenery. Or we could go back to London with her and stay a while in the flat. She's going to have to get back to work at some point. They've been extremely supportive of her at the office, very much more compassionate than many places might be. What do you think?'

'Not in college?' she queried.

'No. Not this week,' he confirmed. 'There are other priorities.'

And Maggie was deeply grateful.

When Kate woke some hour or so later – and yes, it did appear that she had slept reasonably well – the next few days were already planned.

'We've both got appointments at the hairdressers,' announced her mother.

'The hairdressers!' echoed Kate uncomprehendingly, turning to face her, clearly stunned.

'Yes and before you can voice any objection, I quite understand that you probably don't feel that bothered for yourself, but perhaps you'd better take a critical look at your poor old mother.'

Slowly, raising her eyes, Kate examined her mother's appearance. She noted the grey strands in her dark, unkempt hair, its dry texture and increased length, but most of all, she noticed the acutely visible strains and tension, evidence of the suffering inflicted on them all.

Kate stared out of the window as they drove into town. It seemed incredible that life still appeared so normal and she began to feel angry with Martin for destroying any hope of normality for her. Yet it was strange to feel furious with him because he fell off a ladder. His friend was to blame. He should never have asked for Martin's help in the first place.

'It's nobody's fault,' said Maggie.

Kate visibly started. She had said nothing. How had her mother guessed her thoughts? Was she now so nakedly transparent?

With the colour now applied to her roots, Maggie flicked through a pile of magazines, despite the fact that the articles were predictably and unvaryingly repetitive. She stole a glance at Kate beside her who was turning pages haphazardly, indifferently, but then gave way to gazing at the street scene and then upon those captive within the salon. Everything was the same and everything was different.

Yet it was almost possible, if not exactly to enjoy the morning, at least to accept that perhaps she felt marginally more positive as they retraced their steps and had an early lunch and a walk down the lane. The grey day had given way to surprisingly warm sunshine and Kate felt more part of this ordinary world she had observed earlier that morning, even able to exchange a few pleasantries with people they knew.

They walked the next day too, a longer walk that helped them all to feel more physically tired, and later opened a bottle of wine as they sat talking. Richard was about to broach the subject of Kate's return to work, with their offer to accompany her back to London, when they were interrupted by a phone call from Sarah. Kate disappeared from the room to talk at length with her friend.

Her parents looked up expectantly at their daughter's return.

'She's organising me again,' commented Kate, but seemingly in acquiescent mood. 'Bless her, she's a good friend. She's persuaded me the best thing now is to return to the flat and she's moving back in with me for the next month. Somehow I've got to get back on my feet. I've told her that I think at times I'm going to be rotten company and she agrees that may be the case. But she's adamant.'

Maggie and Richard were incredibly relieved and plans were made to drive down to London in a couple of days' time when Sarah would be there.

They did not linger long in London. Sarah rustled around to make coffees, but they soon found themselves on the homeward route.

'This will be so difficult for her,' sighed Maggie, glancing at the line of traffic ahead on the motorway. 'All his things are still there.'

'It will be better when she's back at work on Monday,' said Richard and there was little further talk between them as they drove back.

A week passed. Richard went back to college, returning quite promptly at the end of the day. Maggie kept very busy. She threw herself into projects around the home and garden and caught up with many of her friends. She drove to Gloucestershire to see her parents, a long rather exhausting day and was concerned, as Richard had been, to see her mother's increasing lack of mobility of which she had not been particularly aware at the time of the funeral. It was wearing to try to remain so positive for the sake of everyone else when she too sometimes felt like wailing and beating her breasts. She was just so incredibly tired.

One evening, after an early supper, with the central heating turned on for the first brisk, cool day and with her not so new looking rucksack now packed away in the loft space, Richard pulled his wife close to him, as they sat together on the settee.

'We seem to have forgotten all about your trip away,' he said. 'None of us have really had time to ask you about all your adventures and there must have been so many of them before that wretched call home. We would all have been out there, you know, come Christmas, very much in the pipeline. Where would you have been by then I wonder? Perhaps you'd better start at the beginning and tell me all about it.'

So Maggie thought back to that other world and started with Sydney and its delights, and as she recounted her early explorations she felt again the warmth of the sun on her back. She remembered how it felt to be physically fit, tanned and with time to oneself, time to linger at cafés, beaches and parks. She recalled days of pure, selfish indulgence.

Of course, she did not tell all. The incident in the cemetery did not feature in her account, but the stories of her Manly friend were recounted almost word for word. She could hear his warm Australian drawl and see his comfortable, welcoming smile.

'And what about central Australia?' asked Richard, pleased to see his wife relaxing at last and beginning to look more like her former self.

Maggie paused. 'I've probably got some things to show you.'

She went upstairs for her guidebooks and a few selected photos. Careful here, she thought to herself.

'Look at that!'

So Richard too stared at Uluru and he also was amazed. 'Some bit of rock that,' he agreed. And Maggie told him some of the stories she had heard so that he too could feel the heat and the dryness and imagine the crumbling earth in his hand. She spoke of the camp, of its privations and splendours and of the members of the group. They were all mentioned. It was simply that she omitted the core, the essence, the momentousness, because that was how it had to be. She showed some pictures – the group taken by Mike, all squashed up with arms intertwining and all grinning because Mike had nearly come to grief with the tree stump.

'Amazing. You'll have to take me!' exclaimed Richard. 'She's pretty. Is that the French girl? And he looks a nice chap.' Richard pointed to Jim and Maggie's heart raced as she looked upon her former lover. But no one was ever to know. Here was something she could never ever share. Nor somehow did she feel able to share with her husband her new found knowledge in respect of Tina's death and this she found hard to justify and explain – the ultimate treacherous act. Richard was Tina's father. He had a right to know. Was it that she could not face possible criticism of Jim? How would you voice such a bombshell anyway? Oh, by the way, I met the man whose brother drove that car that killed our daughter? And actually, it went further than just meeting him. No, such admissions were way beyond the possible. They must be forever buried deep, deep. They must forever lie low. She must forever suffer guilt. For everything there is a season, a time and a price.

'Then after that, it was Queensland, wasn't it? Was that with the same group?'

And intertwined with the season, the time and the price come the lies, like roots in grotesque contortion, twisted and gnarled, rampant and ripe in evil propensity for replication and re-growth.

Maggie moistened the roof of her mouth with her tongue.

'Just a few of us. For some the holiday was over and others went on their way. Those of us left swam and snorkelled on the Barrier Reef and then explored the interior and saw something of the rainforest.'

She made a mental note as to which members of the party she would include, and decided upon Mike, Dee, Jim and also Henriette as an additional – and particularly attractive – single female. So the framework of deceit took shape, one in which she was both inexperienced and ill at ease.

However, Richard remained absorbed in her descriptions and was particularly fascinated by her reminiscences of the awe- inspiring vegetation of the rainforest.

'Have you any more photos?' he asked.

'I didn't take that many. We were so busy just gaping at all we saw, and anyway, the effect of the canopy means that in reality, it is actually quite dark.'

Richard put the photos to one side. 'We'll have to go back there together. I can see that.'

He pulled Maggie closer. 'I missed you very much, you know that. It was hard not to worry about you, particularly when you were out of touch. It wasn't the same here without you and not having you around made me very conscious of all the things out there I'd like us to do together. For a start I need to think about work and how much longer I'll give it. But as for now…..'

He left his sentence unfinished as his arm encircled her shoulders, their faces drew close together and their lips met.

Now they were in bed together. They had not made love since Maggie's return. On the one occasion that Richard tried, he early on sensed his wife's lack of response and so he refrained. Events that had overtaken them all would readily account for her lack of arousal, he reasoned, and he accepted her fatigue and weariness of mood. But now, she appeared in better spirits and the occasion seemed more opportune. He wanted to re-establish the links and closeness of man and wife that had been denied him, that they had possibly subconsciously denied each other, even before the departure for Australia.

He pressed her body to his. His hand cajoled the small of her back guiding her to that familiar locking of form. She was aware of his erect penis insistent upon her pubic bone and then searching for that soft point of entry. She tried hard to suppress emotions. This has to be, was the thought she cradled within the curve of her body, wishing to banish thoughts of susceptibility and excitability. Yet, to her surprise and relief, she was touched by a sense of tenderness and sentimentality as she lay beside the man to whom she had once pledged her commitment, whose life she had shared and whose children she had born. She did not climax, as he did, but for the moment it was enough. Then they slept.

Kate found sleep difficult. But then, everything about her return to the flat had proved difficult because everything about it reminded her of Martin. But it was the toothbrush in the mug that finally defeated her and torrents of tears fell as Sarah did what she could to comfort her friend.

'No decisions tonight,' ruled Sarah. 'Then we take stock tomorrow. Some things you need to clear away, but you don't have to dispose of anything in a rush. There are items here that Martin's parents may wish to have and there are some that you shouldn't make hasty decisions about. Then we'll get out in the afternoon, and make sure in the evening that you are as ready for your return to work as you can be. That will be much better than you can possibly imagine, I assure you,' said Sarah, who hoped, rather than believed, that what she so adamantly declared would prove to be true.

And after a week back at work, Kate did begin to realise that her life would continue. It was never to be the same, but it would go on. Many of her colleagues were friends of long-standing, proving supportive and compassionate and some of Martin's work colleagues called one evening and insisted upon on taking the girls out for a drink.

As for the practicalities of the new state of affairs, Kate in discussion with Sarah and Jen too who came over for an evening, leaving Callum in the care of his grandma, reached the conclusion that she would both prefer and need to find alternative accommodation.

'I don't know whether I ought to offer to get a place together,' confided Sarah to Jen, with Kate out at the corner shop for milk and coffee. 'I haven't long been in my present place, which I really like and which suits me fine. Also, my new man is very much still around, sacrificed somewhat for the moment.'

'No. That would be a bad move. Sad though it is, Kate has to stand on her own feet. You've done an enormous amount for her already. We'll help her find a smaller apartment, if that's what she wants, but more than that would be a big mistake.'

Sarah was greatly relieved.

Jen extended her stay over a long weekend, fretting a little about the well-being of Callum from whom so far she had rarely had a night away, and a new flat was sorted, a little nearer Kate's office and significantly reduced in rent. Kate would move there the following month.

But before the month was up, there was a further development.

'Come on, Kate,' urged her friend. 'You've got to eat, you know. You've lost quite a bit of weight already.'

'But I just feel so nauseous all the time,' she objected.

'It's stress. Try smaller meals – eat what you fancy – but at least eat regularly. Or get yourself to the doctor's. I know you don't like the idea of antidepressants and all that stuff, but they must work for some people, otherwise presumably they wouldn't exist. You'll be in Stanley Road next week, and I'll be back in my own place, unable to nag you all the time.'

'Phew!' said Kate, smiling for once. However, she did follow up her friend's suggestion.

But when she returned from the surgery, she did not have any antidepressants.

'He said what?' exclaimed her friend in total disbelief.

'I can't keep telling you. You heard. Pregnant. That's what he said. Pregnant. It means having a baby, in case you don't know. I'm having a baby.'

'I just don't get it! But you were on the pill.'

'Of course I was on the pill!'

'You must have forgotten to take one!'

'I didn't bloody forget, you idiot.'

'Well then!'

'Well then!'

'Sit here,' ordered Sarah patting the couch, 'and tell me exactly what he said.'

So Kate told of her consultation, of the understanding doctor who knew all about broken hearts; the way in which he listened attentively and compassionately and his careful questioning of her symptoms. Next he examined her briefly and expertly. Then, when she was once more seated beside him at his desk, he removed his glasses, leant well back in his padded chair and asked further questions relating to her parents, their support for her in her recent loss, Martin's parents, her network of friends and the nature of her work.

He sat quietly for a moment or two, as if in thought. 'Has it occurred to you that you might be pregnant?' he probed gently.

Now, whilst waiting for Sarah to return from work, and having had time to digest some of the implications of the news she had received, Kate began to make some sense of her present state. She recalled the Indian meal and her subsequent incapacitating sickness. Apparently, it was possible that this could have affected the efficacy of the pill, she had been assured. But more significantly, she now had to think how this diagnosis affected her health and future plans.

At first she had felt utter disbelief, more denial. Then she felt fear welling up within, the sheer panic of how she would now cope with this eventuality, once its reality struck home. Then once again, this sense of fury with Martin. How could he do this to her? And finally, back at home, after making herself a cup of tea, she was able to acknowledge a minute possibility of anticipation, a tiny seed of hope.

'So?' said Sarah.

'So?' echoed Kate.

'Well, well!'

Then Kate laughed. 'I haven't seen you at such a loss for words for a while.'

'It is a bit difficult to know what to say,' agreed Sarah. 'Most friends would say how pleased they were on hearing such an announcement. Are you pleased? I know your situation is not easy at the moment, but now that your news is sinking in, I'm beginning to think that I am very pleased for you. But you need to tell me first, Kate! How do you feel?'

'I think I'm beginning to feel the tiniest speck of something quite delightful. It's really hard to explain, to find the words. I think I'm beginning to feel that this could be all right, no, not just all right. It could be good, very good. Oh my god, Sarah, this is Martin's child! I haven't got my lovely Martin, but I will have his child. How amazing is that!'

Then there were a few tears and much mopping of eyes with tissues. Sarah poured herself a drink. 'Sorry, one of the few occasions when I desperately need one. You can't, of course, 'cos of baby, one of the first of the many privations to come. But very exciting. This will be good for you, Kate. You'll cope. It will be hard, but you know you'll have your parents' support,' which you'll certainly need, she thought privately to herself.

So Kate was at the start of another roller coaster of emotions, but she now had something outside herself to give purpose to her life.

She stood once more on the threshold of another life-changing experience, like her mother before her when she gazed from on high at the edge of the gorge.

Chapter 26

'It must be good news,' concluded Judy, with hands cupped around her coffee mug as she and Maggie sat together in the kitchen.

'I think so. After her initial shock, I think Kate now feels this way too. But it won't be an easy ride.'

'What does Richard think?'

'As the two of us have just being saying, that she'll need well supporting along the way, but we're delighted she feels so positive about it all. She talked for ages on the phone last night and much of what she was saying is now inevitably forward looking. She's moving out of the flat soon into a smaller place nearer the office, planning to keep on working as long as she can so as to take as much maternity leave as possible after. As for then, well, we'll have to wait and see. It's all early days as yet.'

'And Martin's parents?'

'His mother was very emotional, many tears at first, but now I think it's something for them to cling on to as well. Denis is giving a hand with the actual move and then they want her to spend a weekend with them in Surrey.'

'Well, well,' said her friend. 'It's certainly been all change since your retirement do last summer. A lot has happened since that momentous flight of yours.

It sure has, thought Maggie, and that afternoon as she sat on the settee, with the paper put to one side, she allowed herself to think of Jim.

She went upstairs to find her gum tree sketch, still roughly wrapped in paper in the drawer under the bed, for this was one item that as yet she had not shown to her husband. She walked back slowly into the living room, sank back on to the settee and allowed her eyes to travel the paths of the delicate lines that fringed the dappled shading of the trunk and hinted at the tremulous leaves that flipped and turned in sudden breeze. She saw beyond gradating shades white and black, through silver and ivory, to recall celestial blue, earthy ochre and turquoise greens. Her eyes travelled every line, from the strongly robust and coarsely delineated markings of the trunk with its roughly adhering curling bark, to the pearly delicate tracery of the leaves.

With eyes closed and the picture lying loosely on her lap, she remembered every detail from that day in the creek. In her mind's eye she saw the 4WD roughly parked by the red river gum defeated by the final rough boulder, the narrowing rocky path and the green growth by the pool where there were more of the eucalypts. She heard voices, Werner calling to Eric and Henriette's laughter. She remembered where she and Jim had lain together at some distance from the others in the shade of an overhanging rock with the dust and ants tickling her hot damp skin. That must have been when Werner created the sketches that later found their way into Jim's possession.

What had become of Jim? He had been so loving, so caring and undemanding and she hoped from the depths of her heart that life was being kind to him. How often did he think of her, she wondered?

Jim thought of her very often; indeed, in those early days following her abrupt departure, she was constantly in his mind.

Witnessing the departure of her flight tore him apart. He understood this to be a final parting, yet some small voice that would not be stilled cried within him, 'Perhaps, just perhaps…' At the very least he needed to know how she was, particularly in view of the circumstances of her departure. But how was this to be?

In fact, he knew that this could be managed relatively simply, should he so choose, since he had her address. But they had promised each other that they would never make contact. But, he wondered, how long is 'never?' Could 'never' change according to circumstances? Here he had to suppress his wicked thoughts, the evil beasts that stalked in the night. Suppose that Richard...

Here he checked himself and drank another whiskey.

At first, it seemed dangerously possible that he would become another lost soul wandering the globe, as he took flight first to the Northern Territory and became increasingly dependent upon alcohol. However, he soon realised that he owed it to Maggie to do better than this, and anyway, Darwin became decidedly less appealing as the Australian summer took hold.

He went back home to London.

Then, one damp November day, on a day trip to Brighton and longing for Maggie, he walked along the seafront with head lowered against the wind, and, on another of those occasions of unbelievably rare and utterly amazing coincidence, he bumped into Marlene.

Actually, it was a little unclear as to who bumped into whom. Both had their heads down, Jim because he was walking into the wind and Marlene because she was in the process of tying on a headscarf as it was starting to rain.

'Sorry,' muttered Jim, striding on.

The woman acknowledged his apology as she also continued on her way. Then suddenly, she stopped in her tracks and turned to look. But now, she could not see the man's face and she could hardly run back to stare at him more closely. She hesitated, then walked on, but slowly, uncertainly. Then she stopped again, scrutinising Jim's rear view.

What must it be now? Thirty, forty years? She thought she had seen him once or twice in the past, but had always been mistaken. But the way he walked whilst hurrying when the usual ambling gait accelerated into a faster lopsided stride... Soon the man would be out of earshot.

'Jim, Jimmy!'

It was the second call that caused him to pause. Surely this was a voice he knew, but couldn't yet place. He half turned.

It was the woman he'd bumped into.

'Jimmy!'

He quickly ascertained that as there seemed to be no one else around she must have been addressing him. Still he did not recognise her. He stood still and she approached.

'Oh my god, Jimmy, it is you!'

'Marlene!'

They were now facing each other.

'My god,' she said again. 'After all this time. And you haven't changed at all!'

'Nor you!'

This is what they always say, but of course, it isn't true.

They stood together, slightly awkwardly, for what do two people who once shared a life say to each when they meet again?

However, Marlene and Jim had not parted acrimoniously. They realised early on in their marriage that they were perhaps too young and not ideally matched for this commitment and Jim did not blame Marlene for wanting out. He had become poor company anyway after Gary's accident and probably Rob, for whom Marlene finally left him, had more to offer her. But equally, they had shared some good times together, in addition to the not so good, and Jim had been sorry to hear for her own sake that she was no longer with Rob either.

'How's life with you?' asked Jim.

'If you've time to spare to get out of this miserable rain we could catch up a bit, if that's all right with you.'

So they found themselves in one of those seaside cafés that looks somewhat greasy and suspect from outside, but which serve surprisingly reasonable coffee and cake and are useful for drying out damp clothing.

'I've been with Des, now for some twenty years or so, although we never seem to have got round to being married. Perhaps twice is enough anyway. No kids, although Des has a grown-up lad from his first marriage who does his own thing, isn't around that much and causes no hassle. But we see him from time to time. We're just on the outskirts of town, quite handy really. I think I stopped hearing anything of you about the time your mum died. Sorry about that.'

Here she paused.

'Never got over Gary, did she? I don't think any of us ever did.'

They both looked down at the plastic cloth and Jim idly traced a dribble of spilt tea with his index finger.

'I always thought of myself as the jinx,' she continued. I never forgot what I said when you lent him the bloody car. Years later I kept thinking…'

'Then we'd better exorcise that one here and now forever,' interrupted Jim patting her gently on the shoulder. 'These things happened a long time ago. Life moves on.'

Marlene pursed her lips.

'So how has it moved on for you, Jimmy? What have you been up to? Did you ever get to be that famous doctor? You should have done. You had the brains, my share too!'

So Jim gave a brief account of his life in administration and talked of his early retirement and travelling. Marlene too had travelled extensively in Europe and they talked of places they both knew, realising that in their holidaying they still had much in common. However, Marlene had never been to Australia and listened avidly as Jim talked of the places he had visited. Some things, however, like Maggie, he could not yet share. He could not trust himself with a description of Uluru's majestic sunrise and sunset, nor of some of the expeditions he had undertaken with her. However, when talking of well-known attractions such as the Barrier Reef he spoke with great enthusiasm, so that Marlene returned home that night and persuaded Des of their next holiday location.

'So no lucky woman?' ventured Marlene.

Jim hesitated. He'd been tempted during the course of their conversation to speak of Maggie and his love for her and even of the connection with Gary if he dared. However, he simply couldn't find the right moment. All this would be too much for a chance encounter with his ex-wife.

He simply said, 'I grew very fond of someone in Australia – much more than fond. But it is too complicated.'

They both looked out to sea. The early drizzle had turned to persistent light rain and they found themselves glancing simultaneously at their watches.

'Well, Jimmy, this has been very strange but it's been good to catch up with you. I guess there are things you want to keep to yourself, but I hope all goes well for you. Des and I are fine and we rub along pretty well, but there've been a few surprises on the way and I guess that's the same for you too. Maybe we'll meet up some other time for a few more reminiscences?'

'It's been good to see you, Marlene,' was his reply, as they pushed back their chairs and gathered their belongings together. At the café entrance they paused, for their paths now lay in opposite directions. Jim placed his hands on the sleeves of her anorak and they exchanged the formal kiss on the cheek of near strangers and ex-lovers.

It was only when Marlene was back at the car park that she realised they had not exchanged addresses. In later years when she thought back to this chance meeting she was never sure whether this had been intentional on Jim's part or whether he too had simply forgotten. In the event, however, they never met again, although, many years later, their paths passed within feet of each other, but as one was ascending the escalator at Finsbury Park, the other was descending, and both were absorbed in their papers.

That night Jim looked at his holiday photos, lingering long over each individual picture. There were many relating to sights and scenery and a few of Mike's group ones. A couple of Maggie were especially dear to him, one at the roadside in central Australia with the endless red dusty road to the horizon beyond in which she was peering into the distance, looking out for the camels that had been spotted by Brad. The other showed her in relaxed mood on a beach fringed with spiky grass and palm trees. Putting the photos aside, he picked up Werner's sketch and after studying it for a while, found himself drifting round his flat wondering where to locate it. In the end, he removed his English pastoral scene from over the fireplace replacing it with the eucalyptus tree that had now become the focus from the most comfortable armchair in his living room.

Before he went to bed, he opened the curtains wide to the night sky and stared out over the illuminated suburbs beneath a sky almost devoid of stars. But he was not in the mood for artificial incandescence, so drew close the curtains with an almost imperceptible shudder and climbed into bed pulling up the duvet so that it almost covered his head.

As he slept fitfully, he thought he heard the faint sound of didgeridoos. He saw a mosaic of Aboriginal style dots, vivid in colour, arranged in concentric circles. There were four of these and he found that by concentrating hard he could cause them to move. As they moved, they interlocked but in order to make this happen, he had to concentrate with every ounce of energy he possessed and if he also rubbed his eyes almost until they were sore, he could cause the patterns to change in direction, intensity and colour. In the morning, he awoke with reddened eyes.

Werner's sketch was still on the coffee table when Richard returned from work.

'Haven't seen this before,' he said as he bent down to view. 'It's quite a fine drawing. You presumably bought this in Australia? Where's it been hiding? We ought to have this up somewhere.'

'I didn't buy it. I was given it. You remember I told you about the German lads? One of them was quite an artist. In fact, as far as I could make out, it seems he has already had some modest recognition in his own country.'

Maggie approached to look over his shoulder. 'He did this one day, or got the idea for it, I'm not quite sure which, when we had a trip along a dried-up riverbed that eventually led to a small waterhole.'

'Where do you want it? Over on this wall where there is some space?'

Richard held the picture up to the left of the window.

'Not sure. There'd probably be too much reflection on a bright day.'

'Our bedroom perhaps?'

But this suggestion left her even less sure. So, whilst she prepared supper, the picture was wrapped up once more and put away in the drawer under the bed.

After supper and a brief phone call to check on Kate, now feeling less nauseous and coping reasonably well, they sat in the lounge with a coffee.

'You haven't told me much about life here whilst I was away,' ventured Maggie.

So Richard in his turn began to describe some of the events that had taken place in the intervening months between his wife's departure and her premature return. He told her about his visit to Roger Carter and how his hunt for the overnight case resulted in him finding a whole box of family photos he had almost forgotten existed. Here he hesitated, but Maggie just smiled. 'Funny, I had Tina – as all of you – very much in my mind, but Tina especially, the day we explored the rock. I just felt there and then that it's all alright.'

Richard felt relieved.

But more than that, Maggie could not say.

Richard went on to describe the exhibition in London and how, when he arrived at Kate and Martin's flat, there was no one there. He told her about the time Tom, Kate and

Martin visited and how delighted he was to hear of the engagement but how concerned he felt about Tom's response to redundancy. At this point, both parents were quiet for a while. Events had overtaken all of them so very speedily.

'Well, as for Tom's decision, good luck to him. He'll be fine. For Tom, that's the right decision. Your children are adults, you have to remember. And you can be proud of them!'

'Indeed we can. Tom was incredibly helpful over the burglary. I just couldn't have managed without him!'

'What burglary?'

And that was another story.

As for the future, Richard spoke of possible retirement for the following year, but perhaps with the option of some part-time lecturing elsewhere that had been a suggestion of Roger's. However, he and Maggie were both now aware of possible more significant future commitments to Kate.

Time did not heal, but it moved on. There were good and bad days for them all and Maggie personally had to confront a particularly dark period in the second week of November. At that point, life was beginning to recover a semblance of normality and there was this new life on the horizon that offered hope and encouragement. Yet on this particular Armistice Day, with the ceremony at the Cenotaph on the television, Maggie was more than usually overcome by thoughts of sadness and despair. She thought of all the country churches with their chilling, alphabetical lists of young boys' names; parents who lost children, wives husbands, and babes in arms who would never know a father. Nothing, she felt sure, was ever learned from the mistakes of others and the misery is perpetuated, as revenge now scales new heights, taking to the air indiscriminately to destroy towers, and pervading the depths to maim and destroy. There are those who hunt for the limbs of their beloved to find only the head and there are children lost.

She turned off the television for she could watch no more.

Yet there were good days too. Kate's pregnancy progressed smoothly and Martin's parents gave her a happy weekend in their home. Tom kept in touch regularly by email and Maggie and Richard re-established their life together. Even Christmas that year was much more successful than Maggie had thought possible, as they rented a cottage in the Lake District that was a new experience for them all. Tom flew back to join them and they walked, ate and sat by the big log fire in the cosy sitting room.

It was New Year's Eve.

The future looked more hopeful than had once seemed possible.

Chapter 27

Emily Martina was born at noon on Midsummer Day.

'It's a girl!' shouted Maggie from the phone.

'A very auspicious date,' commented the new grandfather.

'Six and a half pounds and all's well with both.' Maggie's face shone with excitement and delight. 'We must get down there. We'll just about make evening visiting time.'

But the journey seemed to take forever.

'Looking at your watch all the time won't speed things up,' commented Richard. 'Anyway, we're making quite good progress. See if there's anything on the radio, or put on a CD.'

So they listened to music as they drove down the M1, with Maggie hardly able to contain her excitement as her thoughts raced ahead.

Kate's pregnancy had been relatively straightforward, although there were times when she felt very much alone. It seemed that everyone else with whom she came into contact had a partner, someone with whom to share the hopes and fears of this awesome new event, and as her pregnancy advanced, her moods swung violently from elation to despair.

One day, in early spring, she found herself walking in St James's Park with Jen and Matt, who had brought young Callum up to London to feed pigeons and ducks – except that they had not realised that the former were now heavily discouraged from Trafalgar Square. Anyway, they had now found ducks in plenty and Callum was happily occupied adding his offering of crusts to a surprisingly wide range of species. His dad was giving him a nature lesson, but his son was more interested in what was going on around.

'Why don't you two girls go and have a coffee?' suggested Matt. 'Callum looks set to be here some time. I'll bring him over when he's had enough.'

'Good thinking,' replied Jen.

Seated at an outside table, the first opportunity to do so after the cold spell earlier on in the year, Kate shared some of her worries with her friend.

'Of course, not every one at the ante-natal sessions is married; in fact, probably more of them are single than otherwise. But they all seem to have a man in the background somewhere. Now the midwife is talking about birthing partners! What am I supposed to do? Produce the token man from somewhere? Where would you get one from, anyway? Is there an agency or something? Perhaps there's a list somewhere and you choose the sort you want. I think I'll go for 'does not faint at the sight of blood'.'

'I think you should go for 'delights later on in getting up for night feeds and a dab hand with the nappies',' added Jen, pleased that Kate could still find some humour in the situation. 'But seriously, Kate, it is something Matt and I are also aware of, and before you object, just listen to our suggestion, bearing in mind that we've talked this over very thoroughly.'

Jen would not allow Kate to give an immediate response to the suggestion so willingly offered in the park that day, yet the more Kate considered it over the next few days, the more acceptable it seemed.

As her very dear friend had advised, she first rang her mother.

'I know you would be with me at the birth,' said her daughter. 'I only have to ask. I know that. And I hope I am not upsetting you if I say that Jen has made a suggestion that I really think I would like to go along with.'

Maggie listened to her daughter with mixed feelings. As Kate guessed, she half expected that her daughter might wish her to be present at the birth of her first baby. However, she knew there would be plenty of opportunity for her own future involvement in the life of a grandchild, and it was good to know that Kate was so well supported by her friends.

'Jen will come over as soon as I call her, 'continued Kate, and her mum will be on call for Callum.'

Moreover, Kate even managed to find a token father for her child, to be around in the days leading up to the arrival of the baby, to visit whilst she was in hospital and to undertake a few of the household chores around the flat when she came home. But the token father flatly refused to be present at the birth.

'No, that's for Jen. No way. Don't even think about it!' declared Tom decisively.

'No, I don't think I will,' giggled his sister.

So when Maggie and Richard arrived at the hospital on a beautiful summer evening, it was to find Kate, Jen and Tom in a curtained bay of the hospital ward devouring chocolates and a small, cocooned wrapped-up bundle asleep in a cot beside the bed.

'Want a cuddle?' asked Kate after hugs and kisses had been exchanged.

'Perhaps I'd better not disturb her,' said Maggie, eyeing her little granddaughter lovingly.

'Go on. She wants you to!' urged Kate. 'Pick her up, Tom!'

Maggie watched in secret astonishment at the relative confidence with which her son extricated the infant from her cot and extra blanket, and placed her on her lap. Tom's willingly volunteered involvement in the arrival of his new niece or nephew had surprised them all.

When Tom first heard about Kate's pregnancy, by email when in Tasmania, he somehow contrived a lengthy phone call to his sister and was relieved and pleased to find her in positive mood. Later on after digesting her news more fully, he realised that he too felt inexplicably delighted and considerably moved by the new situation. Then, after thinking things through in much more considered and thoughtful fashion than was his usual style, he came up with the proposals that accounted for his presence in the hospital and a current address in London.

'But Tom,' remonstrated his sister, when he next called, 'you don't have to come back early for my sake. I've got plenty of help lined up for the last stages of pregnancy and I've even got Jen to be with me at the birth. Then I'm staying in London for a while, possibly going up to Mum and Dad's a bit later on. I've got a year's maternity leave sorted out anyway, so you come back whenever you'd originally planned and do your uncle bit then.'

Initially Maggie and Richard were equally dubious.

'He's never been much of a one for the domestic scene,' said Maggie, raising her eyebrows, 'and he doesn't know anything about babies.'

'But he loves his sister,' said Maggie's mother, when she heard of the plan. 'They've always been there for each other. Why shouldn't he stop gallivanting around and come back to help her out? As for not being any good with a baby, you just wait and see.'

Kate made one further attempt to dissuade her brother, not because she would not appreciate his support and his company, but because she felt this impinged so much on his own plans.

'Martin would approve,' said her brother, and that was that.

So, in May, Tom arrived back in London where he readily found employment in a computer software company taking up residence at first on the sofa in Kate's living room. He helped his sister spring clean the little flat and gave the bedroom a fresh coat of white paint, creating an alcove with a partial, moveable screen where Kate positioned the self-assemble swinging cot. He carried back a flat-pack chest of drawers and accompanied Kate on some of her shopping expeditions to purchase the immediately necessary items, of which there seemed to him to be an excessive amount. He shopped for basic provisions, cleaned the shower and bath and stowed all his empty beer cans in a tidy pile near the bin.

'Anyone would think it was you having the baby!' commented Kate, bemused, but grateful for the practical help.

After a three or four weeks, he moved in with a colleague from his new workplace who was looking for someone to whom he could rent out his spare room, an arrangement most welcomed and beneficial to all three.

One Friday evening, calling in on Kate on his way home, he found her ready, she thought, to make the necessary phone call to Jen, and then the various plans swung efficiently into action. In the end, Matt drove the four of them to the hospital, where he left the young mother-to-be, his wife and the token father, although the latter was sent away, advised to return later. So when Maggie and Richard arrived, Kate and Jen had spent the night at the hospital to be joined by Tom in the afternoon. To the amusement of the girls, the other mothers in the ward and even Rani, one of the nurses, accepted him as the baby's father.

'She's the image of her dad,' commented Rani, nodding towards Tom as he cradled the baby on his knees, and even Dr Patel on his rounds made a similar observation.

Eventually, the three visitors departed and Kate was finally alone with her firstborn, Martin's child, the child the father would never know.

She edged herself gingerly, now feeling a little sore, to the side of the bed and scrutinised every visible detail of the sleeping child beside her, searching for any possible resemblance to either parent, but as far as Kate was concerned, Emily was already decidedly her own little self. She bent forward and scooped the child from her cot, protecting the over heavy head, attached in so fragile a manner to a virtually non-existent neck. The infant, jerked, half woke then searchingly, with barely opened eyes, latched on to her breast.

'Good baby, you know what to do, don't you?' said the young mother, bending to kiss the dark damp spiky hair and to marvel over the perfectly formed fingers and toes. The baby sucked and the mother stroked.

Quite suddenly, everything became simply too much to bear and it was then that the first teardrop formed, detached itself and fell. Kate was unable to help herself. More tears gathered and then there were tears in profusion as she cried hopelessly for Martin, head buried in a damp pillow, weeping for what might have been and for the deep, sad, irreparable loss.

Rani paused on her way down the ward. 'There, there,' she said, making supposedly comforting, clucking noises. 'Let's put her down now. She's fed well the little beauty, and mum needs her sleep.'

Certainly the mother was in need of sleep, but she was in even greater need of something she had no hope of ever having.

She leant back, exhausted, against the pillows, between deftly smoothed and straightened sheets and allowed her eyes to close. Sleep came and she dreamt of their tiny island in the midst of a deep blue sea. At first, it was far away in the hazy distance, but as her gently rocking boat approached, it rose majestically before her eyes in slow motion to take shape and form. She saw rocks, small inlets and a curving bay with deep eddying pools from where a twisting path lead upwards between rough grass and low bushes. Her gaze followed the tortuous route of the path to the craggy summit where, lodged between two boulders was the tiny white abandoned chapel, with a heavy arched, wooden door. She pushed the door open with great difficulty, but there seemed to be someone helping her, so eventually it yielded with much creaking. They were now inside, unable at first to see anything until their eyes had become accustomed to the dark interior and the one flickering candle. There was a musty aroma of incense and damp foliage and a sense that no one had visited for years and years. Yet they were mistaken, for on a wooden rail of what might once have been an altar rail was an exquisite bunch of the whitest of lilies, with the sweetest of fragrances. Now dressed in white in shimmering fabric of lightest gossamer, she threw back her veil to see Martin and as he took her in his arms, the light of a thousand candles flooded the chapel, resplendent in the dazzling sunshine of the light of the day.

There was less dreaming for Kate as the weeks passed and the reality and responsibility of caring for a new being occupied all her time and energy. Tom, as he had promised, undertook many of the more mundane chores around the flat, which now seemed rather on the small side. In addition, his role within his new computer software company seemed to suit him and he was clearly well respected by his new colleagues.

'God, where does all your energy come from?' asked his sister wearily. 'I don't do the night-time bit,' was his reply, 'and I have time for my own things too. You ought to grab a bit of time for yourself too.'

Fat chance, thought his sister, but she made an effort the following weekend when Sarah visited and after Emily had been cuddled and her progress duly recounted, the girls left Tom in charge briefly and went out for an, albeit somewhat hasty, pub lunch by the river.

Kate was again struck, as she had been when visiting the hairdressers after the funeral, by the continuing normality of everything else around.

Whilst Sarah ordered at the bar, she scanned the nearby tables and a family party with a young woman rocking a buggy with one hand, whilst doing her best to manipulate her fork with the other, particularly caught her eye. The baby, as far as Kate could see, appeared to be much the same age as Emily, which suggested that here was someone else who had probably spent the previous night without much in the way of sleep. Yet nothing about the young mother visibly indicated her sleep deprivation, which made Kate wonder whether she too looked much better than she felt. Strange, she thought, as she studied diners at other tables, that nowhere were there visible placards waving above heads, flashing lights or blaring sirens to proclaim a recent bereavement, newly diagnosed terminal illness or, for that matter, a night of wild ecstatic sex.

'Just as well, really,' laughed Sarah, as she rejoined Kate at the table and questioned her friend's train of thought.

'Some you can read a bit,' she added, after examining the scene around. 'That chap there looks a bit gloomy, don't you think? Possibly last night was not up to much for him. But I agree. By and large we all put on the face that's required of us.'

'Since we seem to be on the subject of sex, how's Paul?'

'We won't go into his sexual expertise or otherwise,' answered her friend, 'but I must say that we seem to be getting on famously well. We need to be careful, I think, in the work situation, and I'm now actively engineering a modest change in my contract so that he won't continue to be my line manager, as neither of us find that a very satisfactory situation. I know you've met him once or twice, but I'm planning on a get together soon amongst friends and hope you will be there. It's easy enough to bring Emily while she's so little and you could stay overnight.'

'I'd like to come and I agree it should be easy enough at this stage. It's just that I seem to be making heavy weather of it all. The initial euphoria sort of wears off, and frankly I simply feel so tired all the time. Yet I've had a lot of help from everyone – Tom's absolutely amazing – and I'm just so grateful to Jen and Matt and to you. Anyway, let's eat up now because we'll have to be making tracks back pretty soon. Young Emily seems to require endless feeding.'

The two girls, Kate grateful for the break, duly arrived back at her flat to relieve token father of his duties.

'How was she?'

'Fine.'

'Did she need changing?'

'Nope.'

'Did she cry?'

'Nope.'

So off went Tom to play football and Sarah settled herself on the settee with her goddaughter, an honour she shared with Jen.

'She's absolutely gorgeous,' she declared. 'It's enough to make me feel quite broody myself.'

'Yes, she is quite perfect,' agreed Kate, as Sarah handed her over. 'But despite everything, it's hard on my own. God, I miss Martin desperately! Sometimes I long so much for him to be here with Emily and me that I almost kid myself he'll pop his head round the door, just as if he's gone round to the corner shop to pick up some milk or something. Sometimes I feel furious with him, angry, so angry that he has deserted us when we most need him. How could he have been so stupid to fall off a bloody ladder? How dare he do such a crass thing? I hate him for it. And then I feel so awful and so guilty when I have these thoughts towards him. Sometimes I even wonder whether I might be going mad. Then I look at our beautiful baby and love her to pieces and feel scared for her. How can I be sure I can keep her safe?'

Sarah contemplated her friend as she sat on the settee feeding her baby. Emily was not sucking quite as well as usual as if she sensed her mother's distraction. It was difficult for her to grasp Kate's engorged nipple in her tiny mouth. Kate shuffled her position and guided her baby as best she could to her uncomfortably full, swollen and leaking breast.

'Perhaps a visit to your lovely Dr Harvey wouldn't come amiss,' suggested her friend. 'I advised him once before, if you remember!'

So Kate acted on Sarah's advice once again and Dr Harvey speedily diagnosed the mastitis for which he wrote out a prescription to make his patient more comfortable. Then, as previously, he removed his glasses, leant back in his chair, and asked more general questions about Kate's welfare and how she felt she was coping.

'You are doing very well with your fit and lovely baby,' he commented finally. 'The mastitis will clear quickly but you must ask immediately for a repeat prescription should it return. However, I have no medication for a broken heart. I do not expect you to believe me, but I can assure you that things will eventually improve.' He paused. 'Didn't you say you might return to your parental home for a while? Why don't you go now and accept some pampering? Then, when the time is right, you will be ready to work and to create a home for your little daughter.'

In later years, Kate thought back to this consultation and how grateful she felt that in a world of modern medicine there was still a place for the likes of dear Dr Harvey. At the time, she was simply grateful to find herself back in the home environment in which she had grown up, with the capable and loving hands of her own mother to help her through the immediately demanding period ahead.

There were indeed some difficult years before them: As Richard prepared Tom's old room for Emily, and Maggie cooked and cleaned ready for the arrival of their daughter and granddaughter, none of then guessed that Kate would never return to London, and that Woodbridge Lane would become her permanent home.

It was clear that Kate was suffering postnatal depression, but with medication, support and determination on the part of them all, the dark years faded and finally lay mostly behind them.

Maggie, opening the curtains to a magical sunrise one morning nearly a year later, struggled to recall a long lost phrase deep in her subconscious mind. Her heart stirred, as she stood hypnotised, watching as the sun rose and cast its spell. The magic of Uluru! Then she remembered the phrase. She thought she had heard it first from the lips of an Aboriginal elder as he told the story of his ancestors to a younger more impetuous member of the tribe – maybe in a film she and Jim had watched together, rather than in the flesh. 'Until the black is over! Until the black is over!' It seemed possible at the dawning of this most beautiful day that their own black might perhaps be over.

She stood still, watching. Richard came behind her to watch too, his arms encircling her waist. Together they stood in silence. Gently, insistently, her husband tightened his hold, squeezing Maggie to his chest. She looked up to rest the back of her head on his shoulder, aware of the tightening of his body and the tingling of her own. She closed her eyes momentarily and imagined herself back on the beachfront where she first sighted the amazing, motionless bats in the velvety darkness of the warm night. She felt the proximity of her lover's body. She remembered other antipodean evenings, as the sun set, and the splendour of one spectacular dawn. And here, from her bedroom window was that self-same sun; the one and the same.

Richard too watched, as he held his wife close. Whatever now lay ahead of them both, he wished to share only with her.

Moments passed, and to Maggie, it was as though, in some strangely inexplicable manner, her two lovers had become one.

Today was Emily's first birthday. Tom, who had moved into Kate's flat when she decided to stay in the Midlands to carve a new life for herself, was to arrive later. Maggie's parents were currently with them for the weekend, and could be heard making moves towards the bathroom. They were a household of early risers.

It was, felt Maggie, a significant milestone for them all. Emily predictably enjoyed the attention lavished upon her and chewed and demolished the wrapping paper from her numerous presents with great relish. However, the adults were all quite pleased when she finally accepted the idea of her after lunch sleep and the rest of them could enjoy some civilized conversation and uninterrupted eating and drinking beneath the shade of the trees in the garden.

It was another glorious June day. Judy and Karl dropped by with a present for Emily and stayed a while to chat and eat cake.

'Must now be a couple of years since we were here to celebrate your retirement, Maggie,' recalled Karl.

'I think I rather messed up the great Australian venture,' commented Kate, wryly.

'We won't have you saying things like that, not today on Emily's birthday,' said Maggie. Then more gently, turning to her daughter, 'Of course we'll always be sad that Martin isn't here, but you've got a beautiful little daughter of whom he would be very proud. And he'd be proud too of you, Kate, of how you're coping.'

'A toast to the future, to the birthday girl – who is at this very moment thankfully asleep- and to her old mummy – my lovely sister,' chimed in Tom, deftly opening a bottle of champagne and filling the first glass which he handed to Kate.

'Australia?' quizzed Paul, turning to Maggie, when glasses had been raised and conversation resumed. 'Whereabouts did you get to? Our company is expanding long-haul and Australia will be on the programme soon. We're doing an alternative to the well-established holiday firms, more of a 'build it yourself programme', involving greater elements of personal choice and exploration in smaller groups. Everyone's on to the eco-friendly, support the local economy venture, and we need to secure a share in this development. We're looking to some forestry lodges within the belt of tropical rainforest. This would fit in well with the Great Barrier Reef, which is a must, I'm sure. Did you get to the reef?'

Paul and Sarah, together with the great-grandparents, listened with interest to Maggie's never-endingly enthusiastic descriptions of the rainforest and the reef, and Tom too recounted some of his exploits whilst in Thailand and Tasmania. Judy and Karl were currently planning a Mediterranean cruise and Paul and Sarah had decided to give boating on the Norfolk Broads a try. Conversation was in full swing, when a cry from within reminded them that one-year-old Emily wished to be part of the proceedings.

It was the last family occasion to be celebrated together by both the great-grandparents and the little granddaughter, and, as such, another event to remain firmly etched in Maggie's mind for many a year to come.

Chapter 28

Kate, breakfasting alone in the kitchen with the paper propped up against the coffee jug jumped when she heard the shrill tones of the phone. Instinctively she was concerned, as it was rather early for a call from one of the family. Emily, in her last year at Durham, would probably still be in bed, and Tom usually rang in the evening. She had been with her mother just a couple of days ago, so was not expecting any phone call from Orchard House. So she was totally devastated when she heard the news.

Whilst Eileen spoke, she remained relatively composed, unbelieving. 'But I was with her the other day! She seemed fine! In fact, we were all there last weekend!'

'Peacefully in her sleep,' Eileen was saying.

Numbed, Kate put the phone down and sat heavily amongst the debris of her half finished breakfast. With hands clasped to cheeks, and head bent low, her lower lip began to tremble and her jaw to quiver uncontrollably. Tears welled in the corners of her eyes and she wept, sitting at the kitchen table, as she had wept before for the loss of a loved one. She cried despairingly for her mother, her father, and her lover, howling like a wild animal as violently, angrily she pushed her chair away to pace the living room and the hall.

With sore, reddened eyes and damp strands of uncombed hair clinging to her cheeks, despite the dankness of the day, she made her way into the garden. There, exhausted, she sat on the old bench by the apple tree where a fragment of frayed rope that had once supported Emily's swing still hung. This was where her father had been sitting when he suffered his unexpected heart attack, now some ten years ago. Later, sitting on this same bench, her mother had shared concerns relating to her own personal health with her son and daughter.

'So you see,' she had said, 'I think the time has come for me to look for some sort of alternative living arrangement.'

Kate shivered. The morning was cool and damp.

She returned indoors, still tearful, as she recalled that particular conversation. Their mother had remained adamant, despite their many objections. Moreover, she continued, she wished Kate and Emily to remain in the family home. Tom, with his own substantial home in France, she felt sure, would support her in this. In view of this, in due course, all other assets would come to him.

Reluctantly, as a result of this conversation, Kate and Tom researched various possibilities of care for their mother and their efforts finally took them to Orchard House.

More tears fell as Kate realised that she would never visit her mother there again. Except for this one last time.

But first, there were calls to be made. Thankfully, she got straight through to Tom at La Chapelle, relieved that she did not have to speak first with Sophie or the children. Her brother was equally devastated. 'I'll be with you,' he said. As for Emily, she left a message on her mobile asking her to phone home.

She then made arrangements to visit Orchard House. As she backed the car out of the garage, a light wind blew an eddy of autumn leaves around the flower tubs, finally emptied of their summer geraniums but still awaiting some bulbs or wallflowers for the spring. Kate shuddered. This time of year, when others enjoyed the autumn colours and the promise of cosy nights with curtains drawn and warm central heating, brought her no comfort. Falling leaves and falls from ladders were for her inextricably linked. Time heals nothing. All it does is to move on. And movement involves direction.

Kate had not known which way to turn with the loss of her beloved Martin, but the arrival of Emily forced her to be forward looking. She settled into her parental home – an arrangement that proved to be surprisingly successful from all points of view – and in due course looked to the means of supporting herself and her little daughter. Courses in childcare eventually resulted in nursery work and finally in the acquisition of her own day care nursery, the first of the three she now owned. Whilst the financial rewards were not great, they were certainly adequate, but more importantly, Kate found an occupation that was deeply satisfying and helpful too in the practicalities of bringing up Emily.

At one time, they moved out of the Woodbridge Lane house into a flat still within the catchment area of Emily's school. Initially, Maggie made the suggestion thinking that it might give her daughter more freedom, perhaps even to find a new partner. But Emily missed her grandparents and the child-friendly garden, and apart from a couple of men friends, Kate seemed content to remain celibate, with her energies directed to her daughter and her new career.

Another gust of wind caused the yellowing leaves around the tub to scatter and disperse. Kate sniffed, wiped her eyes with a sodden tissue and gripped the steering wheel, ready for her drive to Orchard House.

She turned into the drive. There stood the eucalyptus that her mother had so admired, but there was little colour in the rest of the garden. The roses had long since finished and the recent rain had left much of the foliage and greenery limp and bedraggled.

Eileen was waiting for her on the steps and took her straight to her office where Helen arrived with a cup of tea.

'I'll take you up now, if you're ready,' said Eileen. 'I will be outside the door if you want me.'

Together they climbed the stairs. Kate hesitated at the door. Eileen patted her arm. Kate turned the handle.

She stood still on entering. A pale and struggling November sun now lightened the room. Kate turned her eyes first to the back window and the misty outline of hills beyond the orchard.

Then she turned towards the bed where her dearly loved mother now lay. She approached tentatively, softly.

The bed was orderly, the duvet straightened and the pillow smoothed. Her mother lay on her back, with only her head and neck visible and her newly combed hair fanned out on the pillow. She appeared peaceful. Kate, encouraged, now bent nearer to scrutinise the so familiar face. How strange then that she saw two faces – the face of the mother she loved and the other, unknown face of an old lady. She leant further to kiss the face of the one she knew and in so doing, she saw the faces to be one and the same. None of them had noticed that Maggie had aged.

Kate drew up a chair to the bed, and without disturbing the bedding, placed her right hand across her mother's body to caress her shoulder and her left hand to rest on her near shoulder. She leant close to whisper the words she wished to whisper.

Then, withdrawing, motionless, she sat for a while to gaze again upon that face, and shed her silent tears.

Then she rose.

Kate had said her goodbye.

Then there were certain formalities to address in Eileen's office. A funeral now required organisation and her mother's body would be taken to whichever funeral parlour as advised by Kate.

'There's something else to ask you,' pursued Eileen gently. 'Dan has asked to be able to say his own farewell to your mother. Is that acceptable to you?'

'Of course,' responded Kate. 'Dan has been a friend to all the family. Each time Emily has visited, right from the time mother first came here, Emily and Dan have been buddies. She still has the sketchbook he gave her years ago. I ought to speak with Dan now. I know he will miss my mother. She always spoke very fondly of him. I think, both having lost their partners in similar circumstances, they came to understand each other very well.'

'Then we'll ask him to come here in a moment and you can have the privacy of this office. But before that, I'm afraid I need to speak to you about your mother's room. Would it be possible for you to clear it by the end of next weekend? Does that give you and the family enough time?'

Kate, who had not given a single thought to the clearing of the room, now began to realise there was quite a lot to do.

'Wednesday, isn't it? My brother Tom will soon be on his way from Paris. Emily can get home easily enough from Durham. Yes, we can be over here on Saturday to sort out Mum's things.'

So Kate met with Dan, who escorted her slowly and falteringly to the front steps. She closed the car door and drove down the gravel drive. She did not look back.

When she next approached Orchard House, she had Tom and Emily with her. Tom sat beside her in the front, staring grimly ahead, with Emily behind him, sniffing periodically into a tissue.

Unusually, Eileen was not at the door to receive them, so they rang the sonorous bell that reverberated in the emptiness of the tiled hall within. Helen was quick to answer.

Kate was first to enter her mother's room. It was already depersonalised. The bed was stripped and the curtains removed, presumably for cleaning. There were no fresh flowers, but instead, the whiff of cleaning fluid or disinfectant.

They were at a loss as to how to begin. However, Emily, turning back from the large front window, soon had them organised.

'Why don't we leave Uncle Tom to collect together the heavier items that belonged to Grandma? Wasn't that rocking chair hers and the rugs? They could go over here, near the door. We can put the clothes into the cases and then all the pictures and things into those big cartons. I'll empty these drawers here.'

So the sad task was started.

After a while, Helen brought up some coffee.

'What's all this, Helen?' asked Emily, as she moved some packaging on the coffee table to one side.

'Oh, I meant to tell you. It came on Tuesday, just after you'd visited,' turning to Kate. 'She started to open the parcel whilst I was here, but I got called away.'

'God, I really like this!' exclaimed Emily, holding up a picture.

'Let's see,' said Kate, moving closer.

'This is an exquisite sketch, quite beautifully executed,' commented Tom. 'It reminds me of ....Have I seen this before?'

'Not quite, Uncle,' replied his niece triumphantly, 'but what could be its twin is over there on that wall.'

Emily unhooked Maggie's sketch.

'It's the same tree!'

'I don't think so. Not quite. Look here.'

'I still think it could be,' persisted Emily.

'Well, there's no doubt that it's the same artist,' said Kate. 'So who's it from?'

Emily rummaged through the papers and packaging on the table.

'There's just this compliments slip thing. 'Sargent and King' or something.

'It's a firm of solicitors,' said Tom, as she handed him the slip. 'But whatever is this?' Tom held up a plain white envelope on which was written, 'Personal. For Margaret Simpson only.' Hang on, there's this with it.'

Tom studied the letter.

'What does it say, Tom?'

'Well I never!'

'What? What is it?'

'Well, it's a communication from a firm of solicitors on behalf of some client of theirs whose wish, upon his own death, was that this sketch and letter should be given to Margaret Simpson. Should Margaret Simpson predecease him – this anonymous client – the unopened letter is to be destroyed forthwith. The sketch – if she likes it – is for….'

Here Tom stopped. He raised his eyes to them. He gulped. He took breath.

'The sketch – if she likes it – is for Emily.'

Everyone stared at Emily.

Nobody said a word.

Helen's phone buzzed. 'I must go,' she said.

'The sketch is for me?' queried a puzzled and confused Emily. 'Who was this person who seemed to know me?'

Kate was alarmed. Who was this? 'Can something like this be done anonymously?' she asked anxiously.

'Well, well, well, our mother was full of surprises. I've no idea what to make of all this!'

But Emily was quick to offer her own explanation. 'Wake up you two! Good old Grandma! She had an admirer – perhaps a lover – although she loved Granddad – so I don't quite know how that fits in. He was an artist, this boyfriend! Perhaps a very famous artist! But why on earth he should wish to give this amazing sketch to me is a mystery! I love mysteries! Is it signed?'

The three of them bent to examine the indistinct signature on the lower right corner.

'Very difficult to make out. A short name starting with 'S'. Maybe the initial 'W'.'

'Do you like the sketch, Emily?' asked her mother.

'I do, I do!' exclaimed her daughter, 'and if it turns out that it's the work of a very famous artist and worth absolutely loads, I shall never part with it. I think it's amazing! Thank you, thank you, Grandma, from the bottom of my heart! Thank you, anonymous donor!'

'Here you are,' said Tom as he handed Kate the original sketch that had long hung on their mother's wall. 'I think this should be yours. I somehow think this anonymous donor would like the idea that the two sketches are owned by mother and daughter.'

'Thank you, Tom. Like Emily, I shall treasure it.'

'What about the letter?'

'We destroy it.'

'Then we'll never know the answer to the mystery.'

'No, Tom, we'll never know.'

'So what do we do with it?' Tom's eyes moved to the bin.

'Uncle Tom!' remonstrated Emily. 'You can't bin a letter like that! We'll take it home and have a ceremonial burning or something. You can't just chuck it away. Where's your imagination?'

And her mother was in full agreement.

The discovery of the package and letter had rather slowed their progress in clearing the room, but finally the job was done, and a van ordered for the items they could not carry. They went then to the lounge where some residents particularly wanted to offer their condolences. Estelle, as usual, was very confused as to who had died, but one of the nurses, seeing that Kate was finding this very wearing, succeeded in distracting her. Dan pulled on an anorak and took Emily to the stone seat. As he shuffled his way along the path, Emily told him about the picture that she had tucked under her arm.

Dan lowered himself gently, spreading out his legs and placing his stick to one side. He patted the space beside him.

'Sat here many times with your Gran,' he said. 'She loved all of you very much, you know that, don't you?'

Emily nodded, sniffed and squeezed his hand.

'I shall miss her too. We all will. Now show me this picture of yours.'

Dan looked closely at Emily's sketch.

'Yes. Undoubtedly one of a pair.'

'Where did Grandma's come from? Did she say?'

Dan thought hard. 'Not sure that she ever did say. But it really meant something to her. Me too. See that tracery there! Those leaves are just about to twirl away. Red river gums these are. Reminded her of Australia. She'd been there as I'm sure you know.'

'I think she had a lover and I think it was this artist. Maybe she met him in Australia. So it's likely he was an Australian artist. I'm going to do some research because I feel linked to this artist in some way. He knew my name for a start. How magical is that! And I didn't even know he existed.'

Dan was still looking at the picture 'Wish I could draw like that!'

'Mind you, if she had had a lover, that wouldn't have been so good for Granddad. Maybe she met him after Granddad died, although that would have made her rather too old for an affair. No, that's not right if she met him in Australia. Anyway,' here she cast a beguiling smile at Dan, 'I once thought you were her lover!'

'Well, then I should have been a lucky man! You'd best be off now, young Emily. Your mum's probably waiting. Treasure your picture and come and see me from time to time.'

'I will, Dan,' she replied, planting a kiss on his forehead and he watched as she made her way back to the house. He bowed his head. He felt sad and old.

In the months that followed, with Emily back at university and Tom in France, Kate felt very low. She immersed herself in new schemes for her nurseries and cautiously allowed her friendship with Colin, a family friend she had known for a number of years, to develop. She even introduced him to Sarah and Paul, who spent a night with her on the way to visit their son in Manchester.

'We like him,' commented her friend.

Over dinner Kate recounted the story of the sketches that in recent weeks had much occupied her thoughts. Sometimes she felt alarmed as to the identity of this person who somehow knew the name of her daughter. 'It's as though someone has been watching us,' she said.

'Have you still got the letter?' asked Colin.

'Yes,' she replied.

'So you could find out?' asked Sarah.

'Yes. If I opened a personal letter expressly sent to my mother, with the request that it be destroyed should she predecease the sender.'

'You can't open it,' pronounced Sarah.

'No, I can't.'

'What will you do with it?' pursued her friend.

'Emily favours some sort of mystical ceremony involving fire and incense and goodness knows what else.'

'Sounds good to me,' commented Sarah.

At Christmas, the ceremony duly took place.

Kate and Emily had given some thought as to how to spend this first Christmas without Maggie.

'We could go to La Chapelle,' suggested Emily, home for a weekend. Tom had already made this suggestion. 'It's such a huge rambling place and they usually invite masses of friends and neighbours. All Aunt Sophie's side of the family is bound to be there. I like the way the French do Christmas. Give me wild boar and a big Christmas Eve meal any day.'

'Trouble is, I'm not sure whether I'm in the mood for enormous endless festivities,' said her mother. 'And there's the other big disadvantage to La Chapelle in winter.'

They both thought of the vast, draughty rooms in the old château, the hopeless radiators and the huge cold tiled bathrooms.

'There'd be a roaring log fire in the drawing room, and in the sitting room,' suggested Emily. But she too liked her creature comforts. Her cousins were made of sterner stuff and possessed a number of very warm jumpers.

'Maybe Tom would come here. Perhaps Sophie might like an English Christmas for a change. I'll make the suggestion' said Kate finally. Somewhat to her surprise, her sister-in-law was delighted by the invitation.

So on Christmas Eve, Tom, Sophie, Christiane and Marc joined Kate and Emily round the log fire roasting chestnuts.

Colin was to join them for Christmas dinner together with Emily's boyfriend.

'I don't even like the things,' commented Emily, face reddened from the heat, 'but I love the atmosphere. Grandma and Granddad always roasted chestnuts and Granddad actually loved them.'

Tom deftly opened a bottle of champagne.

'From Jean-Michel's vines,' he said. 'We did a big job for him. He's got a very impressive website now.'

'Let's hope his bubbly is equally impressive,' commented Emily, handing round the glasses.

'Let's toast Grandma and Granddad,' said Christiane, raising her glass.

'And one for Anonymous!' added Emily, glancing at the two sketches side by side on the far wall.

For one evening at least, there was peace and harmony. Tom added another log to the fire and Marc poked at the flames to cause a sudden flaring of orange and yellow. All eyes focused on the burning logs, spitting and dislodging in the grate. Suddenly, Kate left the room and her daughter guessed why. She too rose from her knees to light some candles on the shelves over the radiators. Then she disappeared into the kitchen to return with fir cones gathered from the woodland down by the stream and dried rosemary picked from the garden.

Kate returned with the letter, uncreased and virgin white. Her mother's name stood out in strong bold type. Marc moved to one side to give space to his aunt and to his cousin as she threw her offerings on to the fire. There was some smoke and a fragrance of rosemary and memories past. Kate held the letter aloft in both hands, thumb and finger on the uppermost corners, and as she knelt the others stood.

'Margaret Eleanor Simpson, we give thanks for your life,' Kate spoke in a strong unfaltering voice.

'We do, we do!' cried Emily, and her affirmation was echoed by them all. They watched as the letter blackened, curled, then was devoured by a sudden tongue of flame. Then it was over. There was a moment's silence followed by much hugging and kissing and not a few tears.

One evening, when Christmas was over, mother and daughter sat together on the hearthrug to enjoy an evening of reminiscences with the family photos. They now had an additional couple of boxes from Kate's mother.

'What a pity they are not all named!' exclaimed Emily. Who is this, for example?'

Kate took the photo from her daughter. 'Why, it's Tina, the baby who died. Before your uncle and me.' She looked closely, compassionately at the photo. 'What a blow, to lose a child!'

'You lost a partner,' said her daughter, quietly.

'And you a father.'

'I'm sorry I never knew my father,' said Emily. 'Tell me some more about him.'

So Kate found further photos and told her daughter, as she had done before, of the life she and Martin had shared. They laughed together at some of the antics and acclaimed as always the story of the romantic proposal.

'Can't imagine Chris doing something like that!'

'Would you like him to?'

'Don't think so. Not at the moment. I'm not after a permanent man yet. When this term is over, I'm off on my travels. I have a mystery to unravel.'

They examined a few more photos.

'What about you, Mum?' asked Emily, without looking up. 'Do you like your Colin?'

'Do you?'

'I asked you first.'

'I think that perhaps I do, Emily, but it's early days. You have to realise that my life could be quite lonely when you take off.'

They turned over more photos.

'How would you feel?' continued her mother.

'I think that would be OK,' replied her daughter, after a pause. 'What about Grandma's boyfriend?'

'What do you mean?'

'Well. Do you mind that she had one?'

For a while there was no response.

'We don't know that she did. Your picture and the anonymous letter don't necessarily mean she had a boyfriend. A friend, a contact of some sort, yes, clearly so. Anyway, I find it strange to think of my mother having an affair – a difficult concept for a daughter, I think.'

'I think I'm handling it quite well,' said Emily, and they both laughed.

'Look here though. Perhaps this is the evidence!' Emily held up a picture of a group of people with a background they recognised. 'It's Uluru! And there is Grandma! Is that the artist, do you think? He's the one standing beside her. And he has got his arm round her.'

Her mother studied the picture.

'They all have their arms round each other,' she reasoned. 'No, Emily. Your research will have to be more convincing than that.'

'Don't worry! It will be!'

Emily's research had to wait until the following summer. After an absurdly early arrival at Heathrow, she paused at Passport Control for a final farewell to Kate and Colin.

'I'm finally off to unravel the mystery,' she beamed, map in hand 'I'm not quite sure what I'm looking for, but I shall know it when I find it!'

She turned and was gone.

They watched until the plane could be seen no more and the first rays of a watery sun broke through the cloud.